Test of Valor

Also by Keira Andrews

Gay Amish Romance Series
A Forbidden Rumspringa
A Clean Break
A Way Home
A Very English Christmas

Contemporary
Valor on the Move
Test of Valor
The Winning Edge
In Case of Emergency
Eight Nights in December
Road to the Sun
The Next Competitor
Arctic Fire
Reading the Signs
Beyond the Sea
If Only in My Dreams
Where the Lovelight Gleams
The Chimera Affair
Love Match
Synchronicity

Historical
Kidnapped by the Pirate
The Station
Semper Fi
Voyageurs (free read!)

Paranormal
Kick at the Darkness
Fight the Tide
A Taste of Midnight (free read!)

Fairy Tales (with Leta Blake)
Levity
Rise
Flight

Test of Valor

BY KEIRA ANDREWS

Test of Valor
Written and published by Keira Andrews
Cover by Dar Albert
Formatting by BB eBooks

ISBN: 978-1-988260-32-7
Print Edition

Acknowledgements

Thanks so much to Anara, Mary, Leta Blake, and DJ Jamison for their friendship and assistance with this book. Special shout-out to Karen (and her son Sean) for their invaluable assistance with making sure the dialogue of the Australian characters sounded natural.

Chapter One

WHEN PEOPLE ASK if it was worth giving up his Secret Service career to run away with the president's son, Shane Kendrick tells them: *abso-fucking-lutely.*

But this morning in their little tent pitched on the beach, a knot cinched in Shane's gut, his heart thumping. Rafa wasn't warm and mumbling in his sleep beside him, and Shane fisted his fingers in the empty blanket.

The awful dream images were still too close to the surface— Shane's feet hopelessly stuck and Rafa snatched away. Waking alone, Shane choked on panic, bile rising in his throat. Naked, he crawled out of the tent and pushed to his feet, ready to run. Ready to fight.

He released a gasp of relief, instantly spotting Rafa a few hundred yards away by the shoreline. It was a Monday morning on a secluded stretch of beach north of Byron Bay in mid-June, and they fortunately had the place to themselves.

Shane's heart still beat too fast and sweat dampened his brow as he watched Rafa wading through the surf in the distance, foamy water swirling around his ankles. Skin tanned, he looked like a local in a purple hoodie, board shorts riding low on his lean hips. He was fucking *beautiful,* his curls shaggy and wild around his head.

The tide was returning with a steady rumbling gurgle, the sun already up in the cloud-splattered blue sky. Nearby, a gull shrieked and flapped its wings, bickering with another bird over a treat that had washed up on the golden sand.

Shane inhaled the fresh air deeply, willing the lingering tension in his limbs and the thudding of his heart to ease. The dreams—all right, nightmares—were similar but never quite the same. This time it wasn't mud in a rest stop parking lot that turned to quicksand, keeping him mired as Rafa was carried away by masked men, screaming for help.

This time, the quicksand was on a sunny, perfect beach like this one. It had sucked him down, freezing him in place. In the dream, he'd tried over and over to get his feet to move, limbs useless as he'd tasted his own blood. Gunshots rang in his ears as he struggled, and he failed miserably as nameless shapes dragged Rafa out of reach.

As he gazed at Rafa, Shane breathed in the fresh sea air again—brine and seaweed and a crisp sunny sweetness. *You're awake. He's all right. Let it go.*

He closed his eyes, counting to five. When he opened them, the time for letting the nightmare bother him would be officially past. They'd had such a peaceful week away, and he couldn't let anything ruin their last day before heading back to Sydney. At least Rafa had already left the tent when the nightmare hit. Shane didn't want him to worry over nothing.

The dreams had started recently without warning and for no good reason, and Shane didn't see why they wouldn't disappear just as quickly. No sense in making a big deal out it.

Well, okay. Maybe they hadn't started completely unprompted. The first had come the night after Shane had been told he'd have to testify at a special inquest in DC. His former partner— former *friend*, his clenching stomach reminded him—had pleaded guilty to treason and was serving life with no possibility of parole. Alan had been lucky to escape the death penalty. He likely only had because Rafa had pleaded for leniency.

Shane's heart swelled watching him kick at the surf. After what Alan had done, most people would hate him, but not Rafa. Digging his toes into the warming sand near the shrubbery and trees growing at the edge of the beach, Shane watched him and tried not to think about the damned inquiry.

It was reasonable that the Secret Service needed to understand just how such a massive breach of security had occurred under their noses. How one of their agents had been turned by terrorists. Not that Shane could understand it himself.

He tried again to push away the thoughts of Alan's betrayal and how it had nearly cost Rafa his life. The memory of finding Rafa squeezed into that box…

Stop!

The nightmares were weak and useless enough—he didn't need to ruin his days by torturing himself with what-ifs and should-haves. At least the Secret Service had agreed Shane could testify by satellite linkup. He needed to stop thinking about it until his testimony, and then he could put it all behind him. And Rafa would never have to know about the ridiculous nightmares. Shane hadn't disturbed him with them yet, and he needed to keep it that way.

He stretched his arms over his head, the wind tickling his bare flesh. The Aussies might have found this winter morning on the chilly side, but to him it was perfect—a cool breeze offsetting the heat of the sun.

He ran a hand over his stubble. Not shaving every day was a little thing, but it still made him happy. He still kept his head shorn since his hairline was receding more and more with each passing month. Once he launched his security consulting business, he'd be groomed and back in suits, but for now he would enjoy being naked and scruffy.

After pissing by a shrub and brushing his teeth with a jug of water, he once again studied Rafa down the beach, Rafa stopping every so often to crouch and pick up seashells abandoned by the tide. His collection was in a glass jar on the windowsill in their rented bungalow's bathroom. Soon, he'd need another jar, and Shane envisioned the sill being squeezed full as the months went by. He smiled.

Squinting at a flash of movement in the distance, he lifted his hand to shield his eyes, spotting a man and dog. He calculated their distance to Rafa, who was still peering intently at something in the sand, then started to jog over before remembering he was naked.

Stop. Breathe. He's safe.

It was only a man walking his dog—not paparazzi or terrorists. Still, he once again eyed the distances between them all. Shane could be at Rafa's side in approximately twenty seconds running full-out, taking into account the slowing effect of sand.

A lot can happen in twenty seconds.

Although the clouds were fluffy and white, not heavy and gray, for a few thumping heartbeats, phantom rain drenched his skin, the steady rumble of the waves transforming to thunder. Gunshots echoed in his mind as he collapsed to the mud in the darkness, an utter failure, Rafa taken. His breath hitched, and he ran a finger over the scar on the left side of his head above his ear.

He almost expected to feel the hot slick of blood, the bullet somehow only grazing him, mercifully not piercing his skull. The remembered terror of realizing Rafa was gone swooped through his stomach now even as he told himself Rafa was right there, safe and whole and smiling to himself as he waded in the surf.

Shaking his head, Shane resolutely turned away and tugged on his board shorts. He was supposed to be over the nightmare, not dredging it up again. Besides, Rafa might get irritated if Shane raced over like a mother hen.

It had taken weeks before Shane had gotten accustomed to

him being out of arm's reach, and he still didn't like it. But Rafa was a grown man, and Shane had to get over himself.

He sat on the log they'd dragged to their fire pit the night before and pondered starting the fire to make coffee. But for the moment, he simply sat and breathed in and out, watching Rafa throw a rock into the water, still trying to perfect his skimming technique.

The man and black Labrador eventually disappeared back the way they'd come, and the remaining tension in Shane's shoulders dissipated. The paps hadn't bothered them in a while now.

After *US Weekly* had broken the story about the romance between the ex-president's gay son and the older Secret Service agent who'd rescued him from evil kidnappers, there had been a flurry of attention. But they'd laid low, living off Shane's savings.

Now they were old news, and most Aussies either didn't recognize them, didn't give a shit, or were too nice to say anything. Shane had quietly laid the groundwork for his security consulting firm, and Rafa was due to start at Sydney's Cordon Bleu campus next month.

When Rafa's parents arrived all too soon for their first visit, it would probably get stirred up again in the press, but hopefully it would all be short-lived. Shane shifted uncomfortably at the thought of making small talk with the Castillos. *Ugh.* He wondered if he'd know any of the agents on their detail and just how incredibly fucking awkward it would all be.

Before he could run through the litany of horrifying potential scenarios, he forced his mind back to the present. It was just the two of them, miles from anything, with the tide coming in and hopefully bringing breaking waves with it.

He dug his phone out of his duffel in the tent and snapped a few pictures of Rafa silhouetted on the sand. There was barely a cell signal on the beach, but he pulled up WhatsApp and was able to send a pic to Darnell with the caption:

Morning view. Hope it's a good night in DC.

Darnell usually sent him pictures of traffic jams and overflowing trash cans in return, along with at least one frowning selfie and mock complaints that Shane was rubbing it in. Chuckling to himself in anticipation, Shane tucked his phone in his pocket and watched Rafa walk back, grinning when Rafa waved and picked up his pace.

Rafa reached into his shorts pocket when he reached their little camp. "Got some good ones. Look how purple this one is." He carefully extracted the shells and held out his flat palm, bending to kiss Shane lightly.

"Beautiful." Shane ran his finger over the gentle curves of the delicate treasures. "Sure there's nothing living in these?"

Rafa huffed good-naturedly. "No closed shells, I promise. Only needed to learn that stinky lesson once." He slid them into a Ziploc and stowed them. "Ready for breakfast? I was thinking bacon. Because...well, bacon."

Shane's phone buzzed, and he took it out of his pocket and opened WhatsApp. Darnell's face scowled from the screen, his tie loosened, the beige and brown detective squad room visible behind him. His normally short afro was getting a little long, and there were bags under his eyes. As the youngest African-American detective on the force, he often said he had to work twice as hard and be three times as smart as his colleagues.

Caught a triple homicide. Glad to see you're working hard down there, you bastard. Hope you and your boy are good. Stay in touch. Two texts in one week—you're on a roll. I'll send you a vext later.

On his commute, Darnell would sometimes record a voice message on WhatsApp—what he called a "vext." He'd talk about whatever was on his mind, and Shane enjoyed listening to his friend ramble.

"Shane?"

He glanced up. "Sorry, what were you saying? Got a message from Darnell." He showed Rafa the screen.

Rafa's dark brows drew close. "I'm not a *boy*."

"What?" Shane reread the text. "Oh. He doesn't mean anything by it."

"Yeah. It's cool." Rafa thrust his hands in his pockets. "Um, say hi or whatever. And I was talking about bacon."

Shane quickly typed out a response that they were indeed good and not to work too hard, then stood and tugged Rafa near. Rafa was tense in his arms, and Shane slid a hand over Rafa's cheek. "Darnell really didn't mean anything."

Shaking his head, Rafa blew out a breath and melted into Shane's touch. "I know. I'm oversensitive about it. Sorry."

"Don't be sorry." He kissed him softly, then murmured, "Maybe bacon can be dessert."

"I brought passion fruit for dessert." Rafa looped his arms around Shane's neck, eyes wide with faux innocence. "Unless you're talking about something else altogether. In which case, I'm just not following."

"I'm talking about fucking you. Sorry that wasn't clear." Shane ran his hands over Rafa's ass, nuzzling his neck.

"Oh, is that what you meant? Well. I suppose I'll let you." He bit the lobe of Shane's ear and whispered, "How do you want me?"

"Hmm. So many options." Shane leaned back and ran his finger over the freckles that stood out beautifully on Rafa's cheeks and across his nose.

Rafa caught Shane's finger in his mouth, nipping it playfully. "How about I take a ride?"

Shane's cock swelled at the thought, and he ground his hips against Rafa. "Giddy up." He glanced around the still-empty beach. "We should probably go back in the tent."

"Nah. Not enough room in there. I don't want to hide." Rafa shoved down his shorts with an impetuous grin and kicked them free. "No one's around." After peeling off his hoodie, he stood naked, fingers twitching.

Shane knew it was unwise, but he couldn't resist Rafa's loose-limbed enthusiasm. As the president's closeted son, his true self had been bottled up for so long. Shane couldn't deny him anything now.

He stripped off his shorts and wound up flat on his back on a towel with Rafa naked and straddling him, impatiently squirting lube and fingering himself open. Rafa bit his lip in concentration, and Shane ran his hands up and down Rafa's flexing thighs.

"That's it. Get yourself ready for me. You're so fucking beautiful."

Rafa blushed, and Shane knew it wasn't because he was naked with his fingers shoved in his ass on a beach where anyone might stumble along. No, even after five months of being together, Rafa twitched with discomfort when Shane told him how good-looking he was, how perfect.

So Shane said it repeatedly, and would say it over and over and over as long as he had breath. "You're gorgeous, baby."

"*You* are," Rafa murmured, his usual reply.

"Ready for my cock?"

A grin spread over Rafa's face. "Always." Impaling himself, he moaned, the sound shooting right to Shane's balls as heat surrounded his cock.

As the months had gone by, Shane had wondered if the sex would start to get boring. He'd always thought it must after a while in a monogamous relationship. But as he watched Rafa sink down on his cock, squeezing it tightly and sending sparks to Shane's toes, he couldn't imagine how it ever would. Not with Rafa.

He pushed himself up on one hand to lick Rafa's dusky nipples and tease the sprinkle of hair on his chest as Rafa sank all the way. Rafa rocked back and forth, little movements of his hips as they breathed harder. He loved being fucked, and God, did Shane love fucking him.

With his other hand, Shane reached around to where his cock filled Rafa, skimming his finger over Rafa's sensitive, stretched hole. He'd always enjoyed being inside a tight ass. But with Rafa, it was more than merely pushing into his body—Shane imagined he could reach all the way to his heart.

Barking out a laugh at his own ridiculously sappy thought, he flopped back down to the towel, bending his legs and thrusting up. Rafa gazed down at him with a dazed smile and asked, "What?"

He shook his head. "Just happy." He stroked Rafa's cock lazily, glancing left and right to make sure they were still alone on the beach. Pushing down the foreskin, he ran his thumb over the glistening head, gathering pre-cum. Then he lifted his hand to Rafa's mouth and slipped his thumb between his lips. Rafa sucked it clean with an eager tongue.

"You like that, hmm?" Shane asked. "My little cum slut." He could see the pleasure ripple through Rafa as he nodded, sucking harder on Shane's thumb. The first time Rafa had asked Shane to call him that, he'd blushed furiously, eyes downcast.

Shane wondered how much farther Rafa wanted to go down that path of submission, but there was plenty of time for them to explore that. He pulled his thumb free and pinched Rafa's nipples one after the other, making him cry out.

It was a joy watching Rafa bloom out of the shadow of the White House, and it was sure as hell a joy having a front-row seat for his discovery of sex. Shane had never had it this good, and as Rafa rode him with increasing speed, bracing his palms on Shane's chest, curls swaying, Shane was the luckiest goddamn man alive.

But for how long? What if he eventually wants more than me? Someone his own age? I'm only getting older, and he's still so young…

Shane tried to shove the thoughts away, concentrating on Rafa's gasps and moans as he fucked himself, so tight and hot and breathless. Rafa was heavy on top of him, a delicious weight, glistening with sweat, gloriously alive. His cock throbbed in Shane's grasp.

He's starting classes next month. Driving the highways every day. There could be an accident. Anything can happen in a blink. And Jesus, how am I going to face his parents? What if he eventually gives into their disapproval? It's easy to say he doesn't care what they think, but he does.

Shane could hear Darnell sighing in his head and saying, "*The future will take care of its damn self.*"

Rafa frowned down at him, his movements slowing. "What are you worrying about?"

"Nothing, baby. Keep going. I'm close." He stroked Rafa's cock with renewed intent.

But Rafa stayed where he was, stilling his motion with Shane's dick all the way inside him, gently batting Shane's hand off his shaft. He rubbed two fingers between Shane's eyebrows, smoothing out the furrow. "What are you worrying about?" he repeated.

"The future. I know, I know."

Rafa leaned down and kissed him, licking into his mouth. His breath tickled Shane's lips as he whispered, "Whatever happens, it'll be okay. Because we'll be together. It'll be more than okay. It'll be amazing."

Shane nodded. "Glass half full."

"I'll make you an optimist, I swear."

Clutching Rafa's hips, Shane dug his heels into the sand and thrust up, both of them gasping. Fucking raw was still a revelation, the slick grip of Rafa's ass like the sweetest fire. The sun glared above, and Shane's whole body went hot, gritty sand sticking to his slick skin despite the towel.

"You gonna give it to me?" Rafa asked breathlessly, lips parted.

"Fuck, yes." Shane held him still and rammed up, nudging his swollen prostate on every stroke.

Rafa threw his head back, crying out and muttering, "Uh, uh, uh…" His cock bobbed, but Shane didn't touch it now, focusing on Rafa's ass and pounding his gland from different angles. He straightened out his legs, giving Rafa more room to maneuver. "Come on. That's it. Spray your cum all over me."

Rafa's cock strained and leaked, flushed dark red. Leaning his hands back on Shane's thighs, he arched, squeezing his ass, the sight and tight sensation stealing Shane's breath. His tan skin smooth to the touch, Rafa moaned, wild rings of curls spilling over his ears. His cry echoed over the beach as he came, splatting Shane's chest and neck with warm jizz.

After thrusting up a few times, Shane let go, emptying into him with low groans until they were both panting. "Love you, Raf," he muttered, his orgasm leaving him wrung out and vibrating with satisfaction.

Rafa flopped down, and Shane wrapped his arms around him. They were a sticky, sweaty mess, and the cool breeze danced over their skin. His dick softened, and he slipped it out, tenderly caressing Rafa's stretched, wet hole.

"I love the feel of your cum inside me," Rafa mumbled, kissing Shane's neck. "Sometimes I think I'll wake up and be back there in my room with wet sheets."

Shane knew *there* was the White House. "You're as far away as you can get. I promise. That cum in your ass is very real."

Rafa laughed softly. "You sure? I used to have some *very* vivid dreams."

Gently inching a finger inside, Shane played with the wet mess. "Positive." He caught Rafa's mouth in a long, slow kiss, and they broke apart when Shane's stomach rumbled.

"What was that you were saying about breakfast?" he asked.

Laughing, Rafa nipped his shoulder. "I was saying you were going to cook for me for a change."

"Hmm. That's not how I recall that conversation."

Rafa lifted his head, an exaggerated frown on his face. "Maybe you're having a senior moment. Should I be worried?"

"Oh, it's like that, is it?" He shoved Rafa off him, and they wrestled in the sand, rolling over and over and getting absolutely filthy. They raced into the waves, their laughter echoing with the seagulls' cries.

Chapter Two

"*Now that the yolks are room temperature, beat in the sugar until you have a thick, whitish foam.*"

Smirking to himself because he had the sense of humor of a twelve-year-old, Rafa paused the YouTube video on his iPad, which he'd propped up on the windowsill. The whir of the hand mixer filled the small kitchen, and he peered out the window by the sink at their little square of a backyard.

A gray bird pecked at the crumbs on the round patio table in the light from the window. Rafa had opened the sheer curtains, and the corners fluttered in the early evening breeze. It was barely six p.m., but already dark.

Even though the beach was a few blocks away, sand and salt permeated the air. Rafa's shoulders ached, and he rolled his neck as he beat the eggs. The swell alert on his phone had pinged earlier, and he'd tugged on his wetsuit and carried his board down to the water, catching a few good sets.

It was still crazy to think that he was actually in Australia. That he was actually surfing like he'd always dreamed. He wasn't half bad, although he had a lot to learn. Shane had taught him the basics and been so patient. As Rafa turned off the mixer and released the beaters, he realized he was grinning.

He was in *Australia*. *Surfing*. With *Shane*.

He washed the beaters in the sink, drying them with a wave-blue tea towel he'd bought up the coast in Surfers Paradise. How much did he love that there was actually a city in Queensland called *Surfers Paradise*? So far, Australia had been better than he'd even imagined.

Humming to himself, he whisked together honey and warm milk. The kitchen in their little house wasn't huge, and was actually about the same square size as the Diet Kitchen in the White House. No room for a table, and the white cupboards needed repainting.

Ugly, faded beige linoleum covered the floor, but it was smooth under his bare feet. There was a double sink, and even though the oven ran hot, it was good enough. It was *his*. Well, for as long as they rented the house, at least.

It was just a little one-bedroom, single-level bungalow, but it was enough. They'd furnished it with a reclaimed Victorian ash square dining table, a soft leather couch, and a king-sized bed. The floors were pale wood aside from the kitchen and bathroom, and the walls were painted a sunny cream. Sometimes Rafa would just walk around grinning, marveling that this was now his life.

He was about to start the video again when Skype bing-bonged. He stared at his mother's picture on the screen—her dark hair perfectly coiffed in a long bob, lips a deep red, and white teeth sparkling almost as much as the pearls around her neck. Tension snaked up his spine, and he patted at his unruly hair. It was useless, so he tapped the screen.

"Hey, Mom."

"Hello, darling. How are you?"

"Good. Great! Just doing some baking. Need to get more practice before school starts."

"Ah. How lovely. What are you making?"

"A Viennese sponge. Going to do a vanilla buttercream and serve it with fresh mandarin slices on top. They're in season now down here."

"That sounds absolutely delicious. Did I tell you that your father and I had dinner with Christian and Hadley in the city the other night at Bergadine? It was exquisite. The chef is known for his desserts. Trained at the culinary institute here."

"Mmm-hmm. Sounds awesome." One of the many upsides to his relationship with Shane was that Rafa's mother was now *very* interested in his culinary aspirations—particularly in him returning to the States to train, or going anywhere Shane wasn't.

"It's an excellent program, I'm told. If circumstances change, I'm sure we could get you enrolled right away. Or of course you could go to Paris. The original Cordon Bleu would be wonderful to experience. Ashleigh loved it in Paris, didn't she?"

He resisted the urge to roll his eyes. "Circumstances" was code for Shane. "Uh-huh."

"And Ashleigh's having a ball in New York. Hadley was saying they had lunch at the Public Kitchen. It's a real hot spot. I'm sure you'd love the food there."

Breathe. Smile. "I'm sure I would, but I'm happy here, Mom. Everything's amazing. Anyway, what are you up to? Wait, what time is it? Isn't it the middle of the night?" He squinted at the unfamiliar room behind her, which had some kind of framed art on the wall. Head shots?

"Just past four in the morning. I'm doing *The Today Show*. Talking about proper nutrition in schools." She smoothed a hand over her perfect hair. "Waiting in the green room."

"Oh, cool."

"And how are things in Curl?" Camila asked.

"Curl *Curl*. Lots of Aboriginal names are repeated, remember? And things are awesome."

"Excellent. I just wanted to go over a few items on our itinerary for next week. We'll all be having dinner with the prime minister and her family."

Rafa groaned. "*I* have to be there? Why?" He started whisking the milk and honey again. *Is Shane invited too?* Maybe they should cross that bridge later.

"Because you're a guest in her country, and she has three teenage children. You and Matthew will keep them engaged."

"Wait, Matty's coming?" He stopped mid-whisk. "Since when?"

Her smile tightened. "Since he tore his rotator cuff a few days ago. He needs to rest it, and his coaches agree getting him away will be the best medicine rather than moping around his apartment."

"Oh. That sucks that he's hurt, but I'm glad I'll get to see him." Even though it twinged that Rafa's brother hadn't told him himself.

As if reading his mind, she said, "Darling, he didn't tell anyone else yet. Christian and your sister don't know. Matthew's very upset. It could mean the end of his swimming career, and he doesn't want to face that. He's very much in his own head right now. But I know he's excited to see you."

Hurt gave way to a sticky swirl of guilt. Rafa had bottled up so much for so long—he shouldn't begrudge his brother time to figure out his shit. "I'm really excited to see him too. It'll be awesome. Even if we have to make small talk with the prime minister and her kids."

"Yes, it will, and yes, you do."

Chuckling, Rafa registered belatedly that the front door had opened, the wooden floor creaking with steps. As Shane came into the kitchen carrying cloth bags of groceries, Rafa opened his mouth to say he was Skyping, but Shane was already giving him a kiss, his lips dry and stubble scratchy.

"Hey, baby." Shane dropped the bags to the floor, then ran his hand over Rafa's ass. "What's cooking?"

"Hello, Agent Kendrick."

Inhaling sharply, Shane stumbled back and almost tripped

over the groceries. He cleared his throat and stood straighter, tugging at his T-shirt. They both wore jeans and tees most days. "Hello, Mrs. Castillo," he said in his deep, calm Secret Service voice. "And please, call me Shane now."

Which Rafa had reminded his mother of only a zillion times. On-screen, she smiled tightly and pointedly didn't say he should call her by her first name.

Rafa cleared his throat and said to Shane, "I was just making a cake and talking to Mom. Mom, I should get back to it, or I'll have to whip the yolks again. We'll see you next week. I'm looking forward to it."

And he was!

Mostly.

A little bit of the ice cracked free, and there was genuine warmth in his mother's eyes. "So am I, darling. We can't wait to see you. We've missed you so much. Happy baking."

Rafa tapped the red button and sagged against the counter. "I don't know why she has to make everything so…" He waved his hand, milk flying off the whisk. He put the bowl on the counter and grabbed a cloth to wipe the cupboards that had been hit.

Shane snorted as he grabbed a Toohey's Extra Dry from the fridge and twisted off the cap. "Because it brings her a twisted sense of joy?" He took a gulp, then grimaced. "Sorry. Look, if you were my kid, I wouldn't want you shacking up with me either."

"*Shacking up?*" He laughed. "Is that what we're doing?"

"Yep." Shane drew him close and gave him a long, slow, *filthy* kiss that sent blood rushing to Rafa's dick. "Living in wonderful sin. Wouldn't have it any other way."

Rafa's smile froze, and before he could stop himself, he blurted, "Like, not ever?"

"What?" Shane frowned.

Grabbing the bowl and metal whisk, Rafa frothed up the now-cold milk and honey again. "Huh? Nothing. Forget it." It really was stupid. He and Shane had only been together, what? Barely six months. If they were going to get married, it wouldn't be for ages. Probably years. He shouldn't read anything into Shane's off-hand comment.

Shane was still staring at him with that furrow between his brows, and Rafa leaned over and gave him a kiss. "My mom just gets me all worked up. Hey, Matty's coming with them. So maybe it'll be slightly less awkward? Oh, and we have to go for dinner at the prime minister's house. I mean, you don't have to come if you don't want to."

Shane smirked. "I think it'll be better for all parties if I sit that one out."

"Yeah. I guess so." Although Shane was his partner, so why shouldn't he come? If Chris and Hadley were visiting, no one would expect Hadley to stay at home. He whipped harder, the whisk clanking on the sides of the bowl.

Shane started unpacking the groceries. "I'm sure you'll have a good time. Does this go in the fridge or cupboard?" He held up a jar of Vegemite.

"Hmm. Cupboard, I think? We could google it. I imagine Australians will have some very strong views on the subject."

"I imagine they will." He opened the jar and sniffed. "I don't think we're going to like this."

"Me either, but I want to at least try it so I know what it tastes like. Apparently you're supposed to have it on toast with butter."

"Sounds like a waste of perfectly good butter."

Rafa laughed. "It really does."

He finally got the cake in the oven as Shane told him about a potential security contract, then Rafa quickly made the frosting and set it aside for when the cake cooled. He gave Shane one of the beaters from the electric hand mixer, keeping the other for himself.

Shane licked the metal slowly, groaning. "Now *this* is an excellent use of butter."

Twisting his tongue in and around his own beater, Rafa mumbled, "Uh-huh."

"Come here." Shane watched him, his blue eyes avid.

With a low pulse of desire, Rafa closed the distance between them. Shane caught his lips, licking at a blob of frosting in the corner of Rafa's mouth. Their tongues were coated in sugar, the creaminess of the butter lingering in their kisses.

Rafa murmured, "Gives *umami* a whole new level." The so-called fifth sense described aftertaste and "mouth feel," and in that moment, he couldn't imagine anything better.

With a chuckle, Shane licked the last of the vanilla cream from his beater and kissed Rafa with it still on his tongue, the frosting sweet and light, yet thick and rich. "Mmm. The things you do in the kitchen. And with your tongue."

"Only downside to getting a KitchenAid one day. Can't have a beater each like with the hand mixer."

"I can just use a spoon." Shane took another lick of Rafa's lips. "Which color did you want? We can buy one tomorrow."

Of course *we* really meant Shane, since Rafa still wasn't making any money. He'd planned on getting a job in a restaurant, but the media shit-storm once his relationship with Shane was revealed had been more intense than he'd expected. He should have sucked it up and tried to get a job anyway, but Shane had insisted money wasn't an issue. Still, it made Rafa uneasy.

Rafa shook his head. "No, that's okay. I want to buy one when I get a job. Or I guess I could take money out of my trust fund like I did for tuition and my car, but… After school starts, I can figure out when I can work, and I'll pay you back for—"

"For *nothing*."

"For my half of the rent, for food, for gas, for…" Rafa waved his hand around. "Everything. I want to contribute."

Shane took his hands. "Baby, you *contribute* more than

enough just by being here. Don't stress about getting a job. Settle into school first. There's no rush. We're partners. This isn't about keeping score. I don't give a shit about money."

Rafa exhaled, some of the tension easing. He knew Shane meant it, although he also knew the money would run out eventually. "Okay." His timer dinged, and he went to test the cake layers.

Partners.

Rafa rolled the word over in his mind, smiling to himself as he pulled a toothpick out of the center of one cake. It came away still a bit gooey, so he closed the oven door and reset the timer. He would still pay his share when he could so their joint bank account wouldn't only be funded by Shane.

He could ask his parents for more money from his trust—which he couldn't freely access until he was twenty-five, which wasn't for three years. But trust-fund money came with guilt-trips and stress. He told himself that Shane was right. They were partners in every other way. In the ways that really counted.

Shane puttered about, folding clothes in the dining room where their laundry basket always seemed to end up once clothes were brought in off the line. The washer did have a drying function, but it took a ridiculously long time, and Rafa understood why laundry was always flapping in Australian backyards.

He boiled fresh noodles and heated up leftover beef khao soi he'd made, the Thai curry spicy and creamy. When the cakes were on cooling racks, he checked the clock and called, "Can you turn it on?"

A few moments later, the murmur of the TV filled the house. A few ads played as Rafa drained the noodles and cut fresh lime wedges. Then the volume went up and a familiar male voice intoned, "Previously on *MasterChef Australia*."

Rafa listened to the recap and plated their dinner, scooping tender beef chunks and sauce over the hot noodles, then sprinkling crispy fried noodles on top and tucking a lime wedge on the side. He hurried into the living room and passed Shane a plate and cutlery. "Do you want another beer?"

"That would be great, thanks. Mmm, this smells amazing."

"It's just the same as yesterday."

Sitting back on the couch with his feet on the low wooden coffee table, Shane grinned as he squeezed lime juice over his dinner. "It was amazing then too. I could eat this every day."

Returning with two beers, Rafa settled beside him, sinking into the dark leather couch. The contestants were being interviewed about how nervous they were for that day's challenge. He grinned in anticipation. Australian reality shows were on five nights a week, which was completely insane—and completely addicting.

Shane's phone buzzed, and he pulled it out of his pocket. "I need to take this, sorry. It's about that security contract with the Chinese corporation."

"You want me to pause it?"

"Nah, this'll only take a minute and they recap everything a million times anyway."

Shane went into the bedroom and closed the door. Commercials came on soon, and Rafa muted the TV and chewed a mouthful of spicy, milky noodles. He listened to the comforting murmur of Shane's voice and got up to straighten the painting over the TV, pushing up the right side just a hair.

They'd bought the painting of two surfers at a gallery in Bondi. Shane had insisted he wanted real art for the first time, not something generic from IKEA or Bed, Bath & Beyond. Rafa stepped back and made sure it was straight.

The oil paint swirled in rich strokes of blue, green, turquoise, and golden white, depicting two surfers straddling their boards out on the ocean, waiting for a swell, silhouetted against the sun above them. The point of view was from beneath, the sun's rays penetrating the clear water, their feet dangling. Nothing was sharp, instead flowing and soft, dreamlike.

It filled Rafa with peace, and he smiled to himself. The endless commercials were still on, and he grabbed a duster from the drawer under the TV stand and ran it over the framed pictures on a side table.

There was one of his family taken at an event, all straight backs and wide, presidential smiles. His curls were slicked straight and his chinos pressed. Rafa blinked at the image of his former self, remembering how sad and scared that young man had been.

He really needed a new, informal family picture. He'd have to make a point to take some shots when his parents and Matthew visited. Too bad Adriana and Chris couldn't come, but they had jobs they couldn't abandon for three weeks.

There was a pic of Rafa and Ashleigh from their UVA graduation in their gowns and mortarboards, arms slung around each other, her golden hair flowing and cheeks dimpling with her grin. A pang rolled through him. Shit, he really needed to Skype her soon and catch up.

She was busting her butt as an admin for a nightmare, Miranda Priestly type of boss. Apparently it was a necessity to live your own *The Devil Wears Prada* experience to make it in the fashion world.

He ran the duster over the silver frame holding a picture of another college graduation. Shane had a lot more hair and fewer lines around his eyes when he smiled. The Kendricks beamed so brightly Rafa could practically feel the warm glow of their love and pride.

Shane's mom had been short and a little frumpy, his dad balding and paunchy. They'd looked utterly normal in the best way. He knew Shane still blamed himself that they died in a fire and he wasn't home, even though he'd been an adult living his own life across the country.

Rafa ached that he'd never meet them. Would they have liked him? Or would they have thought he was too young? He dusted the frame again needlessly. It was the only picture of his parents Shane had left after the fire had destroyed his childhood home. He shivered. As frustrating as his parents could be, the thought of losing them was unbearable.

Back on the couch, he unmuted the TV and returned to his dinner, getting swept up in the competition. Before long, Shane flopped back down beside him and asked, "Okay, what do they have to do here?"

"See all those light boxes on the long table? Each box has a super thin slice of food on it, and they go in turns and identify which food it is. All the easy ones are gone—kiwi fruit, tomato, lime. First three people who get one wrong end up having to cook in the elimination round."

Shane nodded and took a mouthful of beef and noodles as they watched. He squeezed Rafa's thigh. "Delicious as usual. Thank you."

Rafa shrugged, warmth filling his chest. "Anytime."

As the competition went down to the wire, Rafa grabbed the little notebook he kept on the coffee table and jotted down a few of the food items he'd never heard of, like rambutan.

Shane asked, "Have you used that black garlic? I don't think I've ever had it."

"It's usually in Asian cooking. I'll get some at the market if I can. I have a few ideas for a new recipe." Since he'd be learning the French basics at the Cordon Bleu, he was brushing up on other cuisines in the meantime.

He paused the show before the cook-off, and he quickly iced the cake and peeled a few juicy mandarins while Shane did the dishes. They didn't have a dishwasher, but Rafa had gotten used to that in the Diet Kitchen. Shane didn't seem to mind either, humming softly.

Giving the side of the cake one last swipe, Rafa licked the extra icing off the knife. Shane cleared his throat loudly and cocked an eyebrow. He asked, "Aren't you going to share?"

With a grin, Rafa slid his hand behind Shane's head and pulled him down for a long, sweet kiss.

Chapter Three

"Can you repeat that?" Shane asked, his stomach knotting. The man spoke clearly and confidently. "There's been a change in plans, and we require your testimony at the inquest in person. We realize this is short notice, but the panel feels it's necessary."

Shane sat heavily on the deck chair in the backyard, residual sand gritty between his toes and wetsuit clinging to his body. A bird whistled, the sun peeking out from clouds. "You understand I live in Australia now? That I have business commitments?" *That I have a goddamned life, unlike when I was in the Service?*

The man's tone remained coolly professional and unruffled. "We apologize for the inconvenience."

"Uh-huh." The Secret Service hadn't even had Nguyen or Harris or someone Shane knew call him.

"You understand how important this inquest is? After your many years of service—"

"Enough. I'll come." He sure as hell didn't need a patriotic speech on his duty. "What's the flight info? I presume the Service has it arranged already."

"Yes. We'll forward you everything you need. The flight leaves Sydney on Tuesday morning."

They said their terse goodbyes, and Shane stared at his phone screen. App icons skirted the edges of a background image of Rafa laughing with his surfboard, wet curls hanging around his eyes, waves gleaming behind him. The screen went dark after a minute.

Tuesday morning. So, just before the Castillos would arrive in Sydney. He stood and paced back and forth along the strip of grass beyond the shaded stone patio. The blades of grass were cool between his toes. He tried to fight it, but relief washed through him at the thought of not having to deal with Rafa's parents.

But of course he would—they were visiting for weeks, and his testimony at the inquest wouldn't take more than a couple of days. This would just delay the inevitable and likely upset Rafa. "Shit," he muttered. Rafa would have to face his parents alone at first.

Now a shiver of guilt snaked through him. He shouldn't feel relieved in the slightest to be leaving Rafa alone and vulnerable to the pressure his parents would undoubtedly apply. They wanted him to come back to the States. Of course they did—Shane didn't even blame them for that. Most parents wanted their children near them.

Hell, he couldn't even blame them for not wanting Rafa to be with Shane. The age difference, the way they met—Shane wouldn't like it either in their shoes. Yet his own protectiveness for Rafa rose up, and he gripped his phone as he paced faster.

Rafa was *happy* in Australia. With Shane. What they had together was *good*. There was no way Shane would give any of it up without a fight. Neither would Rafa. He had to be confident in that.

But what if—

"Stop." He breathed deeply, nodding to himself. They would weather whatever storm the Castillos might bring. It was an inconvenience that Shane had to leave for the inquest, but he'd be back before Rafa knew it. It would be fine.

What about Rafa being alone in the house?

Shane forced an inhalation again, wishing the yard had more pacing room. It was ridiculous to have nerves about Rafa sleeping alone in the house. He was a grown man. His father was no longer president—Rafa didn't need protection anymore.

Yet the memory of the bone-shaking terror Shane had experienced when Rafa had been kidnapped gripped him. Even though it was broad daylight, for a moment he was back in the rain and mud in the dark, utterly desperate.

"Fuck!" A bird squawked and flapped away at Shane's exclamation. He had to get control of himself. The nightmares were bad enough—he had to let Rafa live his life and not hover over him. Rafa would eventually resent it, and it wasn't healthy.

But anything can happen at any time. There are a million variables. What if he needs me and I'm not here? What if he gets hurt because I'm not here?

"I can't always be here," he said aloud. "This is the way life works." He wished he sounded more convincing.

Tapping his phone, Shane checked the time. There were still a couple of hours before his business dinner in the city with new clients, but standing around worrying about what might happen wouldn't do anything. Rafa would be safe and sound, and their relationship was solid. The Castillos wouldn't change that, even if they had time with Rafa alone.

Shane snorted, laughing to himself as he peeled off his wetsuit and went inside for a shower, shaking off his ridiculous fears. Did he think he was going to be glued to Rafa's side every moment whenever Rafa was with his family? Of course not. Rafa loved his parents, but he didn't let them control him anymore. And he would lock the doors and be perfectly fine while Shane was away.

After a hot shower and a shave, Shane toweled off and dressed in a suit, padding back into the bathroom. The tiles were still damp, condensation clinging to the edges of the mirror over the sink.

He slipped in his earbuds and pressed play on the podcast he'd been listening to earlier about Chinese-Australian relations to give him background on his new project. Always good to understand the political climate. He splashed some aftershave on his freshly smooth cheeks and brushed his teeth.

Lifting his chin, he straightened his burgundy tie and examined his collar in the mirror as the woman on the podcast detailed a trade agreement. Then Rafa appeared behind him in the reflection wearing the jeans and tee he'd tugged on after surfing to go to the market. Shane's heart skipped a beat. He hit pause on his old-school iPod and pulled out one of the earbuds as he looked over his shoulder. "Hey."

"Hey," Rafa replied, biting his lip.

Ugh, Shane had to tell him the bad news. Or maybe it wasn't actually bad—perhaps it was a good thing to give Rafa a few days alone with his parents. Some quality time to catch up? Regardless, he had to tell him about the change in plans. He turned. "So…"

Before he could decide on the right approach, Rafa stepped back a pace, his gaze sweeping Shane up and down. Rafa licked his lips, sending a spark down Shane's spine. "Haven't seen you in a suit since the White House."

"I guess you haven't." He ran a hand over his charcoal jacket. "I'll be dressing up more now that I'll be meeting with clients."

"Mmm. You shaved too. Agent Kendrick was always perfectly groomed." Rafa walked—no, *prowled*—toward him. He reached up and touched the earbud still in Shane's ear, and Shane realized it was similar to the Secret Service earpiece he used to wear.

He smirked. "Should I put on my sunglasses?"

Rafa's knees hit the tile, and he yanked at Shane's belt, pushing him back against the sink. His voice pitched in a low growl as he demanded, "Fuck my mouth, Agent Kendrick." He pushed down Shane's pants and boxer-briefs and freed his cock, which sprang to life.

Shit, he had to spill the news, but as Rafa sucked him to full hardness with needy little moans and slurps, Shane rocked deeper into his mouth. The rest of the world fell away, and there was only the sweet suction.

He muttered, "Goddamn, baby."

Rafa moaned around his cock, his lips stretched. Shane gripped his head, threading his fingers through the curls as he took control with little thrusts, careful not to go too deep. Rafa gazed up at him with such adoration it made his heart clench. Wearing his suit, Shane could almost imagine they were back at the White House. A forbidden thrill shot through him. "You like eating my dick, Valor?"

Rafa groaned, spit dribbling from the corners of his mouth, his throat constricting wonderfully as he swallowed around Shane's cock and gripped his thighs above where Shane's dress pants bunched around his knees.

"No hands," Shane ordered, and Rafa let go. "Get your cock out. Are you hard for me?"

As Shane continued fucking his mouth, supporting Rafa's skull, Rafa fumbled with his jeans and reached into his boxers to pull out his shaft. Shane could glimpse it—the red, shiny head peeking out from his foreskin. Rafa breathed hard though his nose, wet slurps and smacks filling the air.

"Jerk yourself."

He did, his hand flying as he kept his mouth wide, taking everything Shane gave him. "Uhhh, uhh," he groaned.

"That's it." Shane spread his legs, pleasure building with each push into Rafa's wet, hot mouth. "Make sure you don't come on my suit."

For a moment, Shane thought Rafa was choking, then realized with a skip of his thumping heart that he was laughing. Shane laughed too, and Rafa stared up with his eyes full of light and unwavering trust.

Primal possessiveness drummed through Shane. He thrilled in being the only man who'd ever been lucky enough to touch Rafa.

His chest tightened with affection, his head spinning and breath short.

Balls tightening, he rocked deeper, orgasm taking over. He grunted as he shot down Rafa's throat, Rafa's eyes watering as he swallowed convulsively. Shane pulled out and sprayed the last of it on Rafa's face, the white stark against his freckles and tan skin, a long string of spit and cum hanging between the end of his cock and Rafa's glistening, swollen lips.

"Fuck, you're so pretty," Shane whispered.

With a gasp, Rafa closed his eyes and came, jerking himself rapidly, crying softly, "Oh, oh, oh..." Then he tipped forward, his head against Shane's bare hip, his arms wrapping around his thighs. Shane petted Rafa's soft hair.

After a minute, Rafa sat back on his heels and peered down, chest still heaving. "I think I missed your cuff by, like, an inch."

They laughed, and Shane tugged him to his feet. "It would have been worth the dry-cleaning bill."

Rafa gave him a musky kiss, and Shane licked into his mouth tenderly. The reminder that he had to tell Rafa about the change in plans echoed dully, but soon they were laughing about Shane's wrinkled pants, and he had to change his suit and head into the city to make sure he was early for dinner. There was no point in upsetting Rafa now and then having to turn around to leave. It could wait.

BURNING.

Flames leap from the second-floor windows, his parents screaming inside, trapped. Not just Mom and Dad—Rafa too, calling for him, his voice hoarse, cracking.

"Shane!"

Feet stuck in mud, rain blurring everything, but not dampening the fire at all. Heat scorches his face and hands as he flounders in the muck, everyone he loves in agony. He heaves himself up, useless legs collapsing under him. Mom and Dad and Rafa scream and—

Heart about to explode, Shane gasped awake. He was curled naked on his side, body rigid and aching, throat dry. The blackout curtains did their job, and he was in darkness. Had he shouted aloud?

"Okay?" Rafa mumbled, his cool fingers wrapping around Shane's shoulder.

Can't let him see me like this!

Panic roaring, Shane stumbled up and dove into the bathroom, flipping the lock behind him. Knees jelly, he leaned against the door, the fuzzy terrycloth of their hanging bathrobes feeling too rough against his fevered skin. He didn't turn on the light, the frosted glass window beyond the toilet admitting a silvery glow. Rafa's jars of shells were shadows on the windowsill.

"Shane?" Rafa's knock jarred Shane's bones even though it wasn't more than a gentle tap. "What's wrong?" The door handle jiggled. "Oh. What…" After a few moments, he asked again, "Shane?"

"I think it's something I ate," he scraped out. "Don't worry, baby. Go back to bed." He moved away from the door and stood closer to the toilet, leaning both hands on the counter. His head pounded as if he had a hangover, that heavy feeling of dehydration even though he'd only had two glasses of wine at dinner.

"The portions were so small at that fancy restaurant I went to that I had street meat on the way back to the car. Hot dogs are always a crapshoot. In this case, literally."

"Shit. Um, literally."

Shane managed a strained laugh, his pulse finally slowing as he blinked away the nightmare images. Rafa was right outside the door. He was whole. He was safe.

Breathe.

Yet grief rippled through him, the dream voices of his parents and the vision of their house in flames still fresh, a raw wound.

"Do we have any Pepto or anything?" Rafa tried the door again. "I want to help. I can run out to the all-night drugstore. There'd be no traffic."

"No, no. It's okay." Shane lowered the toilet seat and sat wearily. "I just need to get it out. Trust me, you don't want to smell this."

"I can handle a little shit. Or a lot of it. Whatever."

"I'm good. Go back to bed. I think there is some Pepto. I'll just wait a few minutes and see if anything else is coming."

After a few moments, Rafa reluctantly said, "Okay."

Closing his eyes, Shane sat there until his heart beat normally and the sheen of sweat on his skin had dried. He ran his toes over the edges of the tiles, counting the seconds of his inhalations and exhalations, holding his breath in-between for the same amount of time.

He despised his weakness.

Guilt laid heavily over him like an itchy blanket. It was a stupid little fib to say he had diarrhea, but he hated lying regardless. Still, there was no need to worry Rafa with the nightmares. They were temporary. After the inquest, they'd stop. He could put all that shit to rest again. Rafa had moved past it so strongly. Shane sure as hell wasn't going to drag him back into it.

Fuck. Shane hadn't told him yet about having to return to the States either. By the time he'd gotten home from the long dinner meeting, which had ended with handshakes and a promise of couriered contracts to be signed, Rafa had been asleep in bed, the small TV on the dresser playing an international cricket match. Rafa had stirred when Shane slipped in beside him, but there'd been no sense in waking him for bad news.

But really, was it bad? Maybe it was all for the best. He rubbed his face. No, he knew Rafa would be upset, and that's why he was putting it off. He muttered, "Fuck." He'd tell him first thing in the morning.

After long enough, he flushed the toilet and washed his hands before creeping back to bed. He'd barely touched the mattress when Rafa spoke.

"You don't need to be quiet. I'm awake."

"Go back to sleep. It's late. Or early. Either way." He curled on his side, facing the covered windows.

"Do you feel better?" Rafa didn't sound sleepy at all. He smoothed his palm over Shane's back. "You're so tense. Did you have a nightmare or something?"

"No. Just the shits." As Rafa scooted closer and kneaded Shane's tight shoulders, Shane couldn't help but relax into it, even though Rafa should have been sleeping, not taking care of him. "Mmm. Feels good. Thanks."

Rafa hummed, gently digging into Shane's muscles. After a few minutes, he whispered, "You know you can tell me if something's bothering you."

Shane's heart skipped. "Everything's great."

"So why did you just tense right up?" Rafa massaged him gently, thumbs pressing wonderfully at the base of Shane's skull.

"You just hit a tight spot. Honestly, baby. I'm great."

Rafa snuggled closer, spooning Shane and kissing the back of his neck tenderly. "Do you need anything? Do you want some water?"

I'm the one who's supposed to take care of you. Shane shook his head, trying not to tense as guilt tugged, a fishhook in his gut. "You need to sleep." He wriggled and turned, urging Rafa over as well until Shane was the one spooning him. "Thanks for your help."

"I didn't really do anything."

"Sure you did. I think my stomach's settled now." He kissed Rafa's head. Curls tickled his nose, and the heat of Rafa's body in his arms was familiar and grounding. "'Night."

"'Night. You promise you'll wake me if you need anything?"

"Promise."

The minutes ticked by with Rafa safe and warm in his arms, and Shane willed himself to just go back to sleep. Yet the whisper of guilt grew louder until he said, "You still awake?"

Rafa shifted onto his back and peered up at him. In the faint slice of ambient light from the bathroom window, Shane could just make out his face. "Yeah. What do you need?" He rubbed Shane's arm soothingly.

"I got a phone call today. I have to go back to the States for the inquiry in a few days. I leave Tuesday."

His turn to tense up, Rafa blinked at him in the shadows. "*What?* Why? They said you could testify from here."

"They changed their position."

"But my parents and Matty are coming." His voice rose. "I want—you're not going to be here?"

Shane tried for a light tone. "Hey, I'm sure they won't mind one bit."

"But I want them to see us together. I want to show them they're wrong!" He flopped his arms down at his sides. "This really sucks. I had it all planned out in my head. And wait, why didn't you tell me as soon as you found out?"

"I'm sorry. It didn't seem like the right time."

"Why?" After a moment, Rafa said, "Oh. Fine, maybe right after sex wouldn't have been the greatest timing, but still."

"I was going to tell you first thing in the morning." That was the truth, at least. "But I should have told you right away. Look, I'll be back as soon as possible. It'll be several days at the most. Matthew and your parents will be here a few weeks. I'll hardly miss anything."

"But... You'll be back for sure before we go on the fancy train to Perth?"

"Definitely."

Rafa sighed. "You don't work for the Secret Service anymore.

Can they make you go? It's not a trial; it's an inquiry or whatever."

"I'm sure they could come up with a legal reason. But regardless, I don't want it to become a hostile situation. After what happened with Al, and falling in love with you, they don't owe me any favors."

"What Alan did wasn't your fault."

"He was my partner. I should have known."

Rafa sighed heavily. "He hid it. You couldn't read his mind. You're too hard on yourself."

A memory bloomed—the sight of Rafa stuffed into that box, battered and terrified, eyes wide and wild. Shane shuddered and drew him close again, burying his face in his neck. He inhaled deeply, the faint scent of sea and sand and *Rafa* filling his senses.

"Maybe you should stay at the hotel with your folks instead of here while I'm gone."

"What?" Rafa jerked, and Shane raised his head to see the frown creasing his face.

"It's safer."

Rafa's eyebrows shot up. "And our home isn't? No one's after me. I'm safe here. You realize zillions of people live by themselves, right?"

"I know. But you never have."

"Huh." He frowned. "I guess I haven't. I went from the White House to living with you." He rubbed his hand over Shane's chest, teasing the hair there. "It'll be good for me to spend a few nights here alone. I'm not a kid, and now that I'm out of the crazy White House bubble, I want to be normal. And it's normal for people to be alone sometimes."

"Uh-huh." He was absolutely right, so Shane tried to ignore the persistent tug of worry in his gut.

A little smile lifted Rafa's lips. "I'll still miss you, if that's what you're worried about." He drew him down closer, and Shane rested his cheek on Rafa's chest, the sparse hair tickling. It felt so safe and good, being held, yet guilt tugged again that Rafa was taking care of him.

Rafa held him tightly, running his fingers over the stubble on Shane's head. "Relax. We'll be fine. Everything's all right."

Eventually, Rafa's breathing evened out, and Shane listened to the steady echo of his heart, blinking into the darkness, the threat of nightmares keeping him wide awake.

Chapter Four

"WHOA." ON THE screen of Rafa's iPad in the Skype window, Ashleigh's jaw dropped. "Did I step into a time machine? Are you back in the White House?"

"What?" Rafa fidgeted on the patio chair, resisting the urge to touch his hair. He fiddled with the zipper of his hoodie instead. "Looks like you got a haircut too. I love it! Did you dye it? It's still blond, but…" He squinted at the screen.

Grinning, she turned her head left and right, showing off the sleek bob that swayed just under her chin. "Thank you, and yeah, did burgundy undertones. It's all the rage right now, and I have to keep on the cutting edge, of course. Also, nice deflection from your retro hair." Her eyes narrowed. "Are you wearing chinos? Stand up."

"No! Actually, I'm in my underwear."

She waggled her eyebrows. "In that case, *definitely* stand up."

His laughter helped chip away at the block of ice in his chest that had formed steadily since he'd said goodbye to Shane the day before. He peered around at the dark neighboring houses, the sky turning a light gray on the horizon. "I should go inside, actually. Don't want anyone to overhear. And it's freezing out here." When he hadn't been able to get back to sleep, he'd craved the fresh air.

"Hasn't it been months since you've had paps skulking in the bushes?"

"Yeah, but better safe than sorry. Hold on." He grabbed his iPad and hurried inside, carefully locking the sliding door behind him and putting the length of wood in place on the metal track. Shane had sawed the piece of lumber himself and called it old-school security.

Kicking off his flip-flops, he shivered and went through to the living room. He grabbed a throw blanket from the back of the couch before settling himself.

"You should still be in bed anyway, shouldn't you?" She raised a sculpted eyebrow. A delicate silver chain necklace rested against the tops of her collarbones, and her scoop-necked blouse was black. On the wall behind her desk was a huge framed fashion magazine.

"Yes, but..." He sighed. "It's actually weird being here alone. This is literally the first night in my entire life I have been in a house totally alone. I heard a noise, and I had to get up and figure out what it was."

"And?"

"I still don't know, so I'm sure it was nothing." He glanced over at the empty dining room. "Nothing was out of place, and all the doors and windows are locked. It's not like kidnappers are coming after me again. It's stupid to be paranoid. I mean, I'm a *guy*."

Ashleigh smiled sympathetically. "Trust me, as a woman, I've done the 'what was that noise?' dance plenty of times. And you're allowed to be a little nervous. Men are actually permitted to experience a range of emotions without being deemed 'womanly.' Just for the record."

"You're right, as usual."

She sat up straighter, the top of her head disappearing. "Excuse me? 'Usual'? No, no, that would be 'always.' Okay, except that one time on January twentieth of last year. Approximately three-twelve p.m. Other than that, I'm always right."

"I stand corrected." He chuckled. Ashleigh always had a way of making him feel better. "Seen any good Renaissance exhibits lately?"

She smiled at their old code they'd used when they were closeted. "Sadly, I've been too busy working twelve-hour days to find a woman to talk Botticelli with. At least you're riding your Harley daily now."

He grinned. "Yeah. It's pretty amazing."

Ashleigh glanced left and right. "If I wasn't at work, I'd ask for details. No one's around right now, but still. Alas."

"Isn't Skyping at work risky? I didn't expect you to answer. I assume Miranda's not in the office." Ashleigh's boss was really named Chyler something, but they never referred to her by her real name.

"Obvi." She sipped yellowy soup from a spoon. "Miranda frowns upon any sort of break at lunch. Not to mention the consumption of food. Fortunately for us minions, she's in LA at the moment." With a roll of her eyes, she added, "This morning she called me from the back of her chauffeured Town Car to ask for last-minute lunch reservations at the hottest spot in Beverly Hills. I guess she was feeling contemplative, and she was all, 'These people in Beverly Hills, they're not like you and me, Ashleigh. This is *real* wealth.' She just loves to think of herself as one of the little people. As if Miranda and I are on the *same level* somehow. I mean, she just bought a *horse*."

"Wow. How much does a horse cost?"

"Well, since I looked at the bill of sale, I can tell you this one was a hundred and twenty-five grand. Let's just say that if you compare that to my salary, that horse is *significantly* more valued. I don't think Finian's Glory will have to survive on ramen either."

Concern laced with guilt tugged at Rafa. "Are you sure I can't lend you some money?"

Ashleigh's mouth tightened. "I'm positive. Babe, you and your family have already done so much for me. Chris and Hadley take me out to dinner every couple weeks, and I wouldn't even have this job if it wasn't for Hadley. Or the *Vogue* internship your dad scored me last year in Paris. I'm doing fine. My roommates are cool. I'll make a livable wage eventually. Besides, it's my choice to spend my money on doing my hair and stuff like that."

"Yeah, but in your job you have to. My trust fund—"

"Is *yours*. Besides, aren't you stressing about not 'paying your own way'?" She'd lifted her fingers in air quotes, red nail polish gleaming, and now they dropped out of frame. "Even though Shane doesn't mind?"

He squirmed. "Yes. It's just... I've never had to worry about money—I know how lucky I am. But I don't want to be a kid who can't support himself. I want to be a man. Equal, you know?"

"I get it. But you will be! You're going to be a fabulous chef with a fabulous career."

"I hope so." He shrugged. "We'll see."

Ashleigh swallowed a mouthful of soup and said, "Don't let your folks shake your confidence. Even if that's not their intention, we both know what a number parents can do on our heads."

More guilt flooded him. At least his parents had supported him when he came out. "Have you heard from them at all?"

She shrugged, lips pressed into a tight, toothless smile. "It is what it is. I always knew when I came out, they'd freak. It doesn't fit in their tidy little Christian plans to have a lesbo daughter. They're hoping it's a phase and I'll come to my senses. They blame you, of course. Like it was catching or something." She shrugged again, and Rafa longed to hug her. She said, "Anyway. Back to you. Look, I know it's going to be...challenging to see your folks again. But chill. Breathe. Be yourself."

"I know. I will." Still, his cheeks went hot, and he couldn't stop himself from touching his hair, which he'd had cut to a couple of inches, the ends just waving. "But my hair was getting too long—it was in my eyes." That wasn't a lie, at least.

"Okay." She took another sip of soup and watched him patiently.

He sighed. "Look, I know it's stupid, but I just don't want us to fight about my hair."

"Wasn't it more your issue than theirs? Have they said anything about it the past few months?"

"No, but we have enough contentious stuff to deal with."

A sly smile tugged her red lips. "Like your Secret Service agent *lovah?*" She dropped the teasing tone. "Speaking of, I got your text about him having to go back to DC. That blows, babe."

"Yeah." He tried to smile it off, but in the little window in the corner of the screen he could see it was more of a grimace. "The timing sucks. But he's going to come back as soon as he can. Just go and testify, crash at his friend Darnell's, then back on a plane."

"Cool. Darnell's the cop, right?"

"Uh-huh. He seems nice. Really funny." He also seemed very…adult, but Rafa didn't voice that. He was supposed to be a grown-up too.

Ashleigh's gaze went distant, and she nodded and called to someone, "Yes, that envelope, please. Overnight delivery. Thanks." She looked back to Rafa. "I'd better get back to work. The office is quiet right now since most of them are in LA, but Miranda still has her spies."

"Thanks for picking up when I called. I needed the pep talk." He glanced at the time. "My cab's coming soon anyway. Their flight gets in just after six."

"I thought you got a car?"

"I did, but they'll have an armored limo. They still have their security detail and all that. Not as many agents as before, but when they travel there's still an advanced team, and a detail with them and one behind. As time goes by, they'll probably have fewer agents, but for now, they still get threats and stuff." He snorted.

"Besides, I can't see my mom squeezing into my little used Toyota hatchback with Dad, Matty, and an agent."

Ashleigh laughed. "Now there's a mental image. Maybe an agent could sit on her lap. She might enjoy it."

"On that note…"

They blew kisses to each other, and the call ended. Snuggled under the velvety blanket, Rafa wished he could stay there and not face the day. But hiding wouldn't solve anything, so he reluctantly got up.

He wandered to the kitchen and opened the fridge, but his stomach was too acidy to think of eating. In the bedroom, he opened the closet and eyed his side. It was mostly jeans and shorts, his massive collection of T-shirts shoved in his drawers in the dresser. But there was one pair of chinos hanging there, neatly pressed and waiting.

Squaring his shoulders, he went for jeans, but traded his tee and hoodie for a green button-up shirt, leaving the ends untucked. He checked the time and padded back to the kitchen. Still had twenty minutes.

Being completely alone overnight was strange. Somehow it felt different than during the day. Before Shane had left for the airport the previous morning, he'd told Rafa for the hundredth time to lock all the doors and windows and call the Australian version of 911, which Rafa had programmed in his phone in case he panicked and forgot it. Shane had even toyed with installing a security system, but they were only renting the house.

Rafa smiled to himself, running his fingers over one of Shane's suits hanging in the closet. He'd convinced Shane there was no need to be paranoid, but he had to admit that when he was completely alone and didn't keep his mind occupied, it did start to wander and spin out *what-if* scenarios. Everything from the return of his kidnappers to a random burglary circled his mind.

The memory of waking in the pitch black of that cramped

metal box spiked his pulse, his breath catching. His therapist had given him deep-breathing exercises, and he did them now, inhaling and exhaling steadily. Most of the time, he was okay. But in the small hours of the night and morning, when the world was silent and still, it was harder.

Feeling foolish but unable to resist, he buried his face in the dark fabric of the suit Shane had worn to his business dinner the other day. Shane's cologne lingered faintly—a woodsy sweetness—along with a hint of his body, the musk that was all him and like no one else.

Rafa inhaled deeply. Everything was all right. It would be awesome to see his parents and brother again. He didn't have to freak out. But as he shut the closet, his stomach knotted. It was the first time he'd be truly face-to-face with his Mom and Dad since he'd called to tell them the truth about his relationship with Shane. Did they really accept it?

He was about to find out.

"RAFA! WHERE'S SHANE?"

"Uh…" Just inside the terminal, he stared at the young woman rushing toward him with a cameraman in tow. Shit, was he already so out of practice with the media that he couldn't even get "no comment" out of his mouth?

Fortunately, a middle-aged woman sporting a crisp pantsuit, her dark hair pulled into a bun, appeared seemingly from nowhere and blocked the reporter's path. "Mr. Castillo won't be speaking to the media. Thank you."

As the American reporter shouted more questions, Rafa gratefully let the Secret Service agent lead him away, a man in a suit and earpiece following behind them, familiar sunglasses tucked into his breast pocket.

Rafa had worn a windbreaker since it was still chilly when he'd left the house, but now sweat gathered on the back of his neck. He unzipped his jacket and slung it over his arm, aware of dozens of eyes on him, people gathering in the terminal for private planes despite the security trying to shoo them away.

Running a hand over his hair to make sure the pomade was keeping everything in place, Rafa cleared his throat. "Thanks."

The woman smiled professionally. "Of course. I'm Agent Hernandez, and this is Agent O'Leary. Why don't you wait in the car while your parents have their photo ops? The flight was a little early, and your brother's already there."

"Oh, great."

The armored limo was parked in an otherwise-empty hangar. The agent standing by the vehicle nodded and opened the door, and Rafa climbed in and took the seat opposite Matthew, who raised his chin from his chest and blinked blearily, his dark brown hair falling into his eyes. He said, "Hey, bro." The partition between them and the driver was closed, and the distant roar of jet engines was even more muted in the limo.

"Hey, Matty." After a few awkward beats, they stretched across the space and hugged briefly, Matthew's left arm held snug to his body in a sling that also had a strap around his midsection. The black of the sling was stark against his white hoodie. Rafa perched on the edge of the seat and asked, "Does it hurt?" His cheeks went hot. "Stupid question."

Matthew's small smile didn't reach his eyes. "It's okay. Yeah, it hurts like a mother. Doc said surgery went well, but I guess we'll see. Have to wear this stupid thing for a month. Even when I'm sleeping." He stretched his neck from side to side with a groan. "I shouldn't complain since we had a private plane, but fuck, that was a long flight."

In his pocket, Rafa's phone buzzed, and he eagerly read the message from Shane. "Speaking of, Shane's in LA now. Waiting for his connection to DC. It seems like he left so long ago."

"Miss him already?" Matthew asked with a smirk.

Rafa blinked at the cruel-edged tone. "Yeah, I guess. Lame, I know."

"No, don't listen to me." He rubbed his red-rimmed eyes. "I'm cranky and exhausted, and Natalie dumped me, so."

"Shit, sorry." Rafa desperately tried to remember which one Natalie was. Another swimmer, perhaps? Matthew seemed to have a lot of girlfriends in quick succession.

"Don't be. She loved dating a star swimmer. Now that I might be done, she blew me off." He picked up his phone from the leather seat beside him. "Jesus, they are taking forever. I need to crash."

"How are they?"

Matthew scrolled through his phone. "Same, I guess. You know. They're Mom and Dad." He stopped the motion of his finger on the screen and barked out a short laugh. "Ade says we have to get Mom to hold a koala and pay it in eucalyptus or whatever to piss on her silk blouse."

Rafa laughed, imagining their sister's wicked smile with a pang. "Are they, like… I don't know. Have they said anything about me?"

He snorted. "Are you kidding? You're their favorite topic of conversation. Even Chris doesn't get as much attention these days. I mean, don't get me wrong—they still praise him on the regular. It's just every ten minutes now instead of five."

"Heh." Rafa reached for one of the cold water bottles tucked into the doors and chugged half. "So, what do they say about me?"

Shrugging his good shoulder, then wincing, Matthew answered, "Exactly what you think. Shane's a cradle robber and taking advantage of you. They want you to come home so you can be their good little boy again." He raised an eyebrow. "I see you cut your hair."

"It was getting too long!" Rafa cringed internally at how defensive he sounded.

"Okay. Look, man. You just need to stand your ground. Don't freak. They'll pressure you to come home, but they're not going to throw you in the back of—" He paled, the dark circles under his eyes standing out even more. "Sorry. That was a fucked-up joke."

"It's okay. Really." Rafa tried to smile reassuringly.

"Shit, it's good to see you. I missed you. For a long time now. Which is on me."

"You had your own life away from the White House. It's okay. It's in the past now anyway."

Matthew smiled warmly. "You were always too nice, Raf."

The murmur of voices approached, and they shared a look. Rafa blew out a breath. "Here goes nothing."

The limo door opened, and they scooted over to make room for their parents, Ramon settling in beside Rafa, across from Camila. His father pulled Rafa into an enthusiastic hug.

"Rafalito!"

"Hey, Dad." It felt good to be enclosed in his father's strong arms. Shit, he really *had* missed them. He slid to his knees to reach across and hug his mom, who smelled of delicate vanilla. She kissed his freshly shaven cheek, then wiped the smudge of her lipstick off his skin with her thumb.

Settling back in his seat as the limo left the airport, Rafa asked, "How was the trip?"

Camila sighed. "Long. It'll be nice to get out of these grubby clothes."

"You *just* changed into those," Matthew noted.

Her tan linen pants were perfectly pressed, her white blouse crisp, and her "casual" navy jacket probably cost a couple grand. Diamonds gleamed in her ears, and of course a string of pearls circled her long neck. There wasn't a strand out of place in her straightened hair, which she'd grown to brush her shoulders.

She flicked invisible lint from her knee. "Yes, well. That airplane air is so stuffy. Makes me feel unclean."

Ramon chuckled. "You look beautiful as ever." The gray at his temples threaded all through his short hair now, and Rafa was sure there were a few more lines on his face. It had only been a few months, but his father looked older somehow.

Ramon shrugged out of his light jacket. He wore no tie, but his silky cotton button-down shirt was tucked neatly into his slacks. He crossed his legs and propped one ankle on his knee and said, "It's wonderful to see you again, Rafalito." He squeezed Rafa's arm. "We've all missed you very much."

"I missed you guys too. Did you see Adriana when you went through LA?"

"Yes," Ramon answered. "She's doing…" He and Camila shared a glance before he finished, "Very well."

Matthew rolled his eyes. "She's partying too much and having the time of her life. But pretty soon all those hangovers won't be so cute and she'll have to grow up."

Their parents glared at Matthew, but they didn't argue. Camila said, "And of course Christian's doing wonderfully in New York. He and Hadley are so happy together. Finally talking about having children."

"We'd like some grandkids before we get too old to enjoy them," Ramon added.

"You guys are only in your fifties," Matthew said. "Chill."

"Well, I don't think your sister is mother material—at least not at this point—and you're nowhere near settling down. And obviously Rafa won't be having any. So it's high time Christian got started."

Obviously. Rafa tensed and tried to keep his tone light. "Who says I'm not having kids?"

"Oh." Camila smiled smoothly. "Well, yes, I suppose it's possible."

Ramon added, "You've just never spoken of it, so we assumed

since you're… Now that you're…"

"Do many twenty-two-year-old guys talk about having kids?" Rafa asked. "And gay people can have kids. Plenty of them do."

This brought on a flurry of agreement and placation, which Rafa accepted. There was no point in getting upset about it. He rolled his shoulders. *Focus on the positive.* His phone buzzed again, and he pulled it out to read the message from Shane.

Hey. Are they there? Give them my best and try not to let them drive you too crazy. I should probably sleep when I get to DC, but my body has no idea what time it is. Love you. I'll be back before you know it.

Rafa would have normally replied with a joke about Shane's body, but he could feel his parents' eyes on him. He quickly tapped out a "sleep well and I love you too." Putting his phone back in his pocket, he said, "Shane says hi."

"Mmm." Camila's smile was tight-lipped. "That's nice."

Ramon cleared his throat. "Glad he arrived safely."

"Yeah, he really wanted to be here, but you know how important this inquest is. He'll be back soon."

"Darling, how's Ashleigh?" Camila asked, as if they hadn't talked about her in ages, which they had. "You know we've always adored her."

He almost replied, "*Still a lesbian, and I'm still gay in case you're thinking it's a phase.*" But he got hold of himself and said, "Great. We just Skyped this morning. Well, her boss is horrible and pays her crap, and her parents don't accept her and barely speak to her, but other than that she's good."

"We're sorry to hear that about the Hastings," Ramon said. After a beat, he added, "You know we accept you just the way you are."

"I know." Honestly, Rafa was still a little surprised at how hard they'd tried to be understanding and supportive, even if they didn't always succeed. After so many years of dreading their reactions, part of him was still waiting for the other shoe to drop. He tried to think of something to say and glanced out the window as the limo made its way into the city in the sluggish rush-hour traffic.

"Look, there's Sydney Tower." He pointed to the tall, thin structure with a thick, rounded top. "The view's really great up there. Restaurant was crowded. I guess they decided to make it a buffet at some point, but it wasn't designed that way, so the middle aisle for the food was too packed in. The views are amazing from the windows though. The restaurant revolves, and we got a table by the glass, so it was great."

Stop rambling, oh my God.

Camila said, "That sounds interesting. Did you pack some formal clothing?"

"Pack?" Rafa blinked. "Why would I pack anything? We're not leaving for Perth until next week."

"But of course you're staying with us in the Presidential Suite at the hotel. You'll have your own room." She laughed. "There's no sense in you staying in that little…place all alone."

Gritting his teeth, Rafa blew out a slow breath and kept his voice even. "It's my home, Mom. I'm staying there."

"Don't you want to have some quality time with your brother?" she asked.

Matthew shook his head. "Nope. Don't bring me into this. I'm sure Raf and I will have plenty of 'quality time' in the next few weeks."

"We just hate to think of you all alone out there," Ramon said.

"Don't you hate to think of him there with Shane even more?" Matthew muttered, ignoring their parents' matching glares.

Camila smoothed out her face once more, smiling. "Rafa, we just want to spend as much time with you as possible."

"I want to spend time with you guys too. And I will, I promise. My classes don't start until mid-July. We have the whole next three weeks."

He just had to survive them.

Chapter Five

"THANK YOU FOR joining us today, Mr. Kendrick."

Like I had a choice. But Shane smiled graciously at the panel and said, "Of course."

Wearing a somber black suit, he tried not to shift too much in the hard chair that sat some feet in front of a long table of seven inquisitors. He didn't know any of them. The two women and five men ranged in ages and ethnicities, and an older black man named Donaldson sat in the middle to lead the questioning. The windowless boardroom in the Secret Service headquarters was wood-paneled.

Donaldson began with a recitation of the facts—as if Shane could ever forget them. Then he asked, "At the rest stop, you proceeded into the restroom alone?"

"Yes."

"Had you often spent time with Valor alone?"

"I wouldn't say often. Occasionally. When Agent Pearce was off duty while his son was hospitalized."

Another man asked, "What transpired between you and Valor inside the restroom?"

"We spoke." It wasn't a lie—they had spoken. Shane concentrated on breathing calmly and evenly. Of course they'd ask about more than just the kidnapping and what happened with Alan. This was the first time he'd faced anyone from the Service since he and Rafa had gone public. Not that they'd given any interviews, but they weren't hiding.

"Nothing of a sexual nature took place between you?"

"No." Shane would take it to his grave that Rafa had defiantly jerked off in that bathroom stall, furious at his family and tired of always doing the right thing. Besides, it hadn't technically transpired between them *physically*, although Rafa had poured out his fantasies, and Shane had fought desperately against storming into the stall and fucking him right there.

"Then you were shot the moment you stepped outside?"

He resisted the urge to touch the scar over his ear. "Yes."

Then more facts were recited—Alan's gunshot wound, Shane going after Rafa in the Suburban. An older woman on the panel cleared her throat and asked, "Were your hands tested for gunshot residue?"

His heart skipped. "No. Why would they be? I fired multiple weapons when I confronted the kidnappers." What the fuck were they getting at?

She watched him for a long moment, then simply said, "Mmm."

A man asked, "Did you encourage Valor to run away from Castle that day?"

Shane's pulse kicked up. "Of course not. I tried to stop him from leaving. We both did."

"Why would Pearce try to stop him? This was his golden opportunity."

"I don't know. He was still doing his job. I would have noticed something was off if he hadn't."

The older woman said, "Mmm" again, and the sound grated on Shane's nerves. He fiddled with the laminated guest badge pinned to his lapel.

A man said, "You transferred a very large sum of money to Julianna Pearce earlier this year. Close to a million dollars."

"Is that a question, or did you access my bank records?" Shane snapped. *Shit. Keep it together.* He added calmly, "Yes, I did."

"Where did you get the money?"

"The insurance settlement from the fire that killed my parents."

"Have you spoken to Alan Pearce since he's been incarcerated?"

"No."

Donaldson asked, "Why not? You were good friends, weren't you?"

"We were, before he betrayed me, our protectee, and our country. I said everything I have to say when I elicited his confession."

"Mmm," the older woman said again. "It's still hard to believe Mr. Pearce acted as he did. Without anyone knowing—even you, his partner."

Shane breathed in and out, in and out. "Yes. He had me fooled."

She slipped on a pair of reading glasses and scanned a document as the silence stretched out. Shane resisted the urge to fill it. Finally, she said, "It would have been much easier for Pearce to succeed with your help."

Rage burned white hot, and Shane bit out, "I had nothing to do with it. I was shot when they took R—Valor."

One of the men noted, "As was Pearce."

He wanted to jump up and pace back and forth, but Shane kept very still in his chair, his feet planted firmly, forcing his fingers to unclench. "I had absolutely nothing to do with Alan Pearce's plan. I would never have done anything to harm my protectee."

"Because you were sleeping with him?" the younger woman asked.

"*No.* Because it was my job to protect him. And because what

Alan did was wrong. It was criminal. I had no part in it."

"Yet you still gave his wife money."

"For her son Dylan's treatment. Jules has lost her daughter and her husband, even though he's still alive. He's doing life. We all know he'll never get parole. Dylan is all she has left, and he's just a kid. It wasn't his fault what happened, or his mother's. I care about them. I won't apologize for it."

After a few beats of silence, Donaldson nodded. "All right. And you care about Valor as well, as it turns out."

"Yes." Sweat prickled the back of his neck, and he wanted to loosen his tie. He shouldn't feel an iota of guilt for loving Rafa. Rafa was the best thing that had ever happened to him. Yet the stares of the inquisitors were like hot pokers on his skin. Because the truth was, he'd crossed boundaries and behaved unprofessionally while Rafa was still in his care. He couldn't deny that. There was no excuse for it.

Still, he bit back the apology and stayed silent. *Just answer their questions directly. Nothing more.*

Donaldson asked, "Have you ever entered into a personal relationship with a protectee before?"

"No!" Shane knew he didn't have the right to be offended, yet it simmered through him, his voice going hoarse with anger. "Never."

A man asked, "Would you like some water?" He nodded to a table along a sidewall that held pitchers of water, carafes of coffee, a fruit tray, and mini-muffins.

"No." Shane cleared his throat. "Thank you."

"When did your inappropriate relationship with Valor begin?"

"The night of the kidnapping. After I recovered him." It was mostly true. "I put in for a transfer because I knew it couldn't continue."

The older woman asked, "What happened between you that night?"

"None of your business." Shane clenched his jaw and exhaled slowly. "I acknowledge that I broke protocol and it should never have happened."

"But you don't regret it," Donaldson said.

Shane didn't answer. What could he say? No, he'd never regret falling in love with Rafa. Never.

Donaldson sighed heavily. "The performance reports from your superiors over your entire career were exemplary. Agent Nguyen expressed great surprise when she learned of your relationship with Valor. No one suspected a thing." He leaned forward, his gaze intense. "No one suspected a thing with Alan Pearce either. You've admitted to breaking protocol—to betraying our trust in you as an agent. How can we be sure you're not lying about your involvement in Pearce's plan too?"

Heart thumping, Shane could only answer honestly. "Because I love Rafael Castillo. I'd die for him. I'd kill for him—in fact, I have. I would never hurt him. Not only because it was my job to protect him. I understand why you have doubts. I understand why it's difficult to take my word for it. But I was a damn good agent for seventeen years. I devoted my life to the Service. Then I fell in love. I would never hurt him."

After a few moments, Donaldson sat back in his chair. "All right. That will be all. Have a safe trip back to Australia."

Shane nodded and stood, turning to walk to the door behind him. As he reached it, the older woman said, "I hope it was worth it—throwing your life away for an infatuation that can't last."

Instead of anger bubbling up, now it was joy as he thought of how empty his life had been outside his job before Rafa. He shot her a grin over his shoulder. "It's worth every damn minute."

Outside the boardroom, he closed the door and took a breath. There. It was done. He'd answered their questions and completed his duty, and now—

"Kenny?"

He hadn't been called that since Alan, and Shane's stomach plummeted as he turned to find Jules approaching tentatively down the empty hallway. She'd always been a petite woman, but now she looked tiny and brittle, as if he could snap her over his knee like kindling. Her dark hair was swept back in a listless ponytail, and her eyes were puffy.

"Jules. It's so good to see you." Actually, it made his chest tight and the echo of hurt over Alan grow louder, vibrating through him like a gong. He opened his arms for a stiff hug, the bones of Jules's shoulders too sharp as they briefly embraced.

She stepped away. "I heard you were coming back for the inquest after all. I figured it would be my only chance to see you in person. How are things in Australia?"

"Great. I love it down there. I'm surfing again, and I'll be doing security consulting. Can't beat the weather. It was sixty-three the other day, and the Aussies were wearing scarves and gloves. I went to the beach." He was rambling, and he tried to smile.

Jules nodded. "And how's Rafael?"

"He's doing very well. Starting at the Cordon Bleu soon. He's always wanted to be a chef."

She smiled faintly. "I remember. I'm glad he's doing what he wants. I'm glad he's with you. You're happy?"

"I really am." Guilt tugged sharply. He'd never been so happy, yet Jules's life had been decimated. He should have stayed in better touch with her. "How are you? How's Dylan?"

Hugging her narrow waist, she shook her head. "The experimental treatment hasn't helped. We came back from Sweden last month. I didn't... I want him to die at home. With people who love him."

Fuck. It wasn't fair. It really, truly wasn't. "I'm so sorry."

"All that money you gave me—I'm sorry." Tears flooded her eyes. "I'll never be able to thank you enough. He turned eight last week, and he was able to eat his favorite rainbow cake with that disgusting bubblegum ice cream. That's something. And at least I'll know I did everything possible. I won't have to wonder. I don't think I could bear that. I'll never be able to thank you enough for helping us. So many of our friends stopped calling after the arrest. It's been…" Her worn face crumpled.

Shane didn't have any words. He pulled her into a hug, and this time, she collapsed against him, her hands folded against his ribs as he held her. His throat was thick, eyes burning, but he fought back the tears. They wouldn't help Jules. He murmured, "I'm sorry."

There was nothing he could do to save Dylan or bring Jessica back, and he hated it. He couldn't turn back time and stop Alan from making such a stupid, misguided mistake. At least Jules would still have her husband if he could.

Hurt and guilt and fury stewed together in his gut. How had things gone so wrong? Had he been too distracted by Rafa? Would he have realized something was wrong with Al otherwise?

Shane knew he'd never know the answer, but would likely ask himself the question for the rest of his life.

"Kendrick." Sandra Nguyen's voice rang out as she approached, her low-heeled shoes ringing on the polished floor. She wore a suit, her dark hair pulled back in its customary bun.

Jules stiffened and pulled away from Shane, swiping at her eyes before turning to face Nguyen. They all nodded awkwardly, and Nguyen asked, "How's Dylan doing?"

Shaking her head, Jules backed away. "I have to get back to him. I just wanted to… Goodbye, Shane."

Shane said, "I'll come to the house tomorrow. My flight's not until the evening."

"You don't have to do that." More tears tracked down Jules's flushed cheeks.

"I'll see you tomorrow." He gave her a little smile, and she nodded before fleeing. Shane turned back to his former boss. "Agent Nguyen. How are you?"

She regarded him stonily. "Well. And you?"

"Hoping this inquest will be the end of any lingering suspicion that I had anything to do with the kidnapping plot."

She frowned. "Should be. As far as I know, it's accepted that Pearce acted alone. They were probably just shaking the tree one last time to make sure nothing unexpected would fall out. And to give you shit over the embarrassment you brought the Service."

"Guess I can't blame them."

"It was a real pain in our asses, Kendrick. I almost lost my SAIC post because of the crap you pulled. Pearce was bad enough, and then we have to find out about your relationship with Valor in the tabloids? I got an earful, as you can imagine."

Shane winced. "I can. I'm surprised they didn't transfer you, to be honest."

"Me too. And they would have fired your ass in a heartbeat if you hadn't already resigned."

"What about Harris?" Rafa's detail leader had been Shane's immediate superior.

"Transferred. To the field office in Idaho, even though he'd been asking for California for ages to be close to his family."

"Idaho. Ouch."

"He's lucky it wasn't Alaska." She shrugged. "What can you do?"

"Quit like I did?"

That garnered a small smile. "I suppose so. How's Valor?"

"Rafa's great. He's happy. *We're* happy."

She nodded. "Believe it or not, I'm glad to hear it. He was always a good kid, and you were a good agent. Until you weren't. But I hope it works out."

"Thanks. I think."

"Well, I just wanted to… I don't know what, really. Close the loop." She stuck out her hand, and Shane shook it before she added, "Give Valor my best."

She strode on down the corridor, and Shane headed for the elevator. In the lobby, he could feel curious gazes on him, whispers that seemed steeped in judgment buzzing through the air. At the security checkpoint by the entrance, he unclipped his visitor badge and returned it to the guards with a nod.

He didn't look back as he walked away from the Secret Service headquarters for the last time.

THE SCREEN DOOR leading to Darnell's backyard opened with a low, long scrape of metal. Shane closed it behind him as Darnell turned from where he sat on a padded chair on the patio in shorts, his feet up on an ottoman. He'd been facing the sunset, an orange band in the distance over suburban roofs.

With a flash of white teeth, Darnell stood and pulled Shane into a hug. "Hey, man. It's so good to see you."

Shane hugged him back, enveloped by Darnell's big, strong body. Shane wasn't a small man, but at a muscular six-four, Darnell was huge. He wasn't wearing a shirt, and the press of his sun-heated skin was familiar and comforting. Shane gave his back a pat before they parted.

Sighing wearily, Shane plonked down on the chair waiting beside Darnell's. He'd changed out of his suit into cargo shorts and a tee, and he stretched out his legs to rub his bare feet against the grass.

Wordlessly, Darnell opened the cooler between them and pulled out an ice-cold beer. He popped it into a foam cozy bearing the Baltimore Orioles' logo and passed it over.

For a few minutes, they drank and watched the sun dip out of sight, the clouds dotting the clear sky reflecting red now. Cicadas buzzed their song of summer, the evening air humid and still. The small lawn had been cut recently, the scent of fresh-shorn grass lingering, along with the bushes of puffy flowers that lined the wooden fence along the back of the yard. Someone nearby had a pool; shrieks of childish laughter and splashing echoed.

Finally, Shane said, "Sorry I missed you last night. And this morning. I slept like a log." Too exhausted for nightmares, thank God.

Darnell chuckled. "You sure did. But I was home late and gone early. Poked my head into the guest room this morning, but you were still dead to the world. Jet lag's a bitch."

"Yeah." He rubbed his face. "Tried to sleep on the plane, but you know how it is. There was a baby behind me who seemed to be wailing every ten minutes. Felt bad for the poor mother. She wasn't getting any sleep either, that's for sure. Oh, and thanks for setting the alarm for me." The clock radio on the bedside table had blared at nine a.m., giving Shane plenty of time to shower and get his shit together before he had to be downtown at noon.

"No prob. Bastards could have given you a day to decompress before you had to go in."

"They offered, but I need to get back ASAP."

Darnell sipped his beer. "How'd it go?"

"About as expected. Uncomfortable. Slightly hostile. I get it—I'm an embarrassment to the Service. I broke the rules. No matter how many years Raf and I are together, I'll still be the Secret Service agent who ran away with the president's son."

"Don't forget cradle robber as well."

He smirked. "Thanks for the reminder."

"Anytime." Darnell winked and reached over to give Shane's shoulder a quick squeeze.

"Still." He forced out the words, swallowing hard. "It hurts to lose their respect." He'd tried to stop it gnawing at him on the cab ride back to Darnell's, but his brain had replayed the meeting on repeat, zeroing in on the most sneering expressions and disapproving questions.

"Course it does. That was your identity most of your adult life: Secret Service agent. Respected. Even feared. If I lost my badge, who would I be? I honestly don't know." He was silent a few moments, then asked, "So what about you? Do you miss the job? Who are you, Shane Kendrick?"

Shane drank and pondered it. He was Rafa's lover. Boyfriend, partner—whatever you wanted to call it. Soon he'd be a security consultant commanding top dollar due to his years of experience. He was a surfer again for the first time in too long.

"I'm... I'm *good*. All those years of moving wherever the Service sent me, never putting down roots, making the job my life... It was time to let that go. Rafa or not." He smiled to himself. "I really don't miss it. I bought art for my walls. *Our* walls. It was time."

Darnell nodded. "I think it was. I really do. Like I said before, that boy shook you up and woke you up. And you still want to wake up with him every morning?"

"Abso-fucking-lutely."

"Then the Secret Service can kiss your ass."

Shane laughed. "Yeah. Thanks for putting things in perspective."

"Dr. Darnell is always in session for you, my friend."

His smile faded. "Jules Pearce was there today. Came to see me."

"How was that?"

"Brutal. Her son's dying. The Swedish treatment didn't work."

Darnell blew out an exaggerated breath. "Man. That's awful."

"Yeah. And here I am brooding about my poor widdle hurt feelings because the Service was mean to me."

"Hey, your feelings are still valid. There's always going to be someone in the world who has it worse. You're still allowed to feel like shit when you feel like shit."

"Have you always been this profound?"

"I have, as a matter of fact. I'm glad you finally noticed."

"I hate that there's nothing I can do. I'm going to see them tomorrow before I leave. No idea what to say."

"After everything that went down with Alan, visiting them is probably more than most people have done. You're showing up. That means something. It would to me, at least."

"Yeah." Shane tried to shake it off, but he couldn't get Jules's fragile, haunted face out of his mind.

Memories of Alan crowded in as well—his easy, boyish smile back in the day, the hunch of his shoulders and dark circles under his eyes when Dylan had worsened. In the mud, blood seeping too fast from the bullet hole in his chest that was supposed to kill him. "I wonder what it's like. Prison."

"You could visit him and ask."

He shuddered. "I have enough nightmares already."

"Mmm. About the kidnapping?"

Ugh, he shouldn't have said anything. "I guess. It's not a big deal."

"You talk to anyone about those?"

"Like a shrink?" He scoffed. "Not necessary."

"Okay. What about Rafa?"

"No, I don't want to worry him. He has enough stress. It's stupid anyway."

"To be traumatized by a traumatic event? Seems reasonable to me."

Shane rolled his eyes and chugged his beer. He swallowed and said, "I'm not *traumatized*."

Darnell re-crossed his legs on the ottoman. "Is Rafa?"

"Well, it was hard for him, obviously. He was kidnapped. He was terrified. But he had some therapy, and he's doing amazing."

Pride swelled with a warm bloom of affection. "He's resilient."

"That's great." Darnell was quiet a few moments. "But it wasn't hard for you too?"

Impatience flared, and Shane breathed through it. "I was doing my job. It's different."

"And these nightmares—"

"Are *nothing*. Gimme a break, okay? Everyone has nightmares sometimes."

"Of course. We're all human. Even cops and Secret Service agents. So if the nightmares don't stop, maybe—"

"They will. You're making a big deal of nothing."

"Okay. Sorry, man."

"It's fine. All right, enough doom and gloom. I answered their questions, and I'm officially done with the Secret Service. They're not dragging me back into their problems again."

"I'll drink to that." Darnell took a swig from his bottle. "So why are you flying back down under so quickly? What's the rush? Is it me?" He lifted his arm and gave his armpit an exaggerated sniff.

"You smell like roses in springtime, as always. No, it's that Rafa's stuck down there alone with his parents." He didn't mention his fears about him being alone in the house. Rafa *wasn't* a kid, and Shane didn't want to give the impression Rafa was immature or needy. Because he wasn't—it was Shane who was overprotective.

"Ah, yes, the family visit. The hot swimmer brother went with them, didn't he? Saw a picture of him getting on a plane with his arm in a sling."

"Torn rotator cuff."

Darnell winced. "That's gotta put a damper on his Olympic aspirations. Still, he's got two more years before the next Games. I'm sure he'll be a buffer for Rafa with their folks. Besides, I'm sure Rafa's been alone with his parents plenty of times. For example, the twenty-one years or so of his life before he met you."

"Ha-ha." Shane took a swig of beer. "Point taken. It's just…" He picked at the top of the damp label, condensation wetting his fingers. "This is the first time he's seeing them since we got together. Got together officially, I mean."

"Okay. Dr. Darnell's still in session. What are you afraid will happen?"

"That they'll give him shit. Try and convince him to leave me. And no—I don't think he will. But they'll try, and I won't be there to shut it down."

"To protect him."

"I'm always going to protect him. Always."

"I get it. Still, you can't always be there. He has to fight his own battles."

Shane drained his bottle, shifting restlessly in his chair. "I know. But I don't like it. I don't want him to be hurt or angry or stressed."

"That's called *love*, my friend." Darnell whistled softly. "You've got it bad."

"Fuck off." But there was no heat to Shane's words, and he had to chuckle.

"Still a closed relationship?"

"Yep. Sorry to disappoint."

Darnell laughed. "All right, all right, don't get too full of yourself. I wasn't asking because I want another piece of your admittedly fine ass. Just wondering how that's going for you. Monogamy."

"It's great." He crossed his ankles, rubbing his heel against the grass. One of Darnell's neighbors was barbecuing what smelled like sweet and tangy ribs, and his stomach rumbled. "I know it's still early days, but I have no interest in being with anyone else. We can—" He hesitated. Was this sharing too much?

Darnell waited, twisting the top of another beer and passing it over. Shane exchanged his empty bottle and took a long, cold swallow. Then he said, "Raf was a virgin, and I made sure I was tested. We fuck raw, and man. It's good. It's *really* good." A thread of desire pulled tight in him at the thought of how hot and perfect Rafa felt when Shane was inside him.

"Ah. Yeah, I can imagine. I haven't done that since I was a teenager. Never trusted anyone enough over the years." His laughter rumbled. "I bet that caveman side of you really gets off on being his first and only."

Shane had to grin. "I can't deny it."

Returning his grin, Darnell offered a fist bump, then took another beer for himself. "You hungry? We can order in. Sorry, work's been crazy, or I would have bought some steaks."

"No prob. And yeah, pizza? Whatever's fast and easy."

"Just like me." He pulled out his phone and tapped at it, asking Shane for topping preferences before placing the order. As the day faded into night, moon lamps around the yard started glowing. The kids were still splashing in the pool somewhere nearby, faint cries echoing.

Sitting back again with one ankle propped on his opposite knee, Darnell said, "I was always too busy with the job to really think about anything serious."

After a few moments of silence, Shane asked, "And now?"

Darnell sighed heavily. "Now I'm not so sure."

"Any particular reason? A particular person, perhaps?" When Darnell shifted and sighed again, Shane said, "Out with it. Who is he?"

"His name's Henry Chan. Prosecutor. Forty-four, lives here in the Maryland burbs as well. About a twenty-minute drive away. We've been working a tough case. Child neglect; the kid died. But I think the mother's a victim too. It's all sad and fucked-up. I've seen a lot over the years, but something about this one really cuts deep."

"I'm sorry. And Henry…helps?"

"Yeah. We ended up kissing in his office the other night." He shook his head. "Shit, it makes my stomach all fluttery to think about it. And that's all we did—kiss. Talked. Hugged. Now he wants to go to dinner."

"What do you want?"

"Yeah, dinner would be nice. I mean, I'm getting way ahead of myself even thinking about a serious relationship or monogamy." He took a swig of beer. "But I haven't thought much about those things in ages. He makes me want to."

There was too much light pollution to really see the night sky, but a bright star had emerged, likely a satellite. Shane stared at it as he contemplated. "It sounds like you're falling for him and it scares the shit out of you."

"That's the thing. It doesn't. It feels weirdly right." Darnell laughed. "Hell, listen to me. We haven't even had an official *date* yet."

"Sometimes you just know. Although you have to ask the important questions—one in particular."

"Okay," Darnell said seriously. "What's that?"

"Is he an Orioles fan? Because I don't think you could ever be happy with someone who doesn't bleed orange and black like you do."

Darnell grinned. "He's got a classic Ripken poster framed in his office. Autographed."

Shane held out his bottle and they clinked them together, waiting for the pizza in easy silence.

Chapter Six

CLOSING THE BATHROOM door behind him, Rafa groaned to himself. He'd somehow actually forgotten just how painful it was to smile and nod and be the perfect presidential son. The Australian prime minister was very welcoming, her family was super nice—and Rafa couldn't wait to get out of there.

They'd arrived mid-afternoon for cocktails and barbecued shrimp in the garden, which Ramon thought was hilarious for some reason. He'd kept saying, "Throw some more shrimp on the barbie!" in a terrible Australian accent until Camila had shot him a death glare while their hosts weren't looking.

Rafa had just ducked into the bathroom, but not before making the hosts laugh at his choice of word. He still forgot to call it a toilet like the straightforward Aussies did, and he'd joked that he wasn't actually having a shower or a soak.

Ha-ha-ha, smiles, smiles.

It was exhausting. He glanced in the mirror over the white porcelain sink. He hadn't worn his pale blue dress shirt in ages, or the gray slacks. At least his mother hadn't forced him into a tie. He'd done the dance for so many years because he'd had to, and he wished he could escape home and that Shane would be there.

Soon.

He pulled out his phone and tapped the screen, trying a quick call through WhatsApp. Shane had texted that he was at the airport in LA, so maybe Rafa could catch him at the—

Shane answered, "Hey, baby."

"Hey! Are you boarding soon? I miss you so much." It was stupid—Shane had only been gone a few days. Still. "The bed is too big without you." He laughed. "I sound so lame."

There was lots of noise in the background, the murmur of people and boarding calls. "No, you don't. I miss you too. They just started boarding. Fourteen more hours, and I'll be home before you know it. First thing in the morning. Everything's been okay at the house?"

Rafa rolled his eyes. "Yes. No one's broken in yet."

"Let's not tempt fate. What are you up to right now?"

"We're at Kirribilli House. The prime minister lives here when she's in Sydney. It's surprisingly small, but it's historic or whatever. Amazing views of the harbor. The Opera House is so close."

"Sounds great."

"I guess." He scoffed at himself. "Not to be an ungrateful dick. I know I'm lucky to go the places I've been able to go all these years. I just haven't missed needing to be *on*. You know?"

"Yep. What's the PM like?"

"Nicole's really nice. Down to earth and all that."

"And how's it going with your parents?"

"So far, so good. They were pretty jet-lagged. Matty really crashed. But they all seem better today." He could hear voices in the house beyond. "I'd better get back out there. I think we're going in for dinner. Don't want them to think I'm taking a dump or anything."

Shane laughed. "Heaven forbid. They're calling my section anyway. See you in the morning. Love you."

"Love you too."

After a quick piss, Rafa rejoined the others as they made their way toward the dining room. Matthew sidled up beside him. "What are you smiling about?" He glanced around and lowered his voice. "Phone sex in the john with Shane?"

Cheeks going hot, Rafa tried not to laugh too much. "*No*. But we talked. He's boarding in LA."

"Cool." Matthew nudged him with his good arm. "I really am happy for you. He seems like a good dude. No matter what Mom and Dad think."

Rafa's happy bubble popped as he followed into the dining room, the prime minister's thirteen-year-old daughter, Laura, instructing him to sit beside her. He nodded and smiled as she talked about some painting on the wall in the small, formal room.

Meanwhile, the worry nagged. He knew his parents weren't thrilled about his relationship with Shane, but couldn't they see how happy he was?

He did his part during dinner, making the right noises at the right times as Laura told him about her school trip to China. The food was delicious—perfectly seared loins of Wagyu beef tender-loin, crispy roast potatoes and vegetables, and on top of the meat, a lobster-ish crustacean known as a Moreton Bay bug. It melted in his mouth in a rush of garlicy butter.

"Laura, let Rafa get a word in edgewise," her father admonished. "You're giving him a real ear-bashing."

Poor Laura's pale, freckled face went puce. She had reddish hair like her mother, although the Aussies called redheads "blueys" for some reason Rafa had yet to figure out.

Rafa said, "No, no! I'm enjoying hearing all about it. I've never been to China." To Laura, he added, "So did you climb up the Great Wall? Is it a lot of steps in some places?"

She gave him a little smile, but shot her father a nervous glance. Rafa was totally blanking on the guy's name and had no idea why he was being a dick to his daughter.

Ugh, maybe it was because Rafa hadn't been paying close enough attention and it had shown. Pushing away all his worries, he concentrated fully on Laura and encouraged her to keep talking.

Across the table, Matthew rather glumly pushed his food around, not saying much as their parents and Nicole kept up a steady stream of conversation, Laura's pimply-faced older brothers seemingly content to mow down their meals and not say a thing.

When their conversations lulled, Nicole said, "I hear you're all climbing the bridge tomorrow! Should be perfect weather for it. Clear as a bell."

"Yes," Camila answered. "It should be lovely. We're told it's the thing to do now that we're tourists like anyone else."

Rafa kept his eyes on his plate, because he could just imagine the expression Matthew was making, and he didn't want to burst out laughing.

Sure, because ordinary folks travel with Secret Service agents and a team of assistants. And have dinner with the prime minister.

Ramon said, "I'm told your people have been a wonderful help in coordinating everything, Nicole. Thank you."

"Our pleasure." She sipped a glass of red wine and tucked a copper curl behind her ear. She was a pretty woman in her forties who was known for a boisterous laugh but tough-as-nails attitude in parliament. "Rafa, how are you enjoying yourself? You're up in Curl Curl?"

"Yes. I absolutely love it."

One of Laura's brothers piped up. "The beaches are sick up there. How's the surf been?"

Rafa grinned. "Incredible. Too big for me sometimes. It's a little intimidating. Shane says—" He broke off, suddenly self-conscious. Now he certainly had everyone's attention, and a current of tension snaked through the room. He forced a smile. "He says I need to trust myself more. Stop over-thinking it."

Ramon's chuckle was awkward. "Well, we don't want you doing anything dangerous."

Oh, for fuck's sake. "Yeah, of course not, Dad." Rafa took a sip of his wine, the oak-cherry flavor more acidic than it was before.

"Shane would never want me to do anything dangerous either."

"Why didn't he come today?" Laura asked. "He seems really cool." Her parents shot her daggers, but she either didn't notice or ignored them.

"Oh, he had to go back to the States for a…thing." Bringing up that time he got kidnapped didn't seem like a good idea in front of the PM's kids.

Nicole said, "So, Matthew…" Then she seemed at a loss.

Matthew gave her a too-cheery smile. "Do you want to discuss my busted shoulder and how my swimming career might be over?"

"Why don't we talk about this exquisite meal," Camila said. "This Wagyu is delectable. It's raised here in Australia?"

As conversation turned to the cattle industry, Laura whispered, "Sorry. I didn't mean to make things weird."

He ducked his head closer to her. "*You* didn't. Don't worry about it."

"I think your boyfriend's really hot, even if he's old." Her cheeks flushed again.

Rafa laughed softly. "Thanks. So do I."

"Was it very scary? When those bad people took you?"

"It was. But Shane saved me."

She giggled delightedly. "He's your knight in shining armor. It's so romantic."

He thought of the way Shane had held him safe in his strong arms and kissed him in the rain, their lips pressed together desperately. The sweet relief that the bullet had only grazed Shane's skull, and he was still whole and alive. Rafa smiled. "Yeah. I guess it is."

It didn't matter what anyone thought. He and Shane were together, and nothing would tear them apart.

THE LIGHTS OF Sydney glittered, the illuminated Opera House rising up like a giant seashell. From the hotel penthouse, the view was truly spectacular. Standing at the huge window, Rafa watched a ferry's progress across the dark harbor. It was almost midnight, so he'd reluctantly agreed to stay over at the suite.

He shouldn't begrudge his parents wanting to spend time with him. It would possibly be a year before he saw them again. So he'd make them happy and stay over one night, even if he'd rather sleep in his own bed. His and Shane's, that was. He smiled to himself, his lips curving in the faint reflection in the glass.

"Rafa, darling, would you like a drink?" Sitting on a buttery leather love seat, Camila held the stem of a delicate sherry glass. Beside her, Ramon sipped brandy. Sprawled in an armchair tapping his phone, Matthew gulped from a bottle of beer, which Camila frowned at.

"I'm good. Thanks. Shane's flight arrives first thing tomorrow, so I'll be up early. He's just going to grab a cab home, so I'll do the same."

"Back so soon?" Ramon asked. "He'll be exhausted."

The elephant in the room stomped and swung its trunk side to side. Rafa tried to ignore it, forcing a laugh. "Yeah, he won't know which way is up. It sucks he had to go back in person."

"Well, Mr. Kendrick had to do his duty," Camila said dismissively. *Too* dismissively.

Rafa's spidey senses tingled. "What do you think, Dad?"

"Hmm?" Ramon loosened his tie and looked anywhere but at Rafa. "The inquest is very important, of course."

As his father kept his gaze on his brandy snifter, Rafa tensed. Ramon *always* looked at people when he spoke to them. It was a habit he'd developed over the years as a politician. He made eye contact and listened as if that person was the most important in the world. And right now he couldn't even glance up.

Quietly, Rafa asked, "Did you have something to do with

this?"

Camila tilted her head. "Hmm? With what, dear?" She picked up a file folder from the glass coffee table and flipped through it.

He kept his voice calm, or tried to. "With Shane having to go back to DC for the inquest. They'd said it was no problem to testify remotely. Then suddenly he had to be there in person."

His parents shared a glance, and fucking fuck, Rafa knew that look. He exhaled sharply, a burst of disbelief. "Are you shitting me?"

Camila snapped, "*Language*, Rafael."

Matthew glanced up from his phone. "Wow. You guys suck. You made the dude fly halfway around the world so you don't have to deal with him?"

"The inquest is very important," Ramon said. "He needed to be there to properly answer for his actions."

Rafa had started pacing, and he stopped in his tracks. "What's that supposed to mean?"

"Just what I said."

"Shane didn't do anything wrong." At his parents' raised eyebrows, Rafa insisted, "He didn't! I'm not talking about me and him. That's... Fine. That's—whatever. I'm talking about the kidnapping. About Alan. Shane had no idea. He saved my life. He almost died! If that bullet had hit his head a millimeter to the right, he would be dead. *Dead!* He had nothing to do with it."

"Alan Pearce was also shot," Camila reminded him.

"Yes, but you know he confessed to it all! He was trying to help his dying son. He said Shane had no idea." Rafa paced a few steps by the window, his bare feet digging into the plush carpet. "Shane would never hurt me. He had no part in it. He saved me. You seriously think he was in on it?"

Ramon pressed his lips together. "All right, no. We believe he's innocent of that." He put down his brandy snifter with a loud clink and stood. "But let's talk about the rest of it. This 'whatever' as you call it. You say nothing happened until after you went to meet him in California. Is that the truth?"

His parents stared at him. Matthew had abandoned his phone. The weight of their gazes burned on Rafa's skin, and he shifted from foot to foot, throat dry. "Yes. Mostly. We didn't…"

Camila gripped the leather arm of the love seat. "I knew it. You lied to us."

"Fine, I omitted a few details. Look, I was the one who instigated it, and nothing really happened until I went to find him in California. Just a few kisses and stuff."

"*Stuff*," Camila repeated sharply.

Matthew laughed. "Shit, bro. It really is the quiet ones. That's awesome."

Their father shot Matthew a glare. "It is most certainly not awesome. We trusted that man. He was supposed to protect you, not seduce you!"

"He didn't 'seduce' me! I wanted everything."

Ramon gritted his teeth. "That's what men like that want you to think. Don't be naive."

"I'm not. Besides, you said you accepted us."

Camila came to stand beside Ramon, her sherry abandoned. She'd taken off her high heels, and her flowing summer dress was wrinkled. "We said we clearly had no choice in the matter. What could we do? If we tried to make you see sense, you'd just push us away. So we decided it was better to let you come down here and realize for yourself that this relationship is not right for you."

"It *is* right!"

Ramon shook his head. "You just admitted that you and Kendrick were carrying on while he was protecting you. You were innocent, and he took advantage of that."

"He didn't!"

"Did he go into your room at the White House?" Camila asked.

"*No.*" That was a hundred percent true.

She narrowed her gaze. "How were you alone with him? I know Alan Pearce took time off to tend to his unfortunate son, but that doesn't explain how you and your Secret Service agent spent enough time alone together for this—" she waved her hand, "thing to develop."

Rafa's mind whirled. Was he betraying Shane if he told them any of the truth? But he wanted to show them Shane didn't seduce him. "I asked him to come up to the Diet Kitchen sometimes to taste the food I made." His mother couldn't hide her grimace, and a fresh burst of anger bubbled up in him like lava. "I bet you still hate that I want to be a chef. Admit it!"

She appeared affronted. "Haven't I been supportive? I've asked you about your recipes, about what new dishes you're trying. I've offered to help get you into the finest culinary schools in the world."

Rafa scoffed. "That's only so you can get me back in the States and break up me and Shane."

"Sounds about right," Matthew said, still sprawled in his armchair. He drained his bottle of beer.

"We won't deny we want you to come home." Ramon squeezed Camila's hand. "But we fully support you in this career path. We do. Your mother has really made an effort, Rafa. I'm disappointed you don't see that."

Guilt washed through him. "I know you're trying. But I guess it doesn't quite feel real because you don't want me living here."

Ramon said, "We don't want you living here with Shane Kendrick. There's a difference."

Camila added, "We didn't fight you on this before because… Well, because we assumed you'd come down here, the novelty would wear off, and Mr. Kendrick would realize…"

Blinking, Rafa swallowed hard, his throat thick. "What? That he'd made a mistake? That I wasn't worth it? Because I'm just a, a *novelty?*"

"It's not about your worth, Rafa. Of course you are worthy." Ramon ran a hand over his face. "That's our point—that you deserve so much more than this! We understand that you and he bonded. You shared a traumatic experience. But you have nothing else in common. He's almost twice your age! How could this relationship possibly last? It's best to end it now as you start the next chapter of your life. Think of all the young men you'll meet at school. You said you want to get a job at a restaurant. Again, you'll meet new, exciting people. People you share interests with."

"Why do you think Shane and I don't share interests? We both love surfing. He's teaching me, and I've gotten pretty good. That was a dream of mine for years. And he hadn't surfed in a long time until he met me and we started talking about it. His parents died, and he gave up surfing and threw himself into his work. But *I* helped him deal with stuff and surf again. And he encouraged me with cooking. Ash was in Paris and I didn't have anyone to talk to—"

"You were lonely, darling." Camila stepped toward him, hands outstretched. "We should have seen that. It was our fault."

"*No.* You're not…" He ran a palm over his head, spiking up his gelled hair and missing his curls with a stab of shame. Why did he cut his hair? Why did he care what they thought?

He tried to focus. "It's not about blame. Yes, I was lonely. We all could have reached out more or done things differently. Why do we have to blame someone?"

Ramon nodded. "That's very true."

"Can't we move forward and not blame you or me or Shane? Can't I just be happy? And you guys be happy for me?"

Camila sighed. "Your happiness is our greatest concern. Yours, and Matthew's, and Adriana's, and Christian's. It's very difficult to have you living on the other side of the world with a man we cannot trust."

"What do you think Shane's endgame is?" Matthew asked. "What's in it for him to give up his career and move down here to be with Raf, if he doesn't love him? And don't say he's using Rafa for sex, because that dude could have dozens of volunteers lined up in a heartbeat."

Heat flushed Rafa's face to the tips of his ears, and for a moment, he had to stare at his bare feet on the taupe carpet. Then he forced his head up and straightened his shoulders, waiting for his parents to answer. They scowled at Matthew.

Camila hissed, "There's no need to be crude."

"Well?" Rafa asked. "What do you think Shane's nefarious plan is?"

Ramon answered, "We don't know. We just… He's so much older than you, and he was in a position of authority. It makes us very uncomfortable."

"I get it. I do. We didn't plan on falling in love, okay?" Rafa fidgeted, his fingers clenching and unclenching. "But it happened. Yes, we broke the rules, and Shane felt like shit about that. He transferred, and we didn't talk or email or text even *once*. It was done. He ended up quitting to be with me. Because he loves *me*. Because I'm more important to him than his career."

"Seriously, you guys." Still slumped in the armchair, Matthew rolled his eyes. "Deal with it. Clearly they love each other. Raf's happy. Let it go."

Camila's tone was steely. "It's not as easy as that. Especially when you and Mr. Kendrick lied to us, Rafa. What else have you lied about?"

"Nothing! And you guys are ones to talk about lies. You pulled strings to get the Secret Service to make him go back instead of just dealing with it head on. Dealing with *us*."

Ramon approached Rafa and took his shoulders. "We simply wanted the opportunity to speak with you alone. To make sure you truly are happy. That you're not being…influenced."

"Oh my God, Shane's not, like, holding me prisoner."

"Of course not." Ramon gentled his voice. "But when you're young and in love, you can be taken advantage of. Controlled. Influenced, like I said. You're so far away from us living down here."

"Pretty sure that was the point," Matthew muttered.

Camila smoothed her skirt rhythmically. "We just think you should date boys your own age. You're too young to be settling on one person."

"You'd rather I was sleeping around instead of being in a committed relationship?"

She clenched her jaw. "Don't put words in our mouth."

"Look, this is what it comes down to: I'm happy here. I'm staying here. With Shane. So can we just be done with this intervention or whatever it is? Because it's not going to work. And Shane's going to be back tomorrow. He could have stayed in DC and skipped out on awkward dinners with you guys, but he wants to make this work. He's my partner. He's not going anywhere, no matter what you try."

After a few heartbeats, Ramon nodded. "All right." He glanced at Camila. "Yes?"

She strode over to the sideboard and poured a glass of water. "Rafa, we're only concerned for your welfare." She looked down at the glass in her hand, her voice suddenly thick. "I hope you know we love you."

The rest of Rafa's anger drained away, leaving him with lingering guilt and aching affection. "I know, Mom. I love you guys too."

Ramon pulled him into a hug and pressed a kiss to his head while Camila drank her water, breathing hard. When she put down the glass, her smile was back in place. "Tell Mr.—tell him we'll reimburse him for the flight and hotel if it's not paid for. We'll cover all his expenses."

"No, you don't need to." No way Shane would take their money. "Anyway, he crashed at his friend Darnell's place, and the Service paid for the flight."

Camila nodded. "The police detective, his old lover? Well, I'm sure it was nice for them to catch up."

Rafa's knees trembled, nausea rising along with a returning bolt of anger. He was speechless as his heart thumped. Finally, he got out, "What? Darnell and Shane are only friends."

"Mom, you just said you'd cut the crap." Matthew shook his head. "You can't help yourself, can you?"

Blinking, she opened and closed her mouth, then held out her hands at her sides. "What did I say?"

Rafa sputtered. "You implied Shane was hooking up with Darnell! Darnell's not his *ex*—they're only friends! God, Mom. Seriously, cut it out. Shane's not cheating on me."

Mouth open and the picture of innocence, Camila looked to Ramon, who said, "Darnell Jackson? Rafa... They did have a sexual relationship in the past. Kendrick didn't tell you?"

Humiliation burned through him like wildfire. Here he was insisting he and Shane were perfect together, and somehow his parents knew this vital piece of information and he didn't. *Is it really true?* "How... How do you know this?"

"We had him investigated," Ramon said, as if it was nothing. "You think we'd let you move to the other side of the world with this man without searching for skeletons in his closet?"

"Darling, I assumed you knew." Camila stepped closer, looking him in the eye steadily, beseeching. "I wasn't trying to stir anything up. Truly."

Rafa blew out a shaky breath. For her faults, his mother was usually honest, but his head spun and he didn't know which way was up. *Shane and Darnell were lovers? Why didn't Shane tell me?* Bile rose in his throat, and he choked it down.

Ramon said, "From what I recall of the report, it was nothing serious. Intermittent over the years. I'm sure there's nothing between them now. Not if Shane Kendrick is as trustworthy as you say he is."

"He is!" Rafa was shouting. *Be calm. Fuck, fuck, fuck.* He lowered his voice. "Shane would never do that to me." Oh fuck, he had to get away. His family's eyes bored into him like drills, and God, they looked so horribly sympathetic now. *Stop being a lame little loser.*

"Yes, if he's the upstanding man you tell us he is, then I'm sure he wouldn't lie to you," Camila said.

"He is!" Rafa insisted again, squirming under their scrutiny.

"Then there's no problem. I'm sorry to upset you." Her face pinched. "Honestly."

"Yeah. Okay. I'm just going to…" Rafa jerked his thumb toward the bathroom, managing to walk and not run down the corridor of the suite to shut himself inside.

He thought of the glimpses he'd had of Darnell in the odd photo—tall and bulging with muscles, every inch a *man*. Despite how he protested to his parents that *he* was a man now, Rafa felt so much like a dumb little kid.

Hot with shame, he splashed cold water on his red cheeks. Looking in the mirror, he tried to tamp down his stupid hair, which stuck up in places and wanted to curl no matter how much he tried plastering it to his skull.

"*Ch-ch-ch-Chia!*"

He was a gawky, pimply teenager again, his new friends at school pissing themselves laughing, passing around the internet meme. His throat closed, eyes burning, and his voice broke as he whispered at his reflection.

"Nut up. You're pathetic. You're supposed to be a fucking grown-up."

There was a low knock at the door, and Rafa scrubbed his face with a towel before opening it to Matthew, who squeezed Rafa's arm. "Dude, it doesn't mean he's fucking that guy now. I'm sure he's not. Sounds like they were just friends with benefits. It doesn't mean anything. That's probably why he didn't tell you, because it was just sex back in the day. Lots of people do stuff like that."

"I guess," Rafa scraped out, his voice hoarse.

"Look, Shane loves you, right?"

Shane did love him. Rafa didn't doubt that. But what if it wasn't enough? What if *he* wasn't enough? Shane had been with real *men*. Would he get bored of Rafa?"

"Don't let Mom and Dad make you crazy. You still want to stay here tonight, or should I get you an Uber or something?"

"Uber. I got it." He pulled out his phone and opened the app, tapping for a ride home.

"For what it's worth, I think she means it—that she thought you knew about this guy." Matthew glanced over his shoulder and lowered his voice. "But if they think it's for your own good, that doesn't mean they won't use it to drive a wedge between you and Shane. Don't let them. Stay strong."

Nodding, his throat too thick to speak, Rafa vowed to try his best.

Chapter Seven

THE TAXI'S TAILLIGHTS disappeared in the gray murk of dawn, clouds blotting out the moon and any remaining stars as the sun brightened the horizon. The trip from LA had been almost fifteen hours in the end, plus customs and all that crap. Shane breathed in the cool morning gratefully, hurrying to unlock the squat, brick bungalow's door.

Traffic had been light, and Rafa was probably still sleeping, so he eased inside quietly. Yet Rafa appeared almost instantly in the bedroom door, spine rigid, wearing plaid pajama bottoms and a tank top. Shane dropped his duffel bag, trying to hide his surprise.

His relief at seeing Rafa again—breathing and in one piece, the foolish knot of tension in Shane's gut loosening—was short-lived. "Hey, baby. Are you okay?"

"Uh-huh." In the gray light, Rafa's expression wasn't clear. "How was the flight? Get any sleep?"

"About four hours. Not bad." Shane smiled tentatively, his heart jumping uneasily. He'd expected Rafa to run to him with open arms, but something was wrong. "You cut your hair."

Rafa ran a hand over his head, his wild curls snipped down to a couple of inches, the ends just starting to wave. "Yeah, it was getting way too long. It's hot and stuff."

Compared to the end of Aussie summer when they arrived, June was cooler, but sure, the days still got quite warm. So Shane nodded and let it go, even though he suspected Rafa had cut it because of his parents. "Looks good."

Rafa snorted. "You're just saying that because you have to. My hair always looks like crap no matter what I do to it."

He swallowed a burst of frustration. What was happening? The air felt jagged, all sharp edges in the space separating them. "That's not true. I love your hair—however you want to wear it. It's up to you. You're always beautiful."

Cheeks flushing, Rafa mumbled, "Thanks."

Shane closed the distance between them since it seemed Rafa wasn't eager to. He pulled him into a long, searching kiss, stale breath and all. "You're gorgeous. I wish you would believe me."

Rafa wouldn't meet his gaze. "I do."

He took Rafa's face in his hands. "What's wrong? Is it your parents?"

"Everything's fine," Rafa clearly lied, shrugging out of Shane's grasp. "Want me to make breakfast? Are you having a shower?"

Shane put on a teasing smile. "Is that a hint? Are you trying to say I stink?"

"*No.* Figured you wanted a shower after traveling for, like, two days or whatever." He trudged to the kitchen. "It's up to you."

"I was just… Okay. Yeah, I do feel gross. But I'm not hungry, so if you could just put on coffee, that would be great."

"Sure." Rafa disappeared around the corner.

As Shane stripped off and soaped down, turning the water up nice and hot, he tried to guess what the Castillos had done to upset Rafa so much. The possibilities were endless. He'd just have to coax it out. *Be patient.*

Terrycloth robe belted around his waist, Shane padded to the kitchen, inhaling deeply. The overhead light was on, and rain splattered the window. "Mmm. Smells great. Just what the doctor ordered. Thank you."

Leaning against the counter, Rafa had a green and brown mug

with a koala etched into the side between his palms. He studied the linoleum as if there were something vital written there. "Sure. No prob." His shoulders were practically up around his ears.

Shane gave Rafa a few feet of space even though he wanted to drag him into his arms. He took a sip of hot, bitter coffee and casually asked, "How are your parents?"

A shrug. "The same."

"Matthew?"

"Fine, yeah."

"How's his shoulder doing?"

"It hurts. He's stuck in a sling for a month. Has to sleep with it on too. I think he's kind of depressed about the whole thing."

"Understandable."

Rafa glanced up. "Of course it is. I'm not criticizing."

Shane hadn't seen Rafa wound so tight in ages. *Goddamn it.* What had his parents done to upset him so much? And so quickly? They'd still be in Australia for weeks, a thought that filled Shane with even more dread now than it had before. Instead of trying to ease in, he stupidly blurted, "Did your parents tell you to cut your hair?"

"*No.*" Rafa scowled. "I *am* an adult. It was my decision. I told you, we went to dinner at the prime minister's. I wanted to look good."

"I know you are. And it does look good." It was as though a wall had been built between them during his absence, and Shane couldn't hide a huff of aggravation. "Then what's bugging you? And please don't say nothing, because that's clearly not true."

Rafa took a swig of coffee, then sighed. "Sorry." Looking up, he met Shane's gaze, and didn't pull away when Shane took his hand. Rafa gripped his fingers. "How's Darnell?"

"Good. Working too hard."

Rafa's voice was high and tight. "He's gay too, right? Does he have a boyfriend or anything?"

"He's always been too much of a workaholic. It's a tough job."

"Oh. Right."

"Although there's someone he has his eye on. We'll see."

Looking up sharply, Rafa asked, "Really? He's got a guy?"

"Too soon to say, but hopefully it'll work out."

Rafa squeezed Shane's fingers so tightly. "He's a good friend, huh?"

"He is. I'm lucky."

Staring intensely, Rafa opened and closed his mouth, as if he wanted to say something. But before Shane could ask what had gotten under his skin, the counter jammed into his lower back as Rafa dove for his mouth, the koala mug crashing to the floor. Shane barely managed to get his mug in the sink, warm coffee sloshing over his hand.

He grabbed Rafa's arms, holding him at bay. "Whoa."

"Didn't you miss me?" Rafa's eyes shone with a strange urgency, his lips parted.

"Yes." Shane peered into his big brown eyes, wishing he could understand what was wrong. "Of course I missed you. I love you."

"I love you too." Rafa kissed him again, pushing into his mouth with his tongue, seeking, his hands fisted in Shane's robe.

Shane kissed him back, holding him close, trying to say everything with his lips and hands that he clearly wasn't getting right with his voice. Rafa vibrated with need, achy and utterly desperate in a way Shane had never seen him, even the first time they'd been together in the cave.

It was like holding a bundle of raw nerves, and Shane was afraid he'd do the wrong thing and Rafa would split apart. He gasped and licked into Rafa's mouth, sucking on his tongue and making him moan.

Fuck, that was music to Shane's ears—and dick. He was hard as Rafa rutted against him. He mumbled, "Let's go to bed."

Rafa backed up, tugging him along, pulling at the tie on

Shane's robe. They were both naked by the time they stumbled onto the mattress, kissing and groaning.

On top of him, Rafa tore his mouth free, panting. "I want to fuck you. I want you to be mine."

"I am." Was this what was bothering him? Rafa had asked about topping back in California after they'd made love, and Shane had said he could. Rafa hadn't brought it up again since, but maybe Shane should have? Bottoming had never been particularly great for him, but he'd get on his hands and knees for Rafa in a heartbeat.

Rafa scrambled off the mattress and opened the bedside table drawer. Shane rolled over on his belly and asked, "Is this what you need, baby?"

Nodding, Rafa crawled back, and Shane spread his legs so he could kneel between them. He hadn't offered himself up like this in a long, long time, and sweat prickled the nape of his neck. He couldn't understand the strange tension crackling between them.

It wasn't about bottoming. While it wasn't his usual preference, he wasn't opposed to it. It didn't explain the icicles of fear that persisted. Maybe he should roll over and get Rafa to talk and tell him what was wrong.

That's rich considering you won't tell him about your nightmares. Hypocrite.

Before Shane could think of the right thing to say, Rafa's face was unceremoniously buried in his ass. He spread Shane's butt cheeks and licked like his life depended on it. He kissed and licked from behind Shane's balls and then into his hole, and fuck, it felt amazing. Shane could only groan helplessly. They could talk later. Rafa clearly needed sex right now, and Shane would give him exactly what he craved.

"Oh fuck," Shane moaned. "Yeah. Eat my ass."

Rafa spit a couple of times into his hole, pushing his tongue inside and teasing the rim. Then he shoved in a slick finger, and

Shane focused on breathing and relaxing.

He was tight, but Rafa had fingered his own asshole so many times he knew how to coax Shane open, even though his movements were sharp and impatient, and his breath ragged. The need flowed off him in tense waves, and Shane pushed up to his hands and knees.

"Do it, Raf."

Rafa's fingers dug into Shane's hips, his voice thready. "Do you need me?"

"*Yes*. Always." It was the truth. "Fuck me."

The pain when Rafa shoved into him brought tears to Shane's eyes momentarily, the stabbing, burning sensation more intense than he remembered. He'd never had sex with anyone but Rafa without a condom, and the heat of Rafa's throbbing cock inside him was almost too much to take. His chest tightened with emotion he wasn't sure he understood.

But he blinked the moisture away and breathed through it, pushing back on Rafa's cock, giving him permission to really fuck him—giving him what he needed. "You'll be the first to come inside me. You want that, baby?"

Grunting, Rafa pounded into him, and the discomfort eventually gave way to spirals of burning pleasure. "That's it," Shane muttered. "That's so good." He had a feeling Rafa wouldn't last too long given how agitated and pent up he was, so Shane spit into his hand and stroked himself, pressing just the right spots.

Rafa's little cries and groans sent shivers over Shane, tightening his balls. His ass was on fire, the brushes against his prostate making his legs shake. He craned his neck to see Rafa, and *fuck* he was gorgeous. Lips parted and skin flushed, Rafa pounded him with his eyes closed, holding onto Shane's hips like a life raft.

Then he opened his eyes and their gazes locked. Shouting, Rafa quivered, slamming into Shane's ass as he came. It was wet and wonderful, and Shane finished himself off, spurting over his hand and the sheets. "Fuck, Raf." His arms gave out, and he stretched on his belly despite the wet spot.

Rafa eased out and flopped down on his side, his leg hooked over Shane's. He tentatively caressed Shane's ass cheek. "Was it okay?" His face was flushed, and he went even redder, his freckles stark.

"Okay? It was amazing." He shifted so he could ease his arm out from under him. He brushed his knuckles over Rafa's hot cheek. "Did you like it?"

"Uh-huh. It was... Knowing what it's like when you're inside me, it felt so good being inside you. Sharing that. You know what I mean?"

"I do."

"I don't think I'd want to top usually, but sometimes. If we're in the mood or whatever." His gaze dropped to the sheets.

Shane still wasn't sure what had sparked the mood that had given Rafa that undercurrent of desperation and possessiveness, but he murmured, "Sounds good."

Rafa flattened his hand on Shane's ass. "I liked making you mine."

Shane petted his hair. True, he wished he felt wild curls, but he'd meant what he said: Rafa was always beautiful. He wished Rafa would spill about what was bothering him, but it would come out eventually. "I'm always yours. Whether you stick your dick in my ass or not. You know that, right?"

Rafa nodded, and Shane pressed their lips together, trying to kiss away any lingering doubt.

AS SHANE STIFLED a yawn in the elevator up to the hotel penthouse, Rafa asked, "Are you sure you're up for this with the jet lag?"

"I'm good. I'll take a nap this aft." Truthfully, climbing the Sydney Harbour Bridge wasn't high on his priority list—*high* being the operative word. Heights weren't his best event, but given how mysteriously riled Rafa had been that morning, he wasn't about to leave him alone with his parents.

At least Rafa's jagged, tense edges seemed to have smoothed out since they'd fucked. Shane was a little tender, and when he bent to retie a loose lace on his sneakers, his ass twinged. He smiled to himself as he straightened and arched his back, hands on his waist. They both wore jeans and T-shirts as usual.

"You okay?" Rafa asked.

"Yep. You gave my ass a good pounding."

He frowned. "Does it hurt a lot?"

The elevator doors pinged open, and Shane shrugged. "Just a bit." He grinned slyly. "You know what it feels like."

Rafa stuck out his arm so the doors would stay open, not moving from the elevator into the vestibule. At the end of the hallway straight ahead stood two male agents by the penthouse door. The Service had likely chosen this hotel since the elevator didn't give direct access into the penthouse.

Rafa whispered, "But I didn't mean to hurt you. That's not what I…"

"Of course not. It comes with the territory. I'd never want to hurt you either."

Some emotion Shane couldn't place shone from Rafa's brown eyes. "I know."

He wanted to close the elevator doors and stop it between floors so they could speak privately, but obviously that would put the agents on high alert. At a glance, he didn't recognize them, and they were far enough away that they couldn't hear whispers. Still, their stares were like hot pinpricks on his skin as he took Rafa's hand and threaded their fingers together. "What is it?"

"Nothing." Rafa gave him a little smile. "I'm just being crazy.

Parents, you know?" He winced, gripping Shane's fingers. "Fuck, I didn't mean to… I'm sorry."

Shane extended his arm as the doors tried to close again. They bounced back smoothly. "It's okay. Come on, we'd better not be late."

They squeezed each other's hands and let go, walking down the corridor shoulder to shoulder. The young agents wore bland expressions, and one said, "Good morning" as the other spoke into his wrist and gave the door a double knock. The door opened, and Shane nodded to them as he and Rafa passed over the threshold. For a moment, he swore one of them smirked, but then he and Rafa were inside.

Shane's gaze swept over the room, taking an automatic mental inventory of people, exit points, and potential vulnerabilities. In long shorts and a tee, Matthew slouched in an armchair, holding his phone with his good hand and scrolling rhythmically with his thumb. The brace and sling holding his left arm immobile and tucked against his stomach looked damned uncomfortable. His eyes were bleary, shaggy brown hair a mess.

Resentment flickered through Shane. Why did Rafa feel he had to be perfectly coiffed while his brother had never seemed to give a shit?

On couches by a low coffee table, Ramon and Camila Castillo sat with a young man who was likely a personal assistant, and—son of a bitch—Jennifer Hernandez, an agent Shane had worked with for a time in the Rhode Island field office. It had been years ago, and although there were new wrinkles around her eyes, she was still slim and fit and her dark hair showed no signs of gray. Whether that was natural or not, he couldn't say.

They were all looking at an open folder, and Hernandez was the first to stand and approach them, smoothing a hand over her suit jacket. Of course her expression stayed neutral. "Hello, Rafa. Mr. Kendrick."

Shane's heart thumped as he extended his hand. "Agent Hernandez. Good to see you again." *What must she think of me?* Hernandez hesitated, then shook his hand firmly, saying nothing.

Rafa's mother stood and walked around the couch. She wore some of the most casual clothing Shane had ever seen her in—dark khaki slacks, a black blouse, and black and white Michael Kors sneakers. Of course she still wore pearls, and silver leafs dangled from her ears. She spoke to Hernandez. "You know Mr. Kendrick?"

Hernandez's expression didn't waver. "No. I don't."

Now Shane felt like a fool, and he hated the heat flushing down his neck. He cleared his dry throat. "We both worked the Rhode Island field office. Must be ten years ago now."

"Huh." Hernandez shrugged and turned away, the dismissal clear as Rafa's father joined his wife. He wore a polo shirt and light chinos. Eyeing Shane up and down, silence stretched out for a few heartbeats. Shane fought the urge to fidget.

Then Castillo extended his hand. "Mr. Kendrick." Shane had thought of the president as simply "Castillo" or his codename, "Vagabond," for years, and it was a struggle now to think of him by his first name.

Rafa said, "Dad, it's *Shane*," as Shane shook Castillo's hand. Camila didn't offer hers. From his chair, Matthew glanced up and said, "Hey, man. Good to see you."

Shane nodded to him. He felt like a pimpled teenager picking up Rafa for a date and promising to bring him home by eleven. He was afraid if he said anything, his voice would break.

He'd briefly met Rafa's parents and shook their hands after the kidnapping, when they'd been grateful to him. Now they stared at him with even expressions that couldn't be called particularly friendly. Keeping his head high, Shane waited for someone to say something.

Anything.

It was Camila who did. "We weren't sure you'd be up to the climb after your journey. I hope you understand why we felt it important for you to go back in person."

Tensing, he fought not to show his surprise. Without looking at Rafa, he simply said, "Of course." Rafa was a wall of stress beside him. His parents had been the ones to make sure Shane had gone to DC? Was that what had gotten him so upset? Why hadn't he just told Shane? Of course these questions would have to wait. He didn't want the Castillos to see any lack of communication between them. They had to conceal all weaknesses.

Rafa tugged his arm. "Check out this view."

He followed to the wall of glass, his stomach swooping. He knew he wouldn't fall out, but he still kept his gaze on the horizon, trying not to think about how high they were. The Castillos were speaking with their assistants, and Rafa whispered, "I'm sorry. I was going to tell you they pulled some strings to make you go back for the hearing."

"Don't be. It's done now, and there was nothing you could do about it."

Rafa nodded, and then leaned his forehead against the glass. "The people are tiny."

Looking down at the toy cars and ant-people made Shane's head spin, but he forced a smile. "They are."

The PA mercifully announced it was time to go, and they went down to the limo in the underground garage in awkward silence broken only by the PA's constant patter, going through plans for a future trip, apparently to the UK. Facing forward in the limo, Shane sat with Rafa on his right in the middle, Matthew on Rafa's other side. The Castillos and their PA sat across, seemingly engrossed by their travel plans.

Hernandez sat up front with the limo driver, the partition open. Shane examined the back of Hernandez's head. Not a strand of hair seemed to escape from the tight bun. It nagged that she'd pretended not to know him. As if merely being past acquaintances would be too shameful somehow.

Sure, it had been a decade, but she remembered him. After long days in the office, they'd gone drinking sometimes at a dingy little wood-paneled pub in Providence with cold Bud on tap and bargain wings.

"You know what I like about you, Kendrick?" Hernandez dismantled a honey-garlic chicken wing, sucking meat off the skinny bone.

"My sparkling wit? Ability to name all fifty states without counting on my fingers?"

"That I can be sure you won't play grab-ass like Radinski and Moreland." She grimaced. "Ugh, and fucking Kornikov. Who does he think he's kidding with that comb-over? As if I'd touch him with a ten-foot fucking pole." She chugged from her pint glass. "Of course you're the only one I'd want to get busy with. But it's strangely reassuring to know it'll never happen."

"Glad to be of service."

"Mom, I don't need two hands to walk up a bridge," Matthew huffed.

The PA said, "There are segments that require ascending ladders—"

"I can climb ladders with one hand! I'm not a freaking invalid."

"Language," Camila said.

Matthew barked out a laugh. "I didn't realize 'freaking' was a swear word now."

She leveled him with a Look, capital L. "We all know what you meant. Remember, everyone—we must be on our best behavior." She glanced at Shane as if daring him to argue.

"I'm sure it'll be fine," Rafa said, always the peacemaker. Affection swelled, and Shane stopped himself from pressing a kiss to Rafa's head.

Soon they were piling out, several agents positioned by the car and inside the high-ceilinged reception area/gift shop built at the base of one of the massive bridge supports. Shane swept the room.

There were whispering cashiers behind a long check-in counter trying to pretend they weren't looking. To the right, displays of hats, T-shirts, magnets, mugs, and just about anything you might want to overpay for with the Sydney Harbour Bridge logo on it. A few tourists there, staring openly.

A grinning young woman approached. "G'day! Welcome to the bridge climb! Ready for a once-in-a-lifetime opportunity?"

They followed her upstairs, garnering more curious looks from tourists, whispers slithering through the large lobby. Phones came out, and pictures and videos would surely soon flood social media. The agents assigned to Rafa's parents kept a close watch, and Shane had to stop himself from joining in, expecting a message in his ear any second.

Rafa rhythmically smoothed down his hair, his shoulders creeping up. Shane realized he hadn't seen that automatic, nervous reaction to the attention of strangers in months, and he hated seeing it now. As they climbed a wide flight of stairs, all eyes still on their group, he murmured, "You look great."

Cheeks flushing, Rafa shot him a fleeting smile, and Shane itched to take his hand. He shouldn't be intimidated by the Castillos, but he also wanted to keep the peace and avoid awkwardness, so PDAs probably weren't the best idea.

The Castillos were clearly already struggling to be polite with Shane, so he'd do his part. He wasn't ashamed of his relationship with Rafa, but he wanted to keep everyone on an even keel.

A male greeter with a hipster beard boomed, "G'day! We're honored to have you with us today. Now, I'm told you want to do the climb as part of a normal group with other climbers?"

Castillo answered, "Absolutely. We're just regular people like everyone else."

Rafa and Matthew shared a sardonic glance, and Shane kept

his face carefully neutral. Ramon Castillo had done his "we're just ordinary folk" routine throughout his presidency, but he was really hitting it hard now that he was out of office. Never mind the fact that ordinary people didn't attract paparazzi, or hire themselves out to make keynote speeches for hundreds of thousands of dollars, or have Secret Service agents protecting them.

Matthew leaned in to Rafa and whispered too loudly, "Mom can't *wait* to climb this bridge like a regular tourist."

Shane almost murmured a joke about her looking forward to pushing him off the top, but bit his tongue. *Eyes and ears everywhere. Stay sharp.*

The greeter said, "Awesome. The rest of the group's waiting."

Hernandez and her team had undoubtedly vetted the six people already sitting in a small antechamber with benches built along the walls. They were a pair of German women in their sixties, a young male-female couple from New Zealand, and two young Japanese women. After greetings and some handshakes—Castillo always the first to glad-hand—they took their places along the benches.

Shane counted fourteen of them in the group total, including three agents. They all listened as a staff member went over basic safety and then handed them clipboards with waivers to sign. They had to take a breathalyzer; some people giggled at the request.

When it was his turn, Shane leaned forward and spoke into the device as instructed. "One, two, three, four, five."

They had to take off any dangling earrings or jewelry, including Fitbits from around their wrists, and watches. Camila's face pinched as she reluctantly deposited her earrings into a baggie.

"All right, gang! Time to get changed. Follow me!"

They trouped after the staff into a large changing room with dozens of curtained cubicles. A young woman said, "So now you're going to get out of your clothes and into these jumpsuits."

She held up a blue and gray jumpsuit with a zipper up the front. "It's winter, but a bit of a heat wave's rolled in, and the sun's strong. It might seem a bit odd, but we highly recommend stripping down to your underwear beneath the jumpsuit. Or else you'll get very hot."

More giggles. Then Camila asked, "Have these jumpsuits been laundered?"

The woman laughed. "Of course! Clean as a whistle, don't worry."

Camila smiled tightly, and Shane bit back a snort, sharing a smile with Rafa as they took their assigned jumpsuits and each changed in a small, curtained cubicle.

Shane zipped up the jumpsuit over his boxer-briefs, trying to calm his nerves. He reminded himself that countless people had climbed the bridge and no one had fallen off.

Right? Or am I only assuming that? How old is this bridge? Maybe it happened before the internet even existed.

Taking a deep breath, Shane rejoined the others. He was doing this. If Camila Castillo could do it, so could he, goddamn it.

Their clothes and belongings were locked up, and they were harnessed next, a safety line fastened around their waists. If they wanted to wear sunglasses, which everyone did, they had to be secured with a strap the staff provided.

"Right, now you're all set," said the man with the beard. "You've got nothing on you that could fall onto the road below the bridge, which I'm sure you understand is a great concern of ours. No phones, no jewelry, no gum. I know you all want to bring your phones and take snaps, but we'll take plenty for you. Just enjoy the incredible view. Now let's get your complimentary hats hooked onto your suits, then kit you up with radios and headsets so you can hear your guide."

Then there was a test apparatus—ladders they had to climb up, then step over to another to climb down. The staff watched

Matthew closely as he scaled the metal, but he didn't hesitate going up or down, his expression calm. Shane had a feeling if he was in any pain, he'd do whatever it took to hide it.

They lined up, the Kiwi couple in front, then Rafa, Shane, an agent, the Castillos, the other agents, and so on. The harness around their waists were hooked onto a railing with a sort of carabiner, and they were to simply follow the railing the whole way up and back down again.

Rafa shot Shane a grin as they started, first following catwalks and ducking below cantilevers under the massive pylons. To go to the top side of the bridge, they climbed straight up four sets of ladders in a row. Rafa didn't hesitate as he scaled the first, soon disappearing onto a platform off to the side. Shane glanced down at the vehicles speeding by, and his heart pounded as he imagined the impact he'd make if he fell.

Eyes straight ahead.

He climbed and stepped onto the platform before turning to the next ladder. One by one he climbed them, his stupid heart hammering even though he knew he was locked onto the railing and that the climb operators knew what they were doing. They wouldn't let anyone fall. The ladders were narrow, and he banged his knees and elbows as he powered up, refusing to slow.

Up out on the curving top of the bridge, the wind blew pleasantly, and Shane gulped in a few breaths as they waited for the rest of the group. Rafa stared out at the view of the Opera House and harbor and said, "Look, you can see the ocean over there."

"Uh-huh."

Rafa turned to him, lowering his voice. "What's wrong?"

"I don't love heights." Shane gripped the railing, sweat already damp on his skin beneath the jumpsuit.

Rafa's eyes widened and he whispered, "Why didn't you tell me?"

"Because it's ridiculous. This is completely safe, and there's nothing to be afraid of. I wanted to do it. Prove to myself I can.

Didn't want to let you down."

Rafa took his hand. "You can totally do it. I'm right here. I won't let you fall." He uttered it with such *belief* that Shane's heart clenched. He nodded as the guide—the bearded hipster—began speaking.

They climbed very gradually, the steps up the arc of the bridge quite shallow. The guide stopped them a few times to enjoy the view and listen to some history, and each time they stopped, Rafa reached back and squeezed Shane's hand. Bit by bit, he relaxed.

The view really was stunning—the water deep blue, buildings spread out into the distance. And even if Shane hadn't been hooked on, it would have been pretty damn hard to fall off. Not that he was unhooking himself, but the walk up felt surprisingly safe.

He thought of a weekend years ago when Darnell had talked him into rock climbing. Going up hadn't been an issue at all since Shane had been concentrating on finding handholds and footholds in the craggy rock. It was a beginner's climb, and from the bottom, the ledge they were scrambling up to one by one before rappelling down hadn't seemed high at all.

Of course when Shane had reached the ledge and turned around, he'd felt sucker punched. Darnell and the rest of the group on the ground looked very, very far away. But once Shane had gotten the balls to swing out on the rope and had felt that it would hold him—that the guides were doing their jobs and he wouldn't fall—he'd actually enjoyed being lowered down.

It was the same now that he was on the bridge, and by the time they reached the top and took a group picture, he was able to smile genuinely, slinging one arm around Rafa's waist as the group all crowded in.

Another group was farther along at the top section of the bridge. Music floated on the air, and Shane said, "Are they...doing karaoke?"

The guide chuckled. "Yep, it's an add-on option. Popular for team building."

As the group belted out "Single Ladies," Camila wrinkled her nose. "The appeal is rather lost on me."

"Same here," Shane agreed. There was an agent standing between them who said nothing. Camila gave Shane a tight smile.

"All right, time to record your free videos!" the guide announced. "You've got nine seconds, and what I recommend is that you take a minute now to script out a little message."

The Kiwi couple went first, and Shane asked Rafa, "What should we do? Something totally cheesy?"

"Follow my lead." Rafa smiled. "I know what I want to say."

Then it was their turn, and the guide aimed the camera and said go. Rafa pulled down Shane's head with strong hands and kissed him forcefully. Shane jolted, then kissed him back, because if he wanted to make a statement, Shane would be at his side a hundred percent. Then Rafa broke away, smiling at him before turning his grin to the camera.

The guide gave a thumbs-up and said, "Okay. Next!"

They crossed the catwalk to the other side of the bridge, Rafa practically skipping. Shane glanced back. Matthew smirked as his parents smiled tightly, his dad saying something about how wonderful it was to be in beautiful Sydney.

On the other side, they walked down several steps and took their spots at the railing, looking out over the interior of the harbor. Shane murmured, "That was unexpected."

"What? I'm not allowed to kiss my boyfriend? I'm going to make an Instastory. You know, those little videos you can post for a day? I don't have a Facebook because of the creepy-ass messages I'd get flooded with daily. But I'm going to open an Instagram. It's time."

Shane nodded. "Okay. You know I support you."

Still, Rafa's voice rose. "Why shouldn't I get to post a fun video like everyone else? What, you don't want anyone to see us kissing?"

He glanced beyond Rafa at the young couple from Auckland,

who were strenuously pretending not to listen, then back as an agent and Rafa's parents reached the end of the catwalk. Shane quietly said, "You know that's not it," squeezing Rafa's hand. He looked out over the other side of the harbor, his breath catching, a fresh wave of unease zipping through him.

We're safe. We won't fall. Don't think about it. Stop thinking. It was all going well! Look at the horizon.

Clearly needling Camila, Matthew arrived and asked, "Isn't this *awesome*, Mom?"

She sounded completely calm as she answered, "Yes, it's a lovely view."

Rafa's father added, "Quite a feat of engineering, this bridge. Do you remember how long it took to build the Golden Gate? Which took more time?"

While the rest of the group had their videos done, Ramon kept up a steady, cheerful patter about bridges around the world that Shane half-listened to. On the way back down, it was harder not to think about how high they were. Sweat dampened the band of Shane's baseball cap, and when the guide stopped them halfway down to talk about how many people got killed building the bridge, he had to concentrate on breathing in and out.

Rafa took his hand again and whispered, "You're doing so great. I'm proud of you."

And God, how Shane craved that. Satisfaction smoothed out his rigid muscles, and he leaned down and gave Rafa a peck on the lips, not caring who was watching.

Chapter Eight

CHOPPING THE CREMINI and oyster mushrooms for the risotto, Rafa listened to the low drone of the Aussie rules football game Shane was watching in the living room. Rafa had always found sports noises strangely comforting—the cracks of bats and roars of crowds, the patter of the commentators.

He checked his jotted-down recipe for mushroom and mascarpone risotto—the yellow Post-It was stained with oil from the first time he'd tried it a month ago. He and Shane had both loved his new creation, so he'd decided to make it again and serve it to his family with asparagus and seared sea scallops on top.

Now if only his stomach would stop somersaulting.

But the idea of having his parents here—in Rafa and Shane's space—had him gripping his knife handle too tight, his movements jerky and forced, making a mess of the mushrooms. They'd still taste okay, at least.

"Relax," he muttered to himself as the football fans on TV cheered. "It's going to be fine."

After all, the bridge climb had gone fairly well, hadn't it? There hadn't been any shouting matches. Everyone was trying, although he knew his mother and father still didn't approve of Shane. But they were coming for dinner, and they'd get to see how good Shane and Rafa were together—how happy. Yes. They'd see, and they'd start to truly accept Shane rather than reluctantly tolerate him.

His phone buzzed, and he glanced at the message on the screen from Ashleigh.

OMFG, Miranda lost her wallet at a conference in Milan. Plz enjoy this actual email she just sent me: "Help. My wallet was just stolen. What do I do?" Because God knows she's not capable of canceling a credit card on her own. Sometimes I'm amazed she can wipe her own ass. If she doesn't have her passport she is fucked, which means I am fucked. Pray for me. Also good luck with your mom and dad. I think we both need prayers today. (Not to mention the even more useful 'thoughts,' of course.)

Smiling, he quickly tapped a response and put his phone back on the counter. After he brushed away a stray bit of mushroom stem stuck to his tee, he started frying minced garlic and a diced shallot in butter.

From the living room came a groan. Then another. He hadn't realized Shane had gotten so attached to a particular team. Then there were mumbles, and a ragged gasp. Rafa's heart skipped, the hair on his arms rising.

Bare feet quiet on the wood, he peeked into the living room. The Swans and Dockers played on, but Shane was asleep. He'd curled onto his side on the couch, shoulders hunched and knees up, shirtless and only wearing his board shorts.

He jerked and moaned, muttering words Rafa couldn't make out, brow deeply furrowed, his fingers clenched like claws. Then he sucked in a breath and mumbled Rafa's name in a high-pitched whine that sent a shiver down Rafa's spine. He bent and took Shane's bare shoulder, squeezing.

"Shane? It's okay. Wake up."

He did, gasping and jerking, his arm lashing out and hand catching Rafa on the chin. Rafa stumbled back and plopped his butt onto the coffee table. He automatically raised his hand to his chin, but it had only been a glancing blow with the backs of Shane's fingers.

Shane stared at him with wide eyes. Sweat dampened his forehead, and he pushed up to sitting, clearly disoriented. "Raf? What...?" He looked at his own hands, then back at Rafa. "Did I..." His voice cracked. "Did I hit you?"

"No, no—you barely touched me. You were having a nightmare, and I startled you." He ran a palm down Shane's arm. "What were you dreaming about?"

Shane ignored the question, perching on the side of the couch, eyes searching as he gently took Rafa's cheeks and turned his head this way and that. "Where did I get you?"

Rafa sighed. "On my chin. It's nothing. It doesn't even hurt." It stung a tiny bit, but he didn't think it would bruise or anything. "It was an accident. Don't freak out, okay?"

Shane was still examining Rafa's face. "I'm so sorry. Fuck." He bit out, "I'm *pathetic*."

Startled, Rafa opened and closed his mouth. "What? No you aren't. What's wrong?" He closed his hands over Shane's bare knees, rubbing his thumbs against the sharp bones.

Shane sat back and rubbed his face, eyes closed. "It was nothing. I don't remember."

Yet you said my name, and now you won't look at me. Why was Shane lying? "Talk to me. Please."

"It's nothing, baby. Stupid dream." He opened his eyes and leaned forward again, running his fingers over Rafa's jaw. "Are you sure it doesn't hurt?"

"You barely touched me. I'm fine." Irritation sparked, and he tried to tamp it down, keeping his voice calm. "You know you can tell me anything. If something's bothering you, if you have a bad dream, whatever."

"I know." Shane slid his hand behind Rafa's head and drew him near for a tender kiss. Then he sat back and smiled. "That smells good."

"Shit!" Rafa leapt up and ran back to the kitchen. He grabbed a wooden spoon and stirred, getting there just in time to stop the shallots and garlic from burning. He turned down the stove.

From the hallway, Shane called, "Having a shower."

"Wait, I…" But in place of the TV, now he heard water running from their bathroom.

It's fine. He's fine. He had a bad dream. It was nothing.

Yet Rafa's gut told him there was more to it. He thought back to when Shane had claimed to be sick that night and locked himself in the bathroom. Had he had a nightmare then too? Was this an ongoing problem Rafa hadn't noticed? Or that Shane was trying to hide? Why wouldn't Shane just tell him?

Why didn't he tell me he and Darnell used to hook up?

Grimacing, he checked the time and ordered himself to concentrate on dinner. It had to be good. No, not just good— spectacular. He put the garlic and shallots aside. He'd tested the recipe a few different ways and found that precooking them didn't detract from the overall flavor in the end.

Pulling out the smoked salmon to get it to room temperature, he set about beating the blini mixture together using butter he'd clarified earlier. The little buckwheat pancakes would be topped with the salmon, creme fraiche, and a dill sprig.

As he whisked the blini batter, his mind stubbornly returned again and again to the nagging questions he'd tried to forget. Why hadn't Shane told him the truth about Darnell? Rafa had wanted to ask him, but…hadn't.

Because I'm chicken-shit.

But there just hadn't been a good time. Besides, Shane hadn't *lied* to him, had he? He and Darnell were friends. If they'd been friends with benefits in the past, was Shane obligated to tell him? Rafa didn't know the answer, although it'd been a relief to hear that Darnell was seeing someone.

Dripping water and with only a towel around his hips, Shane padded into the kitchen. "Sorry, I just realized I never asked if you need help in here." He rubbed a hand over his stubbly head. "Damn jet lag really caught up with me."

"It's okay. Just…" Rafa stopped whisking. "You're sure you're all right? We're all right?"

His face creasing with a smile, Shane came close and kissed Rafa slowly, their tongues meeting. He rested their foreheads together. "Baby, we're amazing."

Warmth filled Rafa, and he put down the bowl and relaxed into Shane, not caring that he was getting wet since he had to change for dinner anyway. He nuzzled Shane's neck, loving the low sigh that eased through Shane's muscled body, and the way Shane's big hands slipped under Rafa's T-shirt and settled around his waist.

For a few seconds, neither of them reacted to the rumble of the engine. Then they sprang apart, and Rafa jerked his head to check the time on the microwave as Shane hurried into the living room. He called back, "It's them."

"Oh my fucking God, who comes early to a dinner party?" He muttered, "My parents, that's who." Whirling left and right, he tried to figure out what to do next, anxiety rising, his breath catching in his tight lungs.

Shane returned. "You get the door while I pull on clothes. It's okay. Don't panic. We got this."

Nodding, Rafa patted down his hair, grimacing when he realized there was still flour dusting his hands. "Keep your shit together," he murmured to himself as the doorbell chimed.

Two of the agents stood there on the doorstep in the fading daylight in their sunglasses and suits. Everyone else was apparently still in the limo. One agent nodded. "Hello. We need to come in and clear the house."

Rafa stepped back. "Yeah. I know the drill. Obviously. I mean, it's been a while but…" *Stop talking.* He closed the door after them and let them do their thing. They opened closets and pulled all the blinds, turning on lights as they went. It didn't take long, and Shane followed them out of the bedroom, dressed in dark jeans and a burgundy button-down.

After getting the all-clear, Ramon and Camila walked up the little flagstone path, and Rafa smiled widely. "Hey!" He looked beyond them, only seeing Agent Hernandez, who gave him a nod. "Where's Matty?"

"I'm afraid his shoulder is really bothering him," Ramon answered. "He took some pills this afternoon and is too tired to get out of bed. My assistant is checking in on him."

"I knew he shouldn't have done that bridge climb yesterday." Camila pressed a kiss to Rafa's cheek. "But no one ever listens to me."

Ramon's laugh was strained. "All right, dear. Rafalito, show us the house. It smells wonderful in here."

"Thanks. Sorry, I still need to change." Rafa closed the door after them, his heart skipping. Couldn't they have warned him his brother wasn't coming? Now there'd be no buffer. But it was fine. Everything was *fine*.

"Um, so here's the living room." He toured them through the house, which didn't take long. Shane had closed the bedroom door, and Rafa nodded to it as they passed. "Our room's in there." He willed himself not to blush. Unsuccessfully.

When they were back in the living room, Shane appeared and shook Ramon's hand. "Can I get anyone a drink?"

Rafa almost made a joke that they could all use one, but stopped himself. His mother answered, "Vodka soda."

"Yes, thank you," Ramon said. "I'll take a beer."

Rafa said, "I have to get the risotto on. I'll just…" He motioned to the couch. "Make yourselves at home." It was so freaking *weird* that his parents were here in the living room. That he was playing host for the first time ever. He hurried into the kitchen.

Shane was topping off Camila's drink with a sliced lime. He murmured, "Breathe."

"I shouldn't have picked risotto. I have to be in here stirring the whole time."

Huffing out a small laugh, Shane smiled ruefully. "I'll survive. Probably. I'll keep your father talking."

"Good plan. Thank you. I'll get you to help me sear the scallops in a bit."

As Rafa cooked, he could hear snatches of the painful small talk occurring in the living room. He glanced in and saw that Shane had pulled over one of the chairs from the dining room. His parents sat on the couch, backs ramrod straight.

Fortunately, Ramon seemed happy to take the floor and go on about the state of European politics and the power of the Euro in world markets and blah, blah, blah. When Rafa served the salmon appetizers, Shane was asking Camila about her Healthy Children Foundation. She gave short answers, usually one-word.

Rafa's stomach churned.

But he managed not to overcook the risotto, and Shane "helped"—aka watched—him sear the dry scallops in a pan, and they came out perfectly. Rafa plated everything and was glad he'd set the table that morning, although he'd had to remove his brother's place setting. Shane took care of the wine while Rafa ducked into their room to pull on chinos and a clean Polo shirt.

Then the four of them sat around the square, rustic dining table. It could be extended to seat more, but it had seemed strange to do that with only four people, so he'd put the extra leaf away. Yet now Rafa wished he hadn't. They were all so...*close* to each other.

Ramon said, "Tell us about your recipe. It looks delicious." He cut into a scallop and ate half. "Mmm. Wonderful!"

Rafa knew he was talking too fast, but he blathered on as they ate, telling them about the risotto and scallops and more than anyone wanted to know about mushroom varieties. Shane was on wine duty, and soon he had to go for a second bottle of Chardonnay. He refilled Camila's empty glass and topped up everyone else's before putting the bottle into the stainless steel chiller on the table.

Swallowing a bite of scallop, Camila peered toward the sliding glass doors. They'd closed the blinds, but around the edges, the motion detector light snapping on could be spotted. Likely one of the agents patrolling the perimeter. Camila said, "I noticed earlier you have surfboards outside. Aren't you afraid they'll be stolen?"

Shane answered, "Usually we lock them in the little shed. I'll do it later."

"Oh, good. It would be a shame if they were taken. I imagine surfboards aren't cheap." She smiled at Rafa. "How did you afford one, dear?"

He speared a piece of asparagus with his fork, willing himself not to flush. "Shane bought it for me."

"That's very generous." She was still smiling calmly.

Rafa could sense the shark circling under the surface, but kept his tone even. "He's a generous person."

"Clearly. I mean, look at all the money he gave to the wife of the man who orchestrated your kidnapping."

Ramon hissed, "This isn't the time."

With all the faux innocence in the world, she delicately scooped the mushroom risotto onto the tip of her fork. "It's not appropriate to commend Mr. Kendrick's generosity? After what Alan Pearce did to our son, he still gave almost a million dollars to the man's wife."

Ramon's nostrils flared, his tone steely. "Enough, dear."

Shane sat utterly still with his knife and fork in hand, his jaw clenched. Rafa gripped his own fork, trying to stay the trembling of his hand as rage bubbled up. He said, "I'm sorry to disappoint you, but I knew all about it. Julianna Pearce's son is dying and no, it didn't bother me that Shane wanted to help a sick kid. Alan Pearce's family isn't responsible for his actions."

"Well, I didn't say you didn't know." Camila finished her Chardonnay. Shit, how many glasses had she had?

No, but you were hoping. His mother wasn't usually this transparent. Maybe he'd been wrong the other night and she *had* purposefully mentioned Darnell. *Ugh.* He'd worked to push his jealousy and lingering hurt about that aside, and now he shoved it away again. Focused on the now. "And yes, Shane buys me things."

Evenly, Shane put down his cutlery and said, "We're partners. We support each other. In a few years when Rafa's a chef—"

"He'll probably be too old for you!" Camila snapped, eyes blazing. "And you'll have moved on to your next victim."

Ramon's knife clattered onto his plate. "Camila!"

"*Victim?*" Rafa shouted. His forehead throbbed.

"You don't know anything about our relationship," Shane gritted out.

She huffed. "Oh, for God's sake. This is ridiculous! We're all pretending we don't see the emperor has no clothes! '*Partners*'? '*Relationship*'? It's laughable. Mr. Kendrick, we all know you're not my son's *partner*. You're his, his—sugar daddy!"

Face burning, words tangled on Rafa's tongue, his furious denials jumbled.

"Enough!" Ramon smacked his palm on the table. "We agreed we'd keep an open mind."

Camila hauled the wine bottle out of the chiller and sloshed more into her glass. "Oh, I have kept an open mind." She gulped a mouthful of Chardonnay. "All these months Rafa's been living here with this man, and I didn't fly down and drag him home. We agreed to give him time to regain his senses. To let this farce play out. But clearly we made a mistake, Ramon. He's been drinking the Kool-Aid."

"*He's* right here!" Rafa vibrated with fury. "I'm not a child. Stop talking about me like I'm not even in the room. Like you're not sitting here in *our house.* At our table! And I haven't been drinking any Kool-Aid!" He'd heard the term before, but wasn't a hundred percent on what it even meant. Something about brainwashing. "You've clearly been drinking too much wine, though."

Ramon grimaced. "I agree. You had a few cocktails earlier at the hotel as well." He reached for Camila's glass, but she jerked it away.

"You expect me to sit here at dinner stone-cold sober with the man who seduced our son?"

Rafa's head was about to explode. "Shane didn't seduce me! I knew what I wanted. What I still want. I'm not a kid. I love him, and he loves me. We make each other happy. Age doesn't matter. How many times do we have to go through this?"

To Ramon, again as if Rafa wasn't even present, Camila said, "How did we raise such a naive child? In the *White House* of all places." She narrowed her gaze on Shane. "The place where this man broke the rules and engaged in inappropriate contact with him. Rafa admitted it. We know the truth. We're just supposed to let that go? That we trusted you and you broke that trust? Your employer's trust?"

Shane somehow kept his cool. Under the table, he pressed his bare foot against Rafa's, a warm reassuring weight as he said, "I have no excuse. But I can't turn back time and change it. And Rafa is not a child. He's not now, and he wasn't when I met him. He's a man, and he has every right to make his own choices. Sharing my life with him these months have been the happiest I've ever known. And I'm sure you know from digging into my past that I've never dated anyone so much younger than me before. I'm with Rafa despite his age, not because of it. Your son is kind and intelligent and funny. He makes my life better than I'd ever dreamed it could be. I understand why it's difficult for you to accept our relationship. But you'll have to deal with it. With me. Because I'm not going anywhere."

Throat thick, Rafa reached for Shane's hand over the table. Not hiding. He held on, Shane's palm sweaty against his.

Exhaling slowly, Ramon nodded. "Yes, Mr. Ken—" He took another breath and blew it out. "Yes, Shane. I think you're right. You and Rafa clearly care for each other. Frankly, I don't think you would put up with us, or the circus that can surround us, if you didn't. We know you aren't after money. So I suppose you've passed that test." He took his linen napkin from his lap and wiped his mouth. "The jet lag has clearly caught up with my wife. We'll leave you now and see you tomorrow."

Lips pressed into a thin line, Camila shoved back her chair and dropped her napkin over her plate. She wavered unsteadily for a moment, then drained her wine glass and strode through the living room and out the front door, her stilettos striking the wooden floor in staccato beats. Outside, the agents scrambled, the car engine starting.

Ramon sighed. "I'm sorry." Then he walked around the table and drew Rafa to his feet and into a quick hug. "The dinner was delicious. See you both tomorrow at the train station." He gave Rafa's hair an affectionate ruffle and nodded to Shane. "Please accept my apology. Camila's behavior was inexcusable. She's had too much to drink, but… As I said, it's inexcusable."

Nodding, Shane stood and extended his hand. Ramon shook it ruefully and then he was gone, the limo engine soon fading.

Rafa breathed hard, his pulse still racing. "I'm so sorry." God, his mother had acted so terribly to Shane in his own house. He couldn't lift his gaze from the floor, embarrassment and anger pushing against his ribcage.

"Don't be. It's not your fault your mother can really be a—" He went silent.

Rafa looked up at Shane's sympathetic face. "You can say it. My mother can be a real grade-A bitch. And a half."

"She sure can." Shane grimaced, grabbing Camila's plate and stacking it on Ramon's with a clatter. He blew out a breath. "But she's still your mother, so…"

"I try to make her happy! I make this dinner, and then she goes and acts like that. *Fuck.*" Rafa slammed back into his chair. "She pisses me off so much." He stared at their half-eaten plates of food. "Why did she have to ruin this?" Without warning, his anger transformed into sorrow, and tears pricked his eyes. "*Fuck.*"

"It's okay, baby." Shane pulled his chair close and sat, their knees knocking together. He ran a hand over Rafa's head. "It's okay."

"God, and now I'm going to cry about it?" He blinked rapidly.

"Grown men are allowed to cry. You're allowed to be upset."

Rafa thought of Shane's nightmare earlier. "That goes for you too, right?"

Shane's brow furrowed. "Yeah. Of course."

"Okay." He rubbed his thumb over the furrow between Shane's brows, then kissed him softly.

For a few minutes, they held each other, just breathing. When Rafa sat back, he motioned to his plate. "It was pretty good, I thought?"

"It was *delicious.*" Shane popped a scallop into his mouth. "Still is."

"You should finish. I'm not really hungry anymore." His stomach was in too many knots to hope to get food in there. He wished he could avoid his parents for a while, but nope, he'd see them tomorrow.

At least they'll be going home in a couple of weeks. That's something.

Shane said, "Nah, I'm good. I'll clean up. You relax. Finish your wine."

Rafa managed a little smile. "Could use it, that's for sure." He took another swallow, then helped Shane clear the table. As he wiped the placemats with a damp cloth, Rafa's tired sadness retreated, another wave of indignation rolling in.

"I mean, she's supposed to be so mature? She was the one calling you names."

Shane wrapped around him from behind, his arms strong and secure, lips soft on Rafa's ear. He whispered, "I've been called worse than 'sugar daddy.'"

Rafa had to laugh, some of the tension releasing again. "You must really love me to put up with her shit."

"I really, really do." He kissed the back of his neck, sending a shiver down Rafa's spine.

"And to attack you here! In *our* house. At *our* table." He flattened his palms on the wood. "This is ours. I'm yours, and you're mine." He turned in Shane's arms, taking Shane's face in his hands. "You're *mine*, and no one is ever changing that. Especially not my fucking mother."

An almost frantic, electric energy zipped through him as he kissed Shane's mouth, thrusting his tongue inside. Shane kissed him back, gripping Rafa's hips and yanking him closer.

"Damn right you're mine," Shane whispered against Rafa's lips when they gasped for air.

The anger and hurt coalesced now into lust, Rafa getting hard as he rutted against Shane. Fuck his parents and everyone else. He and Shane were together, and they didn't have to hide. This was *their house*.

He tugged at the button on Shane's jeans and dropped to his knees with a thud, desperate to get Shane's cock in his mouth, because it was their house and *he could*.

Shane palmed Rafa's head, looking down at him with eyes dark and lips wet as Rafa yanked down Shane's jeans enough to take out his swelling dick. Holding the base, their eyes still locked together, he swallowed.

Shane groaned. "Oh, fuck, baby."

Rafa took him almost to the root. He gagged and pulled back, licking and spitting, using his hands to stroke where his mouth couldn't reach.

He loved the stretch of his lips over Shane's meat, how Shane throbbed in his mouth, like Rafa could feel Shane's heart through his dick, like he could kiss it. Loved how Shane watched him like he was the most precious, beautiful thing in the world.

Even though Rafa was the one on his knees, he was in control, Shane caressing his head, never pushing. Rafa wanted to let go and let Shane take over, but he also ached for the taste of semen— ached to give pleasure and show Shane how much he loved him.

Because he did, he loved him so freaking much. He didn't care why Shane hadn't told him about Darnell, or why he was close-lipped about his nightmare. It didn't matter. This was all that mattered—that they were together. That they loved each other.

He was wild with affection, his chest swelling with the need to make everything right after his mother had invaded their space. He hollowed his cheeks, sucking desperately.

Shane seemed to sense his mess of emotions, stroking Rafa's head and murmuring, "It's okay." He gasped as Rafa pulled off to suck his balls, digging his fingers into Shane's thighs through his jeans.

Now Rafa wanted to let go, and with Shane, he could. Here in their dining room where his mother had been so awful, he wanted to reclaim their house. He wanted to *be* claimed.

He licked around Shane's shaft again, spitting and getting it soaked. It was rock hard, and it turned Rafa on even more to know how much Shane wanted him. *Him.* Dorky Rafael Castillo, the human Chia Pet, of all the men in the world. Sometimes he still couldn't believe it.

He pushed to his feet. "Need you to fuck me."

Shane nodded, kissing him again, their tongues meeting, Shane's wet cock poking Rafa through the thin cotton of his tee. Desire pooled in Rafa's belly, hot high-wire tension strung through his body. Through his chinos, he rubbed the heel of his hand over his straining dick.

Breaking their kiss, Shane stepped back. "Get ready for me." He disappeared into their bedroom.

Rafa stripped off his shirt and the ridiculous chinos, kicking off his underwear and sending them flying toward the living room. Shane returned with the lube, a grin spreading over his face. His gaze raked down Rafa's body, stopping on his junk. He swiped his finger over the leaking tip. "You're so hot."

Flushing with pleasure and pride, Rafa whimpered as Shane kissed him long and slow, tongue exploring Rafa's mouth until he whined and rutted against the rough material of Shane's jeans.

Shane chuckled. "Okay. I've got you." With sure, strong hands, he turned him around to face the table, hands firm on Rafa's shoulders. Thank God they'd closed all the blinds when his parents had arrived in case any paps had followed.

Shane ran his fingers down Rafa's spine. "How do you want to come? Tell me again what you need."

Apparently Shane wanted to hear it, and the words spilled out of Rafa's swollen lips. "Give me your cock. Fuck me. Hard. Bent over our table. Please."

Shane urged Rafa to fold himself over the table, and he pressed against the wood, a damp placemat under his belly. Shane was silent a moment, spreading his hand over Rafa's lower back. "You need to come on my cock? No one else's?"

"Only yours," Rafa croaked. "I need it so bad." He reached back and spread his ass cheeks. "Please. Fuck me hard. Give me your dick, Shane."

Shane's slick fingers shoved into Rafa's ass without warning, slicking and stretching him. "You're so good. So beautiful. *Mine.*"

He twisted his fingers, the stretch burning. "You ready for me?"

He groaned. "I'm always ready for you. I'm your cum slut. I used to jerk off imagining this, you taking me hard and—" He cried out as Shane thrust into him, going almost to the hilt. Rafa's legs shook, his cock straining beneath the table where he couldn't reach it. He let go of his ass cheeks, reaching across the table and curling his fingers around the other side, shoving away a forgotten fork.

"That's right, baby. Hold on tight."

"Fuck me. Fuck me hard."

Digging his fingers into his hips, Shane pistoned into him, balls smacking against Rafa's tender ass, their flesh slapping and breath loud and desperate with each thrust. Rafa moaned as Shane grunted, Shane filling him so deeply Rafa thought he might break.

But he didn't, and he knew Shane would never hurt him; would never give him more than he wanted. He didn't care what anyone else thought—Shane completed him. And not just when his dick was in Rafa's ass.

"Oh, baby. So dirty. You love it when I fuck you, don't you?"

"Yes," he moaned, turning his head and pressing his hot cheek to the knotty wood table. "I'm yours."

He blinked at a wine glass that was shaking with every thrust. That he was being fucked at the table where his parents had just sat sent a forbidden thrill through him, followed by a deep thrum of power.

"So perfect." Shane punctuated his words with sharp, deep drives into Rafa's core. "I want to fuck you forever."

"Yes," he moaned. "I need to come. *Please.*" His fingers cramped where he hung onto the table, his knees weak as he was wrenched with every thrust. Shane's cock was so thick and big and perfect, stretching him open. Flayed and vulnerable, he trusted Shane completely to keep him safe. This was their home, and Rafa didn't have to hide.

He reached a hand back, hoping he could snake it beneath the table, but Shane caught his wrist, gritting out, "Give me your other one too."

Rafa did, and Shane circled his wrists with his hands, pulling Rafa's arms back straight at his sides, still fucking him, the push and pull so powerful Rafa could only moan and gasp, words beyond him now. Even though his feet were on the ground, he felt like he was floating. Shane's hands and cock were the only things tethering him to the earth.

Shane pounded his ass, their skin slapping, and even though Rafa wasn't the one in control now, the sense of power flowed through him even stronger. He wasn't a kid. He was a man, and this was *his house*, and he'd get filled with cum while splayed across his dining table whenever he wanted.

Shane's movements became shallower as he angled to hit just the right spot. Rafa cried out as he fucked against his gland, his balls tightening as Shane bent over his back to reach down for Rafa's cock.

He only stroked it twice before Rafa seized up, his orgasm exploding, burst after burst of intense pleasure scrubbing him raw through every pore. He opened his mouth on a silent scream, knees quivering as Shane milked him through it.

Then Shane was fucking him again, and Rafa squeezed down as hard as he could, smiling to himself as Shane came inside him, filling him with long pulses. Rafa mumbled, "Give me all of it."

Shane pressed against his back, mouth open, breath hot on the nape of Rafa's neck, his chest hair scratchy. "I think you've got it," Shane replied, groaning as he pulled out and urged Rafa up to standing, turning him and steadying him against the table.

He traced a finger over Rafa's raw mouth, his gaze searching. "You're sure that wasn't too rough?"

"It was amazing. I felt like I was in a porno." He laughed. "All those times I watched videos on Ash's computer, I never dreamed

I'd actually end up having mind-blowing sex for real." Rafa kissed the old surfing scar on Shane's neck, relaxing against him, his limbs sore and ass smarting. "I really needed that. After the things my mom said… I needed to, I dunno. Take back my power or something."

"I get it. Look, your parents are going to think and feel how they do. We have to stay focused on us." He leaned back, a sly grin lifting his lips. "For the record, I'll be your sugar daddy for as long as it takes. Then you can support me in retirement."

Rafa laughed. "Deal." He squeezed his ass, reveling in the soreness. "Mmm. I love feeling you after. I'll be standing as much as possible on that train tomorrow."

Chuckling, Shane tenderly petted Rafa's butt and nuzzled his temple. He whispered, "I love you so much."

"Me too." Rafa leaned back and pulled Shane's head down so he could kiss the scar the bullet had left over his ear, the reminder of how easily it could all be taken away.

Chapter Nine

"READY?" RAFA ASKED. "The car will be here soon."

"Mmm-hmm." Shane stared at his medium hard-shell suitcase, open on the bed, his clothes rolled neatly inside, toiletries and shaving kit tucked into the corners. *Ready to spend three nights on a train with your parents. Yep.* Well, he was as ready as he'd ever be, so he zipped the suitcase closed.

He turned to where Rafa leaned against the doorjamb, shoulders slumped, eyes on the floor. His button-down was crisp and ironed, tucked into his slacks, and hair gelled. He'd seemed so relaxed when they'd gone to bed, but in the light of day…

There would undoubtedly be photographers at the train station, and Shane understood why Rafa was driven to wear his old White House costume. It still set Shane's teeth on edge.

Even after Camila's performance the night before, Rafa wanted to please her. Shane supposed it was an innate need in most people. Sure, he'd wanted to please his parents—make them proud too. And he had.

The grief that would never go away panged dully. His parents had been generous and kind, not like that bi—

He cut off the train of thought. She was Rafa's mother, and it wouldn't do any good to resent her. *Even if she is a bitch.* Of course he'd shaved and dressed sharply himself, so who was he to talk? If he didn't care what the Castillos thought, why didn't he just wear shorts and flip-flops?

"You don't have to come," Rafa said quietly.

"What? Of course I'm coming." He went for levity. "Don't want to give your parents the chance to talk you around to their way of thinking."

But Rafa didn't laugh. Instead, he blinked, jerking his chin back. He pushed off the doorframe. "You think they could convince me? You don't think I can stand up to them?"

Shit. "No, of course you can. Sorry. It was a bad joke, baby." Shane stepped close and ran his palms up and down Rafa's rigid arms, the sleeves of his blue shirt silky.

"Maybe you shouldn't call me that." Rafa dropped his eyes again.

"Oh." Shane struggled to get the right read on the situation. "Is it… Do you not like it? That I call you 'baby'?" He had to admit he'd miss it, but obviously if it bothered Rafa, he'd stop. "You should have told me ages ago. I'm sorry."

Rafa sighed loudly, shaking his head. He met Shane's gaze. "I *do* like it. But maybe I shouldn't?"

"How does it make you feel? When I call you that?"

A little smile lifted Rafa's full, beautiful lips. "Makes me feel safe. Cared-for. Loved."

Shane traced a finger over the freckles dotting Rafa's nose. "Good. Because I will always love you. Protect you. When you're forty-five, you'll still be my baby."

Rafa captured Shane's finger and kissed the tip, then threaded their fingers together. "I like being your baby. But still your partner."

"Absolutely. We're equals, no matter what."

Rafa looked up at him imploringly. "So you know you can tell me anything. No matter what it is. If anything's bothering you…"

"Nothing's bothering me," he automatically answered, guilt tugging immediately. He dropped his gaze to Rafa's chin before forcing his eyes up. There was no bruise or reddening at all from where his fingers had made contact—he'd checked carefully that morning while Rafa still slept—but he still hated it had happened at all. Despised his weakness. The inquest was over—there was no reason to still be having the fucking nightmares.

Shane forced a chuckle. "Well, obviously I'm not too thrilled with your mother at the moment."

Rafa huffed out a half-laugh. "Me either." Then he raised Shane's hand and kissed the back of it. "But you can always talk to me. About anything. Even if it's how much of a bitch my mother can be."

Shane hesitated. Maybe he should just confess about his nightmares. *What, tell him how I see him bloody and beaten? How I see him in that metal box? How I see him* dead? *What good will that do?* The nightmare images filled his mind, and an icy hand squeezed his heart. What if telling the truth about the nightmares sparked bad dreams for Rafa too?

Rafa was right—they were partners. Still, the urge to protect him above all else warred with the desire to tell the truth. He couldn't bear it if unloading his crap ended up hurting him. Rafa was the one who'd been kidnapped, who'd been shoved in that box. Shane had been doing his job. He should be able to let it all go and move past it.

A car honked, and they both jerked. Forcing a smile, Shane stepped back, and Rafa let go of his hand. Shane managed a light tone as he reached for his suitcase. "Well, our journey awaits. And I'm sure I'll have plenty to say about your mother soon enough."

Rafa laughed and gave him a kiss. "I'm sure we both will." His smile faded.

"Don't worry, baby. We've got this."

WHEN THEY ARRIVED at the platform, Hernandez greeted them briskly, leading them past the clusters of other passengers, who stared and whispered. A man in the center of the wide platform played a folky Australian song on a guitar, and waiters circulated with trays of sparkling water and bite-sized appetizers.

"You vetted the other passengers?" Shane asked. He kept close to Rafa, eyeing the clusters of people and looking for threats.

Hernandez glared. "Of course. And we don't need your input."

It was fair enough—she knew how to do her job. He said, "Sorry. Old habits and all that."

Hernandez ignored the apology and soon they joined the Castillos, who clapped politely as the performer finished a song. Aside from Matthew, of course. His bent arm was immobilized against his stomach, and he didn't crack a smile. Shane inventoried the dark circles under his eyes, the barely combed hair, and grayish pallor. Hungover? Or truly in that much pain? The jury was out.

With hundreds of eyes on them, it was time for a show. Castillo hugged Rafa, as did Camila, and Matthew managed a smile and laugh about something Rafa said. Putting on his own smile, Shane extended his hand to Rafa's father and said, "Good to see you again."

Castillo took his hand firmly. "It is, Shane."

Then he offered his hand to Camila, who had no choice but to take it. Her palm was cool and dry, and she shook his hand steadily, tilting her head and smiling. "So *wonderful* to see you. We weren't sure if you were still able to make it."

"I wouldn't miss it," he answered honestly. *As much as part of me would love to.*

Hernandez, who'd been talking to a young woman in a navy uniform skirt and jacket, striped blouse, and brown outback-style hat, approached. "We're ready to board. We've swept the entire train, and we're doing the cabins now. We'll do Matthew and Rafael's too."

"Wait, what?" Rafa frowned. "I'm sharing a cabin with Shane."

Still smiling, Camila quietly said, "Don't be ridiculous, darling. You're not married. You and Matthew are sharing a cabin. Mr. Kendrick will have his own."

Rafa's jaw clenched. "Are you shitting me?"

With a broad smile for the onlookers, Rafa's father murmured, "Watch your language. Christian and Hadley never shared a room at the White House or on any of our trips. Not until they were married. If it was Matthew and a girlfriend, or your sister and a boyfriend, they wouldn't be rooming together either. This is how it goes."

While on one hand it was a sham since he and Rafa lived together, Shane could understand keeping up appearances in an official capacity. Although the Castillos weren't technically on a diplomatic visit, they might as well have been. Shane said, "Of course. That's fine."

Rafa looked like he wanted to argue as they boarded the train and followed into a lounge area with benches under the windows. There were armchairs upholstered in shiny taupe leather and round gold-rimmed cocktail tables positioned throughout the train car.

Shane held back and whispered right into Rafa's ear, "We'll just have to get creative. It'll be fun." Rafa gave him a tight-lipped smile, still tense.

"Why don't we get everyone settled in their cabins," the young woman from the railway announced, after first giving them a spiel on the Indian Pacific's history of traveling between Sydney and Perth and back again since 1970 or something. Shane barely heard her as he rubbed his hand soothingly on Rafa's back, disappointed that Rafa's pinched expression and angry eyes didn't soften.

Shane followed as they all trouped through the passageways toward the cabins. A male agent trailed Rafa and Matthew, and Shane wondered how many extra bodies they had on duty. He'd counted twenty-six cars on the platform, which was a challenging number to control. Even though Matthew and Rafa weren't under protection now, he appreciated that Hernandez wasn't taking any chances.

The young woman leading them opened a door between carriages, and they followed through into a narrow corridor along the right side. Shane was surprised at the heft of the door as he held it open for the agent on their tail, who took hold of it without a flicker of his flat expression.

As another staff member took Rafa's parents into their cabin, the woman stopped by a door and spoke to Rafa and Matthew. "We have ten platinum cabins, and you'll have a twin. You can see your luggage is inside, and there are refreshments. Right now, the cabin is configured in its daytime setting. While you're at dinner, we'll convert the seats into your luxurious beds. I hope you'll be comfortable. My name's Stephanie. Please don't hesitate to ask if you need anything." She smiled brightly, her gaze catching on Matthew's. Adjusting her hat, she motioned them inside.

Shane stayed in the doorway as she went over the features. The wood-paneled cabin had a wide window on the far side, and an interior window on the corridor as well. Both windows had blinds that were currently open. Shane didn't like that there was glass access to the corridor, but…

It's fine. The Service did their job. It's not yours anymore.

Stephanie said, "The spacious en-suite toilet is to your left. There's a full shower and everything you could need. And you see the cabin has a movable table, two ottomans, and a writing desk by the window. This wood is Tasmanian Myrtle, and the carpet was made in…"

Shane tuned out Stephanie. "Spacious" was a bit of a stretch, but the cabin was well-appointed, and the wood gleamed. When the chairs were converted down into beds, there would barely be a foot between them, but he supposed that was to be expected on a train.

Stephanie said, "Again, please let us know if you have any needs."

"Where's Shane's cabin?" Rafa asked. "Next door?"

Her smile faltered momentarily. "Well, your parents and their staff are in the other platinum cabins. But we have a lovely gold-standard single for you, Mr. Kendrick! I'll show it to you now."

"That's fine," Shane said. "I'm sure it will be very nice."

Rafa looked like he wanted to say more, but bit his tongue. Shane gave him a wink and smile before following Stephanie back through the lounge area.

She said, "Your party will have private use of all our platinum lounges and the dining car. All our other passengers are gold class and won't be in this part of the train. Well, aside from you, of course. How are you enjoying Australia, Mr. Kendrick?"

They made small talk as she led him through the narrow side corridors of the train past gold cabins, double sets of heavy doors at the ends of each car. Shane smiled politely and nodded whenever they passed other passengers. "It's a bit of a hike," Stephanie said apologetically as she opened another set of doors. "But we only have one car of single cabins. Here we are."

They passed a little staff office on the left, and then the hall-way weaved through the center of the car instead of being on the left or right side beside cabins. The walls were rounded, the corridor undulating, single berths on both sides. From the head of the car, Shane couldn't see the end thanks to the curving passage-way.

That made him uneasy, and he reminded himself again that there was nothing to worry about. Besides, Rafa would be safe with the agents standing guard in the platinum cabin.

They passed three toilets on the right, and then Stephanie stopped at the fifth cabin on the left. "Here we go." The door was open, and she stepped farther down the hall to give him a view, since Shane soon realized there wasn't really enough room for both of them inside.

The cabin's wood paneling wasn't quite as lustrous, and the seating upholstery was a little worn around the edges, but it was very clean and the window was wide. The cabin was about seven feet long and four and a half wide. There was a chair and table under the window, and a very narrow cupboard just to the right of the door. To the left, there was a sink that could be folded down.

Stephanie said, "We passed by the toilets, and the shower stalls are at the very end of the car." She lowered her voice conspiratorially. "Although I'm sure you could use your boyfriend's shower." Then she flushed, as if afraid she'd said too much.

Shane smiled. "I'm sure I can. Thank you very much for your help."

"You'll be able to find your way back?"

"I'm sure I will. Really only two ways to go on a train."

She laughed. "Right, yes. Well, your suitcase is there. It's a little large for a single berth, but we checked, and it will slide under the bed. Usually we make you bring your carry-on and stow bigger items in the luggage car."

"I appreciate the consideration."

"Oh, of course! And watch your block if you open that upper cupboard." At his frown, she added, "Your head, I mean. You're tall, so." She glanced down the hall the way they'd come, and her eyes went wide. "Oh! I... Hello, Mr. Castillo."

"Please, call me Ramon." Rafa's father appeared, tailed by two agents who had to stand one after the other in the narrow, curving passageway. "And you are?"

Stephanie told him her name and Castillo asked her a few polite questions about herself, listening as if he truly wanted to know more about her outback hometown of Emerald, Queensland. Shane stood there in his cabin with a fixed smile, dread filling him. He hadn't counted on chatting with Rafa's father one-on-one.

Better get used to it.

Finally, Stephanie went back to work, and Castillo murmured something to his agents before entering the cabin. Shane was already in the corner, and they quickly realized that to close the door, Castillo would have to squeeze close to him to get the clearance behind. They both smiled grimly, barely an inch between them.

Not awkward at all. Nope.

Once the door was shut, Castillo stepped back so there was a foot or so separating them. He cleared his throat. "I hope Rafa wasn't too upset after we left."

"He was. We both were, but we worked through it." Shane focused on keeping his face impassive as flashes of memory danced through his head. He banished the thoughts of the amazing sex.

"Good. I must apologize again for my wife's behavior. She'd had too much to drink."

"Yes, she's usually much better at hiding her true feelings. *In vino veritas*, as they say." The train had started moving, slowly rumbling out of the station.

He grimaced. "Indeed. But as it seems you're not going anywhere, she'll have to accept your relationship with our son. As I'm trying very hard to do. I think you are a good man, despite your inappropriate actions while you guarded Rafa." He raised a hand. "And we must move forward at this point. I'm glad you came on this trip. I don't know if we can be friends, as such, but…"

"Mr. Castillo—"

"Please. Call me Ramon if I'm to call you Shane. Let us get comfortable with that much, at least."

Shane nodded. "Ramon, I appreciate the apology. As I said

last night, I understand why this is difficult for you and your wife to accept. Why *I'm* difficult to accept. But yes, we must move forward. For Rafa's sake. He loves you both very much, and it hurts him that you don't support his choices. He—" Shane stopped himself. Was he saying too much?

"What?" Rafa's father frowned. "Please, I want to hear what you have to say."

"For years, he hid who he really was. He tried to be the perfect son to avoid detection. To gain your approval. He still wants that approval now. Desperately."

Mouth turning down, Castillo—Ramon—nodded and rubbed his face. In that moment without his usual politician's smile, he looked damn tired. "I don't want my son to be hurt. Neither does Camila, which I know might be hard to believe." He smiled ruefully. "I love my wife with all my heart, but she can become…entrenched in her viewpoints. She's certain you're the one who will hurt Rafael. I trust you'll take great pleasure in proving her wrong."

Shane had to smile. "I'll do my best."

"Very good." Ramon extended his hand, and Shane took it. "You'll join us in the lounge shortly? We can drink a toast to moving forward."

He nodded, and they had to do the shimmying dance again to open the cabin door, both of them laughing awkwardly. Ramon took his leave, and Shane lowered himself into the comfy, padded chair, watching buildings flick by. His phone buzzed, and he smiled when he saw Darnell had sent a voice message.

He listened to Darnell talk for a few minutes, the recording taken as he drove home from work, or more accurately crawled due to the traffic he complained about. Darnell opened up some about his case and what a strain it was causing. He was thinking about actually seeing a shrink, which took Shane by surprise. Then he added that Henry thought it was a good idea, and Shane smiled to himself.

"*I can't help but feel, you know. Weak, I guess? Which is macho bullshit. But I know you'll feel me on this. How are the nightmares?*"

Shane wanted to respond and say everything was great and there was nothing to worry about. But it felt too disloyal to lie. *So you should tell Rafa too.* Yet the thought still made his stomach churn. Besides, the nightmares might not happen again. He might be through the worst now. He would wait and see, at least until after the train ride.

He thought of Rafa's tight shoulders and stiff-backed posture. Rafa was stressed enough. Right?

Am I completely full of shit, or only partially?

He pressed his thumb to the little microphone and locked it, holding the phone up to his mouth as he left a recording. He asked for Darnell's advice as suburban backyards soon appeared. After a few minutes, he finished off the message: "Okay, I'd better go be social. At least there'll be booze."

Taking a deep breath, he left his single cabin and went to toast the future.

Chapter Ten

I T HAD TAKEN forever to reach Shane's cabin, and Rafa could feel his blood pressure rising. His mother was acting like nothing was wrong and she hadn't been massively out of line at the house, and Shane having to stay in the back of the train was the cherry on top.

He glanced left and right after knocking softly. The curving corridor remained empty, and as the door opened a foot, he shimmied in to the left and just managed to squeeze it shut behind him, his knees bumping the side of the bed that filled the narrow space.

"This is ridiculous!" Rafa exclaimed. "Fine, I get why we can't share, but you should get a full cabin with a bathroom. Not be stuck back here."

In a T-shirt and plaid PJ bottoms, Shane was on his back on the narrow mattress, his right leg bent, knee leaning against the window. He'd drawn the shade, even though there seemed to be only endless miles of nothing beyond the train in the darkness. He shrugged.

"It's okay. It's actually comfortable. Cozy. And I'll use your shower tomorrow." He reached for Rafa's hand. "They said this was the only cabin left, so let's accept that. Give your parents the benefit of the doubt."

"I guess," Rafa grumbled.

Shane smiled softly, tugging his hand. "C'mere."

Rafa stretched out on top of him, fitting between his legs with a sigh. "Maybe I can just stay here tonight."

He chuckled. "You might get a little heavy after a while." He traced a finger over Rafa's freckles as if he was cataloguing them. When he touched them so reverently, it made Rafa's belly somersault pleasantly. "Besides, we don't want to piss off your parents."

Rafa scoffed. "Am I supposed to pretend that we sleep in separate beds at home? In our one-bedroom house?"

"No, but this is their trip. I'm a guest."

"Yeah, okay." He dropped his head to nuzzle at Shane's throat. Five o'clock shadow rasped against his lips.

"Your dad came to see me after we boarded."

Rafa jerked up his head. "What did he say?"

"He apologized again. Said he wants to move forward. Dinner was pretty good, don't you think?'

Rafa knew he wasn't talking about the food, although the grilled kangaroo had been delicious. "Yeah. It wasn't bad. The conductor was a good buffer." The man had been full of information and stories about the train, and having him join them for dinner meant the rest of them hadn't had to talk much.

Resting his head on Shane's chest, he scooted down and got comfortable. Shane snuck his hand up the back of Rafa's button-up shirt and traced his spine rhythmically.

For a little while, they just...*were*. Rafa closed his eyes, the rocking of the train and Shane's warmth and caress lulling him. Then Shane spoke quietly.

"I saw Jules and Dylan when I was in DC."

Now Rafa was wide awake, but he didn't lift his head. He rubbed Shane's bicep and asked, "How was it?"

"Terrible. He's dying. They say there's nothing else that can be done."

"God. I feel so bad for her. I mean, for the kid too. It's so unfair. Why do such awful things have to happen to good people?"

"The eternal question."

Rafa thought of Shane's parents and hugged him tightly.

"I stopped on the way and bought a bunch of toys, but once I saw him, I realized he's too far gone to even get out of bed. I was standing there with an armload of crap he can't play with. Felt like such an asshole."

The train rocked and rattled, and Rafa pressed kisses to Shane's neck. "You're not an asshole."

"Mmm. Depends on who you ask." Shane's hand was warm and gentle on Rafa's back.

"You're not an asshole," he repeated. He couldn't help a moment of happiness that Shane had confided in him, even if it was about something so sad.

They held each other, Rafa's kisses on Shane's neck turning into long sucks. Shane turned his head, murmuring and rolling his hips up.

When they kissed, it was deep and slow, their tongues meeting, tasting like minty toothpaste. Rafa squeezed his hands between them, up under Shane's tee. He tweaked Shane's nipples and raked his nails gently through his chest hair.

Shane urged him to sit up and straddle his hips, then unbuttoned Rafa's shirt slowly, his gaze heavy-lidded. He parted the soft material and ran his hands over Rafa's chest, only brushing his nipples, then dipping lower to tease the hair on his belly. Back up again. Rafa moaned low in his throat, rolling his hips to get friction on his swelling dick still trapped in his pants.

Shane unzipped him and pulled out his cock, urging Rafa forward to brace on his hands beside the pillow. "Feed it to me." He scooted down.

Rafa crawled up, groaning, Shane keeping him steady as the

train suddenly swayed sharply to the right. Then Shane had his hips, and he sucked Rafa's cock deep into his mouth, almost all the way into his throat.

Rafa couldn't stop the gasps and cries as Shane sucked him. His arms trembled as Shane took him deeply, his tongue running up and down the ridge of the shaft.

"Oh fuck," Rafa mumbled. The wet pressure surrounded him, and he ducked his head to glimpse Shane's lips stretched around his dick.

His heart swelled with so much love he thought he might explode. Suddenly he was desperate to have Shane inside him, to taste him too. "Wait. Need…"

Shane immediately released Rafa's dick from his mouth, his brow furrowing as Rafa clumsily shifted backwards. "What do you need, baby?"

Breathing too hard, his body too on fire to form a sentence, he contorted himself around until he faced the other direction. Right below him, Shane's cock tented his PJs, and he quickly freed it with shaking hands as Shane tugged down Rafa's boxers and pants to his knees.

Shane pressed open-mouthed kisses to Rafa's ass, stroking his thighs. Then they were blowing each other, and he didn't know where he ended and Shane began, like the snake eating its own tail.

There was nothing else but mouths and tongues and hands and breath, the train pitching and shaking. It was like they were one person, and Rafa thought of that cheesy line from that old movie: "*You complete me.*"

No matter what happened, no matter how crappy Rafa's parents were, he and Shane were united. It was them against the world—there was nothing between them. He was inside Shane, and Shane was inside him, and they were *unstoppable*.

Rafa dug his fingers into Shane's hairy thighs and came, a

burst of pleasure crashing through him as he sucked harder. Shane swallowed around Rafa's twitching cock, caressing his balls and milking him through the aftershocks. He groaned around Rafa's shaft.

When Shane shot his load, Rafa swallowed as much as he could from his position, some of it dribbling out of his mouth and down to his chin. He coughed and had to pull up, and Shane gently released him. He shifted around on the narrow bed, sprawling on Shane's feet as they caught their breath.

Breathing hard through his mouth, Shane whispered, "You're so beautiful."

His pants were around his knees and cum streaked his flushed face. But in that moment, Rafa truly *felt* beautiful. His eyes burned with the sudden threat of stupid tears, and he flattened himself on Shane, kissing him and molding into his arms until he could breathe again.

WHEN RAFA ENTERED the platinum carriage, one of the agents stationed outside his parents' room knocked on the door. He wanted to race into his own cabin, but he walked steadily, and when his mother appeared in the hallway, he said, "Hey, Mom!" like nothing was wrong.

Of course everything was wrong and he was still pissed at her, but he was going to be the bigger person if it killed him. When she didn't say anything, he prompted, "What's up?"

Can she tell I was just sixty-nining? Can she smell it on me? Fuck it, I don't care if she can. Deal with it, Mom.

She walked several feet down the corridor, and Rafa followed. The agents could probably still hear them, but that was nothing new. He steeled himself for whatever asshole thing she was going to say.

"I behaved badly yesterday," Camila murmured.

Oh. "Um, yeah. You really did."

She regarded him in the low light of the corridor, steadying herself on the wall as the swaying train rumbled over a bumpy patch. "I was rude and unkind. It was beyond the pale. I'm sorry."

He nodded. "Okay. Um, thank you." He waited for her to add on a bunch of excuses and explanations about how she *was* right, though.

But she didn't. She only leaned up and kissed his cheek, then wiped off the smudge of her lingering lipstick. "I've missed you so much. Sleep well, sweetheart."

She was almost inside her cabin when Rafa could swallow the lump in his throat and say, "You too." His anger was still there in the mess of emotions bubbling in him, but she was trying. It was a start, at least.

IN THE DOORWAY of their cabin, Matthew stumbled. From his bed near the exterior window on the right side of the train, Rafa sat up. He'd closed the blinds on the window to the corridor, but kept the bathroom light on and door ajar, and in the beam of light, his brother swayed. "You okay, Matty?"

"Yeah." He closed the door behind him, slumping against it.

"Do you always drink this much?" The question was out before Rafa could stop himself. He braced, but Matthew only laughed sardonically.

"No. Don't worry, I'm not an alkie. Probably just a chip off the old block. Mom was pretty blasted last night, huh?"

"Yeah. It sucked."

"Dad was pissed. I got the impression she outdid herself." He rubbed his face, yawning. "She just can't help it."

"Yeah. She actually apologized a little earlier. I think she meant it."

"I'm sure she did. She's not, like, *evil*. It only feels like that sometimes."

Rafa laughed softly. "Sometimes."

"I don't know why she can't just accept this with Shane. It's not like you're ruining your life by being with a guy who loves you." He snorted. "If anyone's ruining their life, it's me. I'm a total fuckup."

"You are not! It's not your fault you got injured. You're going to get through this."

Grunting noncommittally, Matthew pushed off the door and shuffled into the bathroom, bracing himself with his good hand, the train rattling and wobbling. Rafa waited, listening to his brother piss, then run the tap for a while, seemingly brushing his teeth, the soft sounds of spitting accompanying the water.

Matthew flicked off the light and stripped down to his boxers before shimmying through the foot of space separating the two twin beds and carefully lowering himself to the mattress. He settled on his back under the duvet, his upper body partially propped up on extra pillows.

Rafa raised the shade on the exterior window so he could see snatches of stars blanketing the black sky.

After a few minutes, Matthew said, "I don't know if I will."

Rafa rolled onto his side facing his brother. "There are still two years until the Olympics. It's not over."

"The thing is, I don't know if I'm good enough. The difference between a medal and nothing is seconds. Hundredths of seconds." He snapped his fingers. "That can be the difference. Just that. All that work for nothing."

"But do you love it?"

"I used to. I could escape in the pool. Get away from the White House circus. Now, I don't know."

"Do you miss it? This must be the longest stretch of time that you haven't been in a pool since we were kids."

"I… I miss the routine. The certainty. The purpose. But do I actually miss *swimming*?" Metal screeched distantly, the train's constant sway and rumble filling the silence. Matthew stared at the ceiling. "I can't tell."

"What else would you do? If you don't want to swim anymore?"

"I have no fucking clue." He swallowed, his Adam's apple bobbing in the moonlight, voice hoarse. "That's what scares me."

Rafa reached across the narrow space between their beds and squeezed his good arm. "Don't be scared. You'll figure it out. I'll help you."

Matthew gripped his wrist as Rafa pulled back. He was still a little drunk, but his eyes were clear in the moonlight. "You're a good brother, and I've been shit. I let you deal with all your crap alone."

"It's okay. It's all in the past now anyway. We're moving forward."

"Yeah. Okay." He nodded, his fingers relaxing, eyes suddenly getting heavy.

"Whether you keep swimming or not, you'll figure it out. We will."

"Thanks, Raf. Fuck, I'm a mess. Sorry."

"Sleep. We'll talk more in the morning." He gently pulled free of Matthew's grasp.

"Right. Yeah."

Yet as the minutes ticked by and Matthew's breathing evened out and deepened, Rafa stayed stubbornly awake. He shivered a little when he sat up and the covers pooled at his waist, so he got up and pulled a Bondi Beach hooded sweatshirt over his plaid pajama bottoms. Knees to his chest, he sat on his bed and stared out at the night.

The steady rumble and rattle of the train as it powered

through the outback was strangely comforting. They were miles and miles from anything now, and beyond the lights of the train there were only dark shapes of hills and the occasional fence.

They'd be stopping in a town called Broken Hill before six o'clock in the morning, where buses would be waiting to take them on an optional excursion for an hour before re-boarding the train.

Rafa knew he should try and sleep, but he was mesmerized, sitting in the dark cabin, looking out at the shadowy landscape passing by. It was so barren and stark and unfamiliar. He spotted the red glare of taillights, and pressed his forehead to the glass, watching the vehicle—a pick-up truck, it looked like—until it disappeared.

Who was driving? Where did they live? Probably at one of the farming stations or perhaps in a tiny town. What was their life like out here? Rafa tried to remember a term he'd heard to describe the outback, and it nagged at him, the words almost within his grasp. He pulled out his phone, but of course there was no signal. He tucked it back in a little drawer between the beds.

Finally it came to him—*back of beyond.* Looking out onto that vast land, loneliness took hold of him, digging in with blunt fingers. There was something about the silence of the middle of the night that made him contemplative, and his mind spun over questions that had no answer—was there life after death? Was there a heaven? Was there anything beyond this planet they lived on?

Huffing softly, he shook his head. He needed to sleep, not ponder the mysteries of the freaking universe. Yet even when he curled under the blankets and closed his eyes, sleep wouldn't come. The constant shaking and occasional whine of metal on metal was pleasant, yet it kept him awake at the same time.

He gave up and slipped on his flip-flops. Maybe a little walk would clear his head and tire him out. Besides, perhaps Shane was awake too. ~~Rafa grinned to himself. Another nice little orgasm~~ would surely help him sleep. He eased open the cabin door and closed it carefully behind him.

He turned and almost immediately walked into one of the agents who stood guard. The man, who was Asian and about thirty, momentarily steadied Rafa with a hand on his shoulder. Then he simply raised an eyebrow.

"Can't sleep," Rafa whispered. "I'm going for a walk."

The agent regarded him evenly, his eyebrow still popped.

Embarrassment and indignation warred. "I'm allowed to," Rafa hissed. He resisted adding, *"You're not the boss of me!"*

The agent simply nodded and turned his gaze away, surveying the empty corridor and then standing there with his hands clasped in front of him. Rafa passed him and took a deep, calming breath. He had nothing to apologize for! Even if he was going to Shane's cabin to fuck, it wasn't the Secret Service's business. Or his mom and dad's.

Another agent was stationed in the platinum lounge, and Rafa nodded to him as he passed, head held high and shoulders back. He made his way along the train, carriage by carriage. There were a few staff members around, and they each smiled and greeted him and asked if there was anything he needed.

My boyfriend's dick would be fabulous, so just get out of my way.

Finally he made it to the car with the single berths. There was no one about, and he traced one hand along the curving wall as he neared Shane's tiny cabin. Over the shake and clang of the train, he heard a deep voice. For a moment he wondered if Shane was talking to himself, but as he stopped outside the door, he realized it was someone else.

It was Darnell.

Confusion reigned for a moment since there was no cell signal and Shane couldn't be talking to Darnell on the phone. Then he realized it was one of the voice messages Darnell liked to send sometimes. It must have downloaded onto Shane's phone earlier while they were still in reach of civilization.

Rafa lifted his hand, fingers curled to knock softly at the door. But his fist hovered there as he listened to Darnell's baritone.

"*Look, man. I really think you should talk to a shrink if these nightmares aren't going away. There's no shame in it.*"

Nightmares? Plural? Rafa's heart thumped. *I knew it.* There had been something off lately with Shane, and…

And Shane had confided in Darnell about it and not him?

Hurt seized him with a sharp, vicious twist, followed by a flood of shame as he thought of how a few hours earlier he'd felt so *connected* to Shane, like they were two halves of one person.

His heart had been so full, and now he stood there feeling like the biggest idiot in the world. Before he could talk himself out of it, he pressed his ear to the cabin door.

"*It makes sense that the inquest stirred all this shit up again. Those dreams sound brutal. Clearly your brain is trying to process. I know you don't want to tell your boy, but—*"

A bolt of fury exploded, and Rafa thumped the door with his fist. *I. Am. Not. A. Boy!* Did Shane even respect him at all as an equal? Did he tell him anything real, or did he save all that for Darnell?

The recorded voice went silent, and the cabin door opened, Shane on his knees on the bed, blinking into the low light of the corridor. He stared at Rafa. "What are you…?"

Rafa pushed inside, squeezing into the corner of the stupidly small space to get the door shut behind him. The blind was up, moon and starlight giving the dark cabin a silvery glow. His fingers twitched into fists, and he shifted his weight back and forth on his feet as he hissed, "I am not a *boy!*"

Sitting on his feet on the narrow bed, Shane gaped at him for a moment before jerking his head back. "Were you *listening?*"

Guilt was obliterated by righteous anger. "Why shouldn't I

hear what Darnell says? We're partners, aren't we?"

"That doesn't mean we don't get privacy if we want it," Shane whispered harshly. "How long were you out there?"

"Why? What did he say that you don't want me to hear?"

Shane huffed out a breath. "It doesn't matter what he said. You shouldn't be skulking around eavesdropping."

"I wasn't 'skulking.' I couldn't sleep, and I came to see if you were awake. Then I heard a voice, and I realized it was *him*."

"Yes, Darnell sent a vext earlier. I couldn't sleep either, so I was listening. I told you, he doesn't mean anything by 'boy,' but I'll tell him not to use that word."

"When you tell him more about the nightmares you won't talk to me about?"

Shane visibly tensed, then rubbed a hand over his stubbly face. "It's nothing to worry about."

"No. It's *something*. Something you trust him with and not me."

He reached out for Rafa's clenched hand. "Baby, it's not—"

"No!" Rafa jerked away, thumping against the door. "Why have you been lying to me? That night, when you said you were sick and locked yourself in the bathroom. Was that true?"

He sighed and dropped his gaze, which was answer enough.

"If you're having nightmares, why won't you talk to me?"

"Because you have enough to worry about."

"That's such a bullshit excuse!"

"Lower your voice!" Shane hissed.

"No!"

He raised his eyebrows and whispered, "You want whoever's in the cabins around here to sell our fight to the media? Want them to record it on their phone?"

Rafa struggled against the ridiculous urge to disagree just for the sake of it. He forced a deep breath, blood rushing in his ears. Then he gritted out in a whisper, "It's still a bullshit excuse. We're supposed to share the stuff we worry about. That's what partners do. You think I can't handle it?"

"You just have so much stuff to deal with right now. Your parents' visit, starting the Cordon Bleu soon. I didn't want to stress you out with this—" He waved his hand. "This whatever. I don't know why these nightmares have started. I'm sure they'll stop now that I've testified and it's all in the past."

"What are you dreaming about?"

He shook his head. "Just stressful crap."

"About the kidnapping?"

"Yes. And *you* were the one who was kidnapped, but you're fine, so it makes no sense that *I'm* having nightmares." He pressed his lips into a thin line, and Rafa could see the guilt in his eyes.

A bit of his anger dampened, like turning down the flame on a gas stove, still burning, but not as powerfully. "I've had nightmares too sometimes. And I talked to a therapist every week for months. Maybe you should see someone when we get back."

But Shane brushed it off. "It'll be fine. I don't need to talk to a shrink."

In an instant, the gas turned up to high again. Rafa spat, "But you'll talk to Darnell no problem?"

"He's a cop. He understands what it's like. We're old friends."

"Is that all you are? Did you have sex with him when you went back to DC?"

Shane blinked at him. His mouth opened and closed before he loudly whispered, "No! Of course not."

"But you have in the past. You've fucked him. Why should I believe you that you didn't this time? I had to hear about it from my *mother* of all people!" The humiliation flooded back. He knew he should be able to talk rationally, like an adult, but his nerves were rubbed raw and jangling.

"Wait, what?" Shane's nostrils flared. "Your mother said I had sex with Darnell last week? If she's having me followed, her PI is feeding her lies." He clenched his jaw, spitting out the words. "You think I'd have sex with someone else? You think I'd do that? Not to mention, then be with you without a condom?"

The swirling mess of anger and confusion became murkier in the face of the hurt shining from Shane's eyes, and guilt rejoined the party. "No. I know you wouldn't." He raked a hand over his too-short hair. "Fuck, I'm just... Why won't you talk to me? Why can you tell *him* what's really going on in your head? Why can't you tell me?"

"You're right. I should have talked to you."

Rafa punched a fist against his own thigh. "Yes, you should have! You tell me you love me, but you don't actually tell me shit! Like how you and Darnell used to fuck, right?"

Shane held up his palms, exasperated. "It's in the past. I honestly never thought about it. It wasn't relevant."

"Not relevant?" His voice rose, and Rafa lowered it again with effort. "I think it's pretty damn relevant when you were sleeping at his house."

"We're only friends now. And it was never more than friends with benefits in the past. It was just sex."

"Well, I'm sorry I can't be so dismissive of it. Sex means a lot to me. It's not nothing."

Shane got his feet out from under him and awkwardly stood in the corner of space left beside Rafa. "Sex with you is different. I'm in love with you." He reached out, but Rafa snatched his hand away.

"I asked if Darnell was gay or seeing anyone—I gave you the opportunity to tell me the truth, and you didn't say anything about your past with him."

Shane's eyes flashed. "If you'd just asked me if I fucked him, you would have gotten an answer to the question you were really asking. I can't read your mind!"

They were almost chest-to-chest now, both of them breathing

hard, harsh pants in the quiet of the tiny cabin. Rafa shook his head. "I need to—I can't—" He squeezed around and tried to open the door, but of course there was no room. He pushed back against Shane. "Move! I need to go. Can't do this right now."

Shane caught his hips, his hot breath putting the hair on the back of Rafa's neck on end. "Wait. Please. Let's talk this out."

But panic clawed at Rafa, and he shoved back, getting the door open a few inches. "Not now!"

Sighing, Shane retreated to the bed, and Rafa was able to escape. In the corridor, he plunged back the way he came, his lungs painfully tight. His flip-flops flapped as he made it to the end of the carriage and hauled open the heavy door. He realized Shane was behind him, and almost started running, holding onto the walls as the train rattled and swayed.

In the next car, an agent was walking farther down the narrow passage. He must have heard Rafa open the door, and he turned and approached. When they met halfway, the man—older, balding, blond hair and dark eyebrows—asked, "Is everything all right?" Then his gaze jerked beyond Rafa, the door closing behind Shane with a thud.

"Raf," Shane called softly as he walked toward them.

The agent frowned. "Would you like me to escort you back to your cabin?"

Rafa was about to tell him he wasn't a kid and didn't need a damn escort, but he stopped, the words dying in his throat. He managed a nod, and the agent deftly ushered Rafa ahead of him and blocked Shane's progress.

"We need to talk this out." Shane spoke calmly, glaring daggers at the agent.

Rafa's head spun, thoughts too jumbled and contradictory to figure out. "Just leave me alone right now." It was a dick move to use the agent to block Shane, but Rafa couldn't deal.

"You heard Mr. Castillo," the agent said. "Please return to

your cabin."

"Are you f—" Shane's jaw snapped shut. He inhaled loudly through his nose. "Okay. I'll talk to you in the morning, Raf. Try to get some sleep." With that, he turned on his heel and stalked away, the door at the end of the carriage shutting with a thud.

"Are you sure everything's all right?" the agent asked.

"Uh-huh." Rafa walked into the next car, already feeling bereft at Shane's absence. He muttered to the agent, "I'm good. Thanks."

"I'll just escort you anyway now that I've completed my patrol."

Rafa wanted to argue, but he'd had enough for one night. Simmering in confusion and resentment, he walked back to his cabin with the agent on his heels, a reminder that his life would never really be normal.

Chapter Eleven

B Y FIVE, MANY of the train passengers were stirring, preparing for the excursion in Broken Hill. Shane stared out the window at the dry scrub, the sky starting to brighten as the train rumbled onward. He hadn't slept a wink, and acid bubbled in his gut. He hadn't even tried to sleep after the fight with Rafa.

Fuck.

It genuinely hadn't occurred to him to tell Rafa that he'd slept with Darnell in the past. Of course now he realized how utterly stupid he'd been, how truly thoughtless. Yet hurt lingered. Festered. How could Rafa actually think Shane would cheat on him?

Yes, Rafa still struggled with insecurity, but it stung nonetheless. Didn't he know how much Shane adored him? More than anything or anyone else on the planet? How much Shane trusted him? They were sharing a life together now.

So why didn't you tell him the truth about the nightmares?

Guilt festered along with the hurt. He'd wanted to protect Rafa, but himself as well. He just wanted the fucking nightmares to stop and go away, but maybe he had to face them first.

Yes, he should have told Rafa the truth. He could admit his fuck-up. But for Rafa to think he'd cheat was still a kick in the nuts. It probably wasn't fair, but the lack of faith knocked the wind right out of him. Part of him wanted to go to Rafa's cabin and make him talk this through, but maybe it was best to give it a little time for both of them to lick their wounds.

He imagined how he'd feel if Rafa went to spend the night with a man he used to fuck—which of course led to thoughts of Rafa with other men. Suffice it to say, Shane's caveman side did *not* like the idea one little bit.

He was unpleasantly reminded of the months they were apart after Shane left the White House. How he had examined every paparazzi photo of Rafa in the tabloid rags, his heart aching at the mere sight of him, his head over-analyzing Rafa's potential relationship with any males near him.

There had been one picture snapped leaving a gay bar in Charlottesville. At first glance, Shane's chest had loosened. Ashleigh was at Rafa's side, laughing, and Rafa was smiling too. But then Shane's gaze had zeroed in on the young man just behind. Rafa's head was turned slightly toward him, this blond, built, frat-boy type. Frat boy had seemed to be saying something, and Rafa was listening.

It was embarrassing now to think of how long he'd stared at that damn picture. He'd finally closed the browser and cleared his internet history, feeling far too much like a creepy stalker. It had taken more effort than it should have not to search for the photo again the next day.

He'd hatched his plan to quit his job and fly halfway around the world on the chance Rafa would still want him. Instead, Rafa had come to him. Stretching out on his bed now and closing his eyes, the train swaying steadily, Shane let himself go back to that moment on the beach.

How his heart had leapt, and it had been all he could do to keep his cool and not race across the sand to sweep up Rafa in his arms. How Rafa had declared his love, how his lips had tasted— sweet from the slushee, with a tang of salt from the sea air. They'd finally been able to go to bed together. In a real bed, where they could take their time, finally unafraid. Where Shane finally fucked him.

His balls tingled now as he remembered Rafa on his knees, ass in the air, spreading himself open with his hands, offering himself, begging for it. Shane spit in his palm and slid his hand into his pajama bottoms, stroking as he lost himself in the memories.

After the argument and unresolved frustration, he ached for a release, and jerking off would have to do. He let himself remember the pleasure and excitement and nervousness and affection that had flitted across Rafa's expressive face the first time. Rafa had been so tight and wonderful, still so unsure of himself.

"You really want me."

Shane bent his legs and dug into the mattress with his heels, thrusting into his fist, breathing harder, flesh slapping. He'd never wanted another man the way he wanted Rafa. Not just with his cock, but his heart. He ached with that tenderness. Rafa wasn't only the first man he'd fucked raw—he was the first man Shane had *made love* to, as corny as it sounded.

He fondled his hairy balls with his other hand, remembering what it had been like to come inside him with nothing between them, how every time, he imagined he left a bit of himself inside like a fingerprint.

He should have gotten up and went to Rafa's cabin so they could deal with their issues, but he was helpless against the onslaught of memories and pleasure. He just wanted to lose himself for a few minutes before reality crashed back over him like a bucket of ice water.

Shane let himself imagine Rafa was there, needing him, wanting to be taken care of.

"Give me your cock. Fuck me. Hard. Bent over our table. Please."

His cock strained in his grasp as he remembered Rafa so vulnerable, begging him for a good fucking after the awful scene with his mother. The remembered rush of power—of being Rafa's protector—flowed, and he came with a gasp, imagining he was emptying into Rafa and not his hand.

Legs flopping down, he groped for the face towel he'd left hanging on the handle of the narrow closet. He had to get washed and dressed and out on the platform soon for the excursion to Broken Hill, but his eyes grew heavy after the sleepless night. Maybe he'd just catch a quick ten minutes before he faced the day and the reconciliation that had to be made.

"FUCK!" SHANE BOLTED up, blinking at the sunlight streaming through the window. The train rattled and swayed as if it had never stopped, but it had to have sat at the Broken Hill station for at least an hour or more that morning. He grabbed his phone and grimaced at the screen. After ten. So not only had he missed the excursion, but breakfast as well.

Why hadn't Rafa woken him? Maybe he'd wanted to let Shane sleep. Or maybe he hadn't wanted to see him at all and was relieved when Shane didn't appear. Rafa's parents were surely enjoying his absence.

"Fuck," he muttered again.

After a shower in the cramped stall at the end of the carriage, his elbows sore from banging them on the walls a hundred times, he squared his shoulders and put on his best placid, no-problem expression. He'd perfected it in the Service over the years, and actually felt some of the tension melt. It was like putting on an old, familiar coat.

It didn't even slip when he nodded to the agent outside the platinum lounge. He didn't bother to see how the agent responded, but felt the man's eyes on him as the door closed.

At the thunk, all eyes glanced his way. Rafa and Matthew were playing a game of what might have been Parcheesi, although Shane couldn't be sure since he hadn't played it in decades.

His gaze locked with Rafa's, and then Rafa looked away and rolled the dice. Sitting with their assistants farther down the car, Ramon and Camila regarded him with open curiosity, clearly aware something was amiss.

Shane nodded to them pleasantly and announced to everyone, "Good morning. Think that jet lag caught up with me." *Again.*

He went and sat in the chair next to Rafa's, ignoring the stares. Hernandez wasn't there, and he kept his gaze away from that of the agent stationed inside the far door. Clearing his throat, Shane nodded to Matthew. "Morning."

Matthew eyed Shane and Rafa. "Morning. We were wondering what happened to you. Broken Hill wasn't that exciting, but it was nice to get off the train for a bit."

"Didn't sleep all night and figured I'd take a catnap. Didn't intend it to be hours." Keeping his tone even, he asked Rafa, "Why didn't you wake me?"

Rafa shrugged, eyes on the game board. "When I didn't see you, I figured you didn't want to come." He glanced up, brown eyes sorrowful, cheeks flushing. "That you didn't want to see me after the things I said. I kind of freaked out, and…" He grimaced. "It's embarrassing."

Shane hated to see him so miserable. "Of course I want to see you. I really did fall asleep. I wasn't…punishing you or something."

Blowing out a long breath, Rafa nodded. "Okay."

Matthew quietly asked, "What's up with you guys? He's barely said two words all morning."

Rafa glared at his brother. "Stay out of it."

"Well, Mom and Dad can smell blood in the water. So kiss and make up."

Shoulders slumped, Rafa glanced at Shane. "Can we talk about it later?" He rubbed his face. "I didn't sleep at all, and I'm just…not ready yet. Although if you want to break up with me, I guess I'd rather get that over with."

Shane's heart clenched. Not caring who was watching, he rubbed his hand up and down Rafa's rigid back. He murmured, "I'm not breaking up with you. We both made mistakes. We'll work it out together. Okay?"

A flicker of a smile passed Rafa's lips. "Okay."

Matthew reached for the dice. "Glad we got that settled."

"Why don't you go have a nap?" Shane suggested to Rafa. Part of him still wanted to leave the lounge so they could talk privately and truly get it settled. But he could wait until Rafa was rested and they could hash it out rationally.

Rafa nodded. "Yeah. I think I might. Then later, we can talk and stuff. We're..." He tentatively touched Shane's thigh, his palm a comforting weight. "We're going to be okay?"

"Absolutely." He pressed a kiss to Rafa's temple. "You rest, and I'm going to see if I can scare up a coffee and toast."

Matthew glanced around the carriage. "There should be a staff person back soon. She was here a minute ago."

"No problem. I'll go to the dining car. I'm sure someone there can help." Keeping calm and steady, Shane squeezed Rafa's tense shoulder. "Sleep well." He wanted to go to bed with him and just hold him, but if Rafa needed some space, he'd give it.

He walked through the lounge, giving Ramon and Camila another nod as he passed, their gazes on him razor-sharp. They had a ream of papers on the low table between them, one of the assistants telling them about something to do with an appearance in Los Angeles with Schwarzenegger.

The agent at the end of the lounge car by the bar stepped aside for him, and Shane told himself he was imagining the tiny smirk on the man's lips.

He pushed into the dining car, and his heart sank. He'd found Hernandez, who was standing in the middle of the car with the other agents having some kind of debriefing. The blond agent from the night before said something too low for Shane to hear, and the others laughed.

It was like being back in fucking high school, and while he ordered himself to rise above it, face burning, he choked on the humiliation. These people had been his peers for most of his life—hell, Hernandez had been his friend—and now their judgment and derision hurt like a son of a bitch.

Hernandez faced him, her expression mocking and bored. "What do you want, Kendrick?"

He responded before he could stop himself. "I want you to go fuck yourself for starters."

She drew herself up taller. "What did you say to me?"

"Guess he's still grumpy after the fight with his teenage boy-friend." The blond agent sneered.

Biting back the retort that Rafa wasn't a teenager, Shane marched toward them as Hernandez shook her head, a vein jumping in her temple. "You've got a lot of nerve, Kendrick. I still can't believe you're even showing your face while Venus and Vagabond are down here. You're an embarrassment."

"So you all get to judge me and—"

"You're damn right we do!" she snapped. She barked to the other agents, "Everyone back to your posts. Chang, Miller, get some sleep."

Just as they left, a young woman working on the train entered from the kitchen side of the dining car. Considering Shane and Hernandez were standing there in the aisle practically baring their teeth at each other, she skidded to a stop and said, "Oh! Um, sorry. I'll just..." She scurried back the way she'd come.

"As I was saying, you're a goddamn embarrassment, Kendrick. Hooking up with a protectee? The president's son, of all people? He's almost half your age, as I'm sure you're well aware. You're a disgrace to the Service. I wish they could have fired your irrespon-sible ass before you quit."

"I didn't plan on falling in love." He winced internally. It wasn't much of a defense.

Hernandez's lip curled. "Jesus Christ, have some dignity. Spare me the hearts and flowers and *falling in love*. You were there to do your job, not get busy with that kid." She shook her head. "I couldn't believe it when the news broke. Thought it had to be some kind of fucking mistake. The Shane Kendrick I knew—"

"So you admit you knew me?"

She lifted her chin. "Sure. Fine, I admit it. I thought you were a great guy. Dependable and capable agent. Solid human. Guess you had me fooled."

It shouldn't have hurt, but it fucking did. "I'm not saying I didn't screw up." He jerked his shoulders in a shrug. "But I'd do it again. For him, I'd do anything."

She scoffed. "You practice that in front of a mirror? Because I almost believe you."

"You can believe whatever you want."

"Thanks for the permission. Now I have to get back to work, since I haven't tossed my career in the dumpster for a piece of ass."

She brushed by him, back toward the lounge car. Standing there, Shane breathed in and out deeply, slowing his thumping heart as a few minutes passed. The young female staff member reappeared and cleared her throat.

"G'day. Can I help you with anything?"

His voice was hoarse. "Coffee, please. Just black."

"No worries. Anything to eat? I didn't see you at breakfast." She clasped her hands in front of her navy uniform skirt, looking at him so earnestly, like she very much wanted to help.

Her kindness tightened Shane's chest, and he swallowed a ridiculous lump in his throat. "Some toast with butter would be great. Thank you." Anticipating her next question, he added, "Multigrain, please."

"Right away! I can bring it to you in the lounge."

The thought of facing the Castillos again so soon had dread sinking through him. "Is it all right if I eat in here? Or am I in the way?"

"Not at all! Choose any table you like."

The tables had already been reset for lunch, the crisp white linen spotless. Shane took a seat by a window, staring out at the landscape, which was starting to feature low hills, the earth not quite as red as they sped south toward Adelaide.

He told himself he shouldn't give a damn what the Secret Service and its agents thought of him. But he could tell himself that all he wanted—he still cared. Their scorn cut him more deeply than anyone else's. After the fight with Rafa, it was like salt scoured over a wound.

The girl returned with not only steaming coffee and buttered toast, but a bowl of freshly sliced fruit. He thanked her and poked at the food, forcing at least some of it down. His mind whirled, trying to figure out a solution to how he and Rafa had had such a breakdown in communication.

He cursed himself again for not telling Rafa about his history with Darnell. Of course Rafa would feel threatened when he thought it was some *secret* Shane had kept. When he had to hear it from his mother. Shane tightened his grip on the coffee cup. No doubt Camila had taken great pleasure in revealing it.

All sorts of words to describe Camila Castillo ricocheted through his head, and he fought to banish them. She wasn't going anywhere, and resenting her wouldn't help a damn thing. He was responsible for not being honest with Rafa about the nightmares, and of course it had hurt Rafa to overhear that he'd confided in Darnell.

Yes, it still stung that Rafa had accused him of cheating, but he'd been angry. Shane had to believe he hadn't really meant it. Now they just needed to sit down and talk it out. Identify where they'd gone wrong and make sure it didn't happen again.

Unfortunately, the next several hours proved impossible to get Rafa alone between Rafa's nap, a late lunch, and the Castillos' insistence on playing a family game of Scrabble. Shane pretended nothing was wrong, flipping through a magazine and not reading a word.

By the time the train neared Adelaide mid-afternoon, the need to talk to Rafa—to make everything a hundred-percent okay again—pushed at him, an expanding pressure against his ribcage.

Hernandez entered the lounge with an older staff member in the full uniform, including the jacket and brown outback hat. He grinned and said, "G'day! How ya goin'? I wanted to talk about your excursion options. We'll be stopping shortly in Two Wells, about forty clicks north of Adelaide. There's a Barossa Valley tour this arvo, but the bigwigs thought we'd offer something extra special for the Castillo family."

Ramon smiled. "That's so kind, but we don't need any special treatment."

"We truly don't," Camila added. "But what were you thinking?"

"Well, how about a helicopter tour? Take you all around the wine country. It'll be sweet as." He grinned.

In the beat of silence, Camila asked, "As what?"

The man frowned. "Sorry?"

"Mom, he just means it'll be really good," Rafa said.

"Absolutely!" The man nodded. "Then you'll have dinner with everyone else in the Barossa before hopping back on the train in Adelaide later tonight. There's room for five along with the pilot, one up front and four in the back."

Camila beamed. "Well, that sounds just lovely. It's been a while since we've flown in a helicopter."

The man grinned. "That's right, you'd be experts at it. But I dare say the scenery here will be hard to beat. Seeing the sunset over the Clare Valley can't be missed."

Ramon nodded. "You've certainly convinced us." He looked to Hernandez. "You're on board?"

She smiled. "Quite literally. I'll accompany you, Camila, and the boys."

"But…" Rafa glanced over to Shane. "I don't want to go without Shane."

Shane waved his hand. "No, no. Of course you should go. I'll see you for dinner." *Another awkward, stilted meal with your parents, hooray.*

Matthew spoke up. "I never liked helicopters. I'll go on the bus with the hoi polloi and Shane can take my spot."

"Really, dear? '*Hoi polloi*'?" Camila raised an eyebrow at her son. "Let's not forget our manners. And I'm sure you would enjoy a sightseeing ride."

"No, I wouldn't," Matthew insisted. "I never liked flying. I can deal with planes, but helicopters? Hard pass. You know I've never liked them."

"Well, that's true." Ramon nodded. "All right, then. Shane, are you game?"

As Camila looked at her husband like he'd grown an extra head, Shane gave them a smile and said, "Always."

Before long, the train had stopped and they were shepherded onto a Mercedes minibus in the waning afternoon sun. Shane and Rafa took the big back seat, Hernandez and three other agents in the middle seats, and Rafa's parents in the seat closest to the front. They made small talk with the driver, sounding cheerful and interested, which Shane had to admit was a skill they had down pat.

He bumped his knee against Rafa's and murmured, "Feeling better?"

"Yeah." Rafa smiled softly. "I really needed a nap and a good lunch." He took Shane's hand, threading their fingers together. Shane squeezed, his lungs expanding a little more easily now that he and Rafa were hand-in-hand.

We're okay. We got this.

They'd hash it out later, and for now, they could enjoy the tour. Shane tuned in as the driver spoke through the radio and pointed out sites of interest as they made their way along a winding road, vineyards and trees spreading out in all directions.

When they boarded the helicopter, Hernandez sat up front beside the pilot, Camila and Ramon on the first two seats, and Shane and Rafa behind. The view of the Barossa Valley from the sky truly was breathtaking, the rows and rows of grapes creating geometric patterns amid the swathes of farmland. Shane and Rafa smiled at each other and held hands again, and he relaxed and enjoyed the landscape.

The middle-aged, balding pilot came on, his voice filling their ears through the headsets everyone wore. "Now we're coming up on a golf course to the left, and golf courses are one of the greatest places to spot roos, especially later in the day. We're having a real heat wave for this time of year—high was all the way up to twenty-six, and the low is going to be about seventeen. So they really enjoy luxuriating on a golf course while they wait for the sun to go down."

"Anyone know what twenty-six and seventeen are in real temperatures?" Hernandez asked.

The pilot laughed good-naturedly. "I'd say it's about high seventies or up to eighty, and down to low or mid-sixties in your crazy Fahrenheit."

"It's usually colder this time of year?" Camila asked.

"Yeah, it can dip down quite a bit in winter here in South Australia. My missus never leaves home without a cardigan or jacket this time of year. But global warming seems to really be playing havoc."

"Oh! I see kangaroos!" Rafa grabbed Shane's arm and pointed out the left window.

They all ohh-ed and ahh-ed, even Hernandez, who should have been keeping strictly professional and straight-faced. Shane couldn't help but grumble to himself after the way she'd laid into him earlier. Although he did admit that seeing the kangaroos hopping across the green lawn, the incredible spring in their back legs powering them along so effortlessly, was magical.

As they headed north past the Clare Valley, the landscape became rougher and less refined, but still beautiful. The pilot said, "You're in for a treat. We had some heavy rains earlier in the week, and there's a little lake in a valley between ridges that is a lot bigger at the moment. No roads to it, so it's absolutely pristine."

They flew over meadows toward a hillier region with more trees. When they crested over a ridge and saw the lake, the sinking sun glittering over the blue water, Shane's chest tightened at the sheer beauty. He looked to Rafa, and they shared a fleeting smile before turning back to their windows.

Everything's okay. We're okay.

The pilot took the chopper lower, the wind from the rotors rippling out across the lake's surface. The pilot said, "Isn't that just gorgeous? I tell you, it may be winter, but I think this can be the best time to see the region. If you look to the right—"

A metal *clang* echoed, then a *screeeeeech* that shot shivers down Shane's spine as they jerked violently. They were suddenly spinning, the helicopter shaking horribly.

He grasped for Rafa blindly, the world a terrifying and bone-crunching blur, screams ripping through the air. Shane latched onto Rafa's vibrating arm as the helicopter pitched nose down and plummeted.

Suddenly Shane's gut was being compressed like a tin can, the pressure unbearable, but in another heartbeat they crashed into the water with a deafening impact. In the twist of metal and glass, he gripped Rafa, refusing to ever let him go.

Chapter Twelve

THE TERRIBLE PRESSURE that had been crushing Rafa's chest and stomach lifted, but what…what was happening? He was on his side—no the helicopter was on its side, the left windows Rafa had been looking out now above him. Everything shook, his teeth rattling, the massive rotor still churning the water.

Get out!

Something gripped his right arm painfully—Shane! Shane was below him, and there was water coming into the helicopter, a window smashed. Rafa jabbed at his seatbelt with his free hand. It came loose and then Shane was shoving at him.

Shane shouted, "Pull the red emergency latch and push the window out!"

The rotor kept them shuddering on the surface, metal scream-ing, the noise unbearable. Rafa grappled for the latch, trying to focus on anything red. He ran his hands over the window frame. *There!* He yanked on the handle, but nothing happened.

"The yellow ring! Lift it first!" Shane was reaching up, stand-ing on his seat. He tugged at a piece of yellow metal, throwing it aside, then turning the red handle. "Push the window out!"

Rafa's heart thundered as he shoved at the glass, fighting gravi-ty. He got one foot on the side of the chair, the other floundering for purchase. He hit something solid, then Shane had his foot in his hands, boosting him up.

Shane's head was barely above the rushing water now, still supporting Rafa's weight. Rafa punched at the window, shoving the glass away, then getting his hands around the frame and hauling himself up, Shane boosting him.

He shimmied out into the lake, kicking and paddling. He turned back to the helicopter, the body of it almost completely under now, the huge rotors slowing but still spraying air and water violently, stinging his eyes.

Oh God! Shane! Mom, Dad!

He scrambled back to the window as his mother appeared, Shane shoving her up and out. Rafa dragged her free, and she clung to him, her fingers digging into his flesh, her weight pulling him down. His head went under, and he kicked wildly, lungs burning.

As he broke the surface, she let go, screaming something he couldn't understand over the blood rushing in his ears and the awful whir of the dying rotor.

His father was half out the window now, flopped over and barely conscious, a terrifying piece of metal jutting out of his chest just below his shoulder. Rafa grabbed his arms, kicking desperately, his feet hitting the side of the sinking helicopter as he pulled his father free, the impaled shrapnel scraping Rafa's neck.

He turned his moaning father onto his back, and Camila grabbed onto both of them, floundering. Her hair streamed about her pale face. She made a horrible sound, a desperate, high-pitched wail. It sent shivers over him, but he couldn't freak out.

"Mom, take Dad! On his back—keep his head out of the water. Go to shore. Now! Go!" He turned back for Shane, but he wasn't there.

No! No!

With a final groan, the rotors stopped, and the helicopter sank below the surface. Rafa took a deep breath and dove under, hands outstretched as he went back through the window. It was so dark, and he couldn't see Shane. The water felt too thick and his lungs burned already.

He felt around desperately, swimming down, finding the edge of a broken window, glass slicing his palms. He turned, something sharp scraping his stomach, and then his hands hit flesh and fabric. *Yes!* He pulled up frantically, swimming back to the distant light of the surface, then sucking in another breath when he reached it.

Hair falling out of its bun, Agent Hernandez was barely conscious, her eyes opening and closing as if she'd been drugged and was trying to fight it. Blood flowed from a gash in her forehead, and her suit jacket bunched in Rafa's hands. Shane was behind her, gasping for air and keeping her head above the surface. Rafa's relief that they were out was short-lived.

"Going back for the pilot!" Shane shouted. "Get her to shore!"

"No!" Panic clawed at Rafa, and he grabbed for Shane, not willing to see him disappear below the dark surface again, as horribly selfish as it was.

But Shane was already out of his grasp, and Rafa had to keep the woman in his arms from drowning. He moved onto his back, rolling her with him, one arm across her chest. She seemed to be breathing all right, at least. He glanced back at his parents, his mother holding his father afloat the same way.

Camila was kicking and swimming with one arm, making for the closest land, which looked maybe sixty yards away, so not too far. She grunted, her teeth bared, struggling with Ramon. The metal jutting from his chest gleamed in the sun, and his eyes were closed. She screamed, "Rafa, come on!"

Balancing Hernandez's dead weight in the water, his sneakers heavy as he kicked, Rafa looked back to the spot where Shane had disappeared. A rotor tip stuck out from the water, sinking steadily. How long could Shane hold his breath? What if he didn't come up?

God, please! Please!

Wheezing, Rafa knew he was hyperventilating, but he couldn't calm his breath, a scream frozen in his throat. Bubbles popped on the lake's surface, and his heart leapt.

But there was nothing. No Shane. No one.

No, no, no! Shane couldn't die! *No!* Rafa's limbs jerked with frantic energy as he waited. He couldn't just stand by and watch! But if he let go of Agent Hernandez, she'd drown, and *fuck*!

With a mighty splash, Shane broke the surface, sucking in a desperate breath, the slumped pilot in his grasp. Tears spilled from Rafa's eyes, his throat wet with them. Shane was okay. Rafa could breathe again.

He kicked and concentrated on getting Agent Hernandez to shore, making sure he could still see Shane. His parents were ahead, Camila splashing in the shallows as she hauled Ramon out of the water, her feet bare, soaked capris and blouse clinging to her. Over the thunder of his own heartbeat and harsh pants, Rafa could hear his mother groaning as she struggled with Ramon's weight.

Land hadn't seemed that far to Rafa, but as the minutes ticked by, it was taking forever. Agent Hernandez's hair got into his mouth. As he tried to spit it out, he accidentally swallowed water, coughing and sputtering. At least it was fresh water, not salt.

He refocused on Shane, who was with the pilot and...kissing him? Rafa blinked at the sight, trying to make sense of it. As Shane pinched the pilot's nose and covered his mouth again, the other shoe dropped with a dull thud. *Mouth-to-mouth.*

Fuck, was Rafa sure Agent Hernandez was still breathing? He tried to get a good look at her pale face. Her lips were parted, and there—her eyelids flickered. He shook her slightly just to make sure, and she moaned. Okay. Good. Now...what was he doing? Right, he had to get her back to shore. Stroking one arm through the water and kicking, Rafa stared up at the blue sky.

Is this really happening?

He watched a cloud, glancing behind him every so often to make sure he was still going straight. The water didn't seem cold anymore, but he wasn't sure if that was a good thing or not. His limbs didn't feel like they were attached to his body the right way—as if they'd been bent and loosened, not answering his commands the way they should.

But he kept kicking, his left arm numb where it was locked around Agent Hernandez, his right cramping as he pulled through the water. Inch by inch, the trees got closer, the swollen lake lapping ten feet from their roots. He saw Camila drag Ramon onto land, her grunts echoing over the water.

That's when he realized how quiet it was aside from splashing and the sound of his own ragged breath and thudding of his heart. He was almost there, and he dipped a foot down, yelping when he hit a rock. It was strange how he couldn't really feel his legs, but they still worked, and he got his feet under him as the shore sloped up, the water to his chest now as he splashed out of the lake, dragging Agent Hernandez.

He stumbled back onto his butt in the wet dirt, water still around her feet, but he managed to get most of her on land. He shouldn't have been so exhausted. He'd surely swam much farther in the past. Matthew was the swimmer in the family, but Rafa had always liked the water too.

Matty. Thank God he hadn't come with them. He was all right. He was safe. *Safe.* Was Rafa? He was out of the water, but all he could do for the moment was sit there shivering, the sun dipping below the western ridge beyond the lake, an incredible purple streaking the blue sky.

The sunset really is beautiful.

Shaking his head, he struggled to focus. *Snap out of it! Wake up!* He scrubbed at his face and breathed deeply. Agent Hernandez was resting heavily on his legs, moaning. He dug his heels into the rocky dirt and managed to push back several more feet until she was completely out of the water.

He focused on Shane still in the lake, pausing in his swimming to blow more breaths into the pilot's mouth, pinching his nose. Shane looked to be in control. He was okay. Then Rafa turned to his parents about twenty feet away down the shore. His heart seized, adrenaline spiking and offering sudden clarity.

"Mom! Stop!" Rafa scrambled over. His father was stretched out on his back, barely conscious, muttering. The piece of metal, at least two inches thick, was lodged under the front of his shoulder, protruding about six inches.

Camila had hold of the end. "It's not supposed to be there! It's not right! I have to get it out." She pulled, and Ramon *shrieked*.

Rafa shoved her away, prying her hands loose. Fortunately the metal hadn't moved that much, although fresh blood seeped from around it. "You're going to do more damage pulling it out! Let the doctors do it." He'd streamed enough episodes of that old *ER* show with George Clooney to know that.

Sitting there on the ground, legs bent beside her and feet bare, she stared at Rafa, then down at her husband. She was wet and filthy with dirt and blood, and she panted softly through parted lips, her eyes not quite focusing the way they should.

With a horrible, sinking sensation, Rafa realized his mother—famously unflappable, with never a strand of hair out of place and an answer for everything—was completely in shock.

She needs you. Keep it together!

He took her limp hand. "Mom, it's okay. Everything's all right. Look at me. *Please.*" With his other hand, he held her chin, smearing more dirt on her skin. Her pearls were gone, the strand likely snapped when she'd clawed free of the wreckage, scratch marks scouring her neck. "Mom. You're all right. Dad's all right. Don't touch the piece of metal. It'll make it worse."

Her fingers twitched against his, and she blinked. Then she

nodded and pulled him into a hug, her fingers digging into his back. "Oh, my darling."

"I'm okay, Mom. We're okay." He held her tightly, still feeling strangely numb. He knew it was shock, and he had to shake it off.

"Raf! Are you hurt?" Shane called from nearby.

Rafa turned to find him kneeling on the ground, arms locked as he performed chest compressions on the pilot, whose face was a horrible gray. When Rafa tried to answer, his voice caught. He cleared his throat. "I'm fine."

He turned back to Camila. "Are you hurt, Mom?" He examined her body, looking for blood or obvious injuries. Her blouse was torn and capri pants filthy, but she seemed okay.

She shook her head. "I'm fine. Your father…"

Ramon groaned, his eyes flickering open. Rafa crawled to his other side. "Dad? You're okay. Just relax. Help will be here soon." As the words left his mouth, he realized he actually had no idea if that was true. But he tried to smile for his parents' sake. "Just rest. Don't move." He lifted Ramon's shirt and looked for other injuries, not finding anything obvious aside from the huge piece of metal impaling him.

So, you know, other than that, we're good.

He choked down the burst of hysteria and tore a strip off the bottom of his father's golf shirt. There was blood pouring too quickly from a gash in Ramon's head, and Rafa tied the makeshift bandage around his skull carefully, making sure it was tight, but not too tight.

"Stay here. I'm going to check on Agent Hernandez."

"I think the pilot's dead," Camila muttered, her vacant gaze on Shane performing CPR.

"Just don't move, Mom. It's okay. Here, hold Dad's hand." He awkwardly threaded their fingers together.

Camila looked down at her hand, then back up at Rafa. After

a moment, she blinked and shook her head a little. "Darling? Are you all right?" Her eyes seemed to sharpen. "Are you hurt?"

"No, I'm all right."

"You're bleeding!" She stared at his arms.

Lifting his palms, he could see blood dripping from the cuts on his hands and some on his inner arms he didn't know he had. "I'm okay."

Camila pulled her blouse out of her waistband and tore at the hem with surprising strength, the fabric tearing with a low *rip*. She bandaged one of Rafa's hands, then the other, before nodding. "You're okay."

He pushed unsteadily to his feet and passed Shane and the pilot. Breathing hard as he pressed on the pilot's chest, Shane glanced up. A red cut marred his temple and cheek, blood dripping, but not gushing. "Hernandez?"

"I'm going to…" Rafa motioned with his hand, continuing on a few steps past Shane to where he'd left her. She was coughing, and Rafa helped her roll onto her left side, remembering a school lesson on first aid and the recovery position. He wasn't sure if it would make a difference since she wasn't completely knocked out, but figured it couldn't hurt. He prayed he wasn't wrong.

Like in the water, Agent Hernandez seemed to be struggling to wake up fully and unable to do it. Her pantsuit was obviously soaked, and Rafa wished he had a blanket to put over her. Of course there was nothing.

He eased off her jacket and wrung it out, his palms stinging. He hung it from a tree branch, hoping it would dry a bit and could be a little blanket later. He also said a quick prayer that *later*, they would be rescued and safe.

Not seeing what else he could do for her, he crawled over to Shane and the pilot, kneeling on the pilot's other side. In the twilight, Shane met his gaze. He was counting under his breath, and stopped compressions to tilt the pilot's head and breathe twice into his mouth. He resumed compressions, counting softly again.

"I can do the breathing," Rafa said, his throat raw. Shane nodded, and Rafa positioned himself.

When Shane said, "Thirty," Rafa puffed twice into the pilot's mouth, pinching his nose and tilting his head back. The man's lips felt cold and rubbery, and in the fading light, the gray pallor of his face looked *wrong* on an instinctive level that made Rafa want to get away from him.

His skin crawled, but he stayed put, breathing twice into the man's lifeless mouth every time Shane reached thirty. Along with lake water, sweat beaded on Shane's forehead and dripped into his eyes. Rafa said, "We should switch." Shane nodded, and Rafa took over after the next cycle, pounding hard in the rhythm of the song "Staying Alive."

Shane said, "I'm counting," so Rafa concentrated on the song in his head, repeating the chorus over and over. *Uh-uh-uh-uh.* Shane counted aloud from twenty-five, then did the breathing after thirty. Then they started the cycle again.

Rafa wasn't sure how many times they went through it, Shane eventually taking over compressions again when Rafa got out of breath. It was shockingly draining—more so than he ever would have thought it could be. The pilot's eyes were closed, and he didn't move or cough or suddenly wake and spit up water the way people did in movies.

No, as darkness settled in, the temperature dipping, the pilot simply laid there as they pounded on his chest, more and more minutes ticking by until Camila spoke, her voice making both Shane and Rafa jump.

"He's dead."

Rafa was doing the compressions, and he glanced at her, his shoulders burning. She shook her head. "Without a defibrillator it's impossible. And it's been too long now anyway."

Shane sighed. "She's right. He'd be brain dead even if paramedics suddenly got here. It's been, what?" He glanced at Camila. "Forty minutes?"

"Yes, I think so," she answered.

Rafa was still singing in his head as he did the compressions. *Uh-uh-uh-uh.* Shane covered Rafa's hands with his own, gently easing them away, threading their fingers together. He murmured, "It's okay. We did everything we could."

Staring down at the pilot in the light of the rising moon, Rafa thought of the man's "missus" and wondered if he had kids. He only realized he was crying when his vision blurred. Then Shane was leading him away from the body, and they hugged tightly, holding each other close.

Shane murmured into his ear, "It's okay. We're okay." His arms tightened, pulling Rafa flush to his body. Shane's belt dug into his stomach. Rafa gasped and jerked at the unexpected flare of pain. The cuts on his hands and arms were stinging now, as if they'd been frozen and were thawing hotly.

Holding onto Rafa's shoulders with tense fingers, Shane took a shaky breath. "What?" His eyes roamed over him, hands following. "Baby, are you hurt?"

Rafa prodded gently at his stomach and lifted his tee. Just above the waist of his jeans there was a long cut he must have gotten going back into the wrecked helicopter.

Shane dropped to his knees in the dirt, inhaling forcefully and demanding, "Why didn't you say anything?"

"I don't think it's that bad."

"What's wrong?" Camila asked sharply from where she sat by Ramon about ten feet away. "Mr. Kendrick, what's wrong with him?"

Shane blew out a shaky breath, the warm air ghosting over Rafa's belly. He spoke authoritatively. "He'll be fine. A gash on his stomach, but it's shallow." He whipped his shirt over his head and pressed it to the wound, then unbuckled his belt with one hand

and wrapped that around Rafa's waist, securing the make-shift compress.

As Shane pressed a kiss to the bare skin over the gash, Rafa caressed Shane's stubbly head and murmured, "I'm fine."

"Sit down. Here, against this tree." Shane got to his feet and led him over to a tree close to his parents, getting him situated. The bark was rough through the thin cotton of Rafa's drying T-shirt. "Rest," Shane ordered.

While Shane went to examine Agent Hernandez and shift her closer to their little group, Rafa watched his parents. His father's head was now in Camila's lap, and she murmured something to him. The air was mercifully still, the surface of the water glassy.

Looking at the lake, one would never know chaos and disaster had just occurred. That there was a helicopter that had just been flying powerfully through the sky, now lost and broken in the depths, the surface calm as if the chaos had only been a dream.

The ridge on the other side of the valley was a jagged shadow against the brilliant stars. It was strangely peaceful, the odd night bird hooting distantly. *Pristine*, the pilot had called it, since there were no roads in or out.

Rafa was reluctant to say it out loud, but asked, "How are they going to find us?"

Shane was still carefully easing Agent Hernandez closer. She still didn't really wake up as Shane curled her back on her side, tucking her knees up to her chest. He said, "I don't think the pilot had time for a mayday, but obviously we'll be reported missing very soon if we haven't already."

Camila nodded to Agent Hernandez. "Her radio?"

Shane shook his head. "It's dead. Can't handle being sub-merged."

"Is there a GPS or beacon or something on the helicopter?" Rafa asked.

"Not sure," Shane answered.

"And what about our phones?" Rafa grimaced. "Although they obviously got soaked. I think mine's at the bottom of the lake."

"Mine's gone too," Shane said.

Camila sighed. "Mine's in my purse back in the car with the other agents. I think your father left his in there too."

"But they'll have every chopper in the state out searching before long." Shane smiled grimly. "One of the perks of crash landing with a former president."

"Glad to be of service," Ramon muttered, then coughed. "Water," he croaked.

Rafa crawled to him. "It's okay, Dad. It's okay."

Shane glanced around his feet. "We've got plenty of water, but how to transport it?" He mumbled, as if to himself. "If there was a rock with enough of a basin…"

"I guess we could use a shoe?" Rafa suggested. "It's kind of gross, but he needs to stay hydrated." He unlaced his sneaker and offered it.

Shane made his way to the water's edge past the pilot's body. He kneeled there, apparently giving Rafa's shoe a good rinse, scrubbing at it until he was satisfied. Then he filled it and crouched by Ramon. "Open up."

Ramon did, Camila supporting his head, and Shane tipped the fresh water into his mouth. He went back to the lake for a refill before Ramon said he'd had enough. He offered the rest to Camila, who swallowed it silently. She smiled wryly. "Tastes surprisingly good given how much Rafa's feet stink."

"Hey! Chris's are way worse than mine. Remember that time he took off his shoes in the limo on the way home from some event and we could hardly breathe?" *What the fuck am I talking about?* Everything was utterly surreal, and he wished he could wake up.

Camila managed a half-hearted laugh, caressing Ramon's hair, his head settled back on her lap. "You raise a fair point, darling."

Rafa asked, "Should we try to give Agent Hernandez some?"

Shane shook his head. "She could aspirate. Hopefully they'll find us soon and she can get IV fluids." He glanced over at the pilot. "I wish we could cover him somehow. But I guess it doesn't matter much to him."

Quietly, Camila asked, "Could you take him out of sight? Not too far that the animals will…" She shuddered. "Just far enough we don't have to look at him?"

Shane nodded and did as she asked, carefully pulling the pilot off to the left, just beyond the next tree. Rafa stared at his mother, and she caught his gaze and frowned before she said, "I'm sorry if it seems cold-hearted."

"Actually, I'm surprised it bothers you at all." *Shit. Did I say that out loud?*

She blinked at him, her face creasing with hurt that made her look so much younger. "Do you really think me so unfeeling? That a dead man would have no effect?"

"I'm sorry. I didn't mean that." He swallowed hard. "I really didn't."

She nodded and turned her face down as she smoothed her fingers over Ramon's hair, her shoulders hunched. Rafa wanted to apologize more, but he was so tired.

He watched Shane walk to the water's edge and crouch to drink, gulping from his cupped hands. His bare torso gleamed in the moonlight. As night set in, it was getting colder, and Rafa prayed again that help was on the way.

Rafa was thirsty too, but he didn't want to move from his father's side just yet. Shane refilled the sneaker and brought it over. Rafa gulped gratefully. He couldn't taste feet at all, and the water was cool and clear. At least they hadn't crashed in the outback or something. His stomach clenched at the thought of surviving the night out there without water.

He took off his other shoe and squeezed out his socks. "If we hang these on a branch, they'll dry better."

"Good idea," Shane said, following suit. "Put both your shoes back on. We'll use Hernandez's Oxford for water since she's not walking around." He kneeled by her feet and took off her shoes and socks, hanging the socks to dry. Camila passed over Ramon's.

Shane settled against the nearby tree, insisting the bark didn't bother him. Rafa leaned back, safe in the V of Shane's legs, powerful arms wrapped around his chest. Shane traced Rafa's elbows with his fingertips.

They sat in silence for a long time, Agent Hernandez moaning sometimes, then falling back into unconsciousness. Rafa had just closed his eyes when Ramon mumbled, "How?"

Shane jerked slightly, and Camila said, "Shh. Rest." She had been rhythmically rubbing his body, keeping him warm.

"How?" he repeated.

Shane's baritone rumbled against Rafa's back. "The way we started spinning like that, I think the tail rotor must have blown. We were so low there was no time for the pilot to recover. Although if we'd been higher, we probably wouldn't have survived the impact."

The fact that they'd very narrowly escaped death was still hard to compute. Rafa said, "If it blew, do you think it was a bomb or something?"

Shane tightened his arms, his fingers caressing Rafa's rib cage on both sides. "Doubtful. The advance team would have inspected the chopper. I just mean something mechanical. A catastrophic failure in the rotor itself."

They all fell quiet again. After a time, a dull, throbbing sound got louder, and Shane tensed and murmured, "Chopper."

Yet the sound never got louder. They waited. And waited. But no one came, and time ticked by slowly.

The temperature had definitely dropped, but with not much wind it didn't feel too bad. "Thank God for the heat wave," Rafa murmured.

"Mmm. We still have to be careful of hypothermia," Shane said.

They did another round of water, and Rafa pushed to his feet and joined Shane by the lake's edge. He winced as he dropped to his knees, his left one smarting. He'd probably banged it getting out of the helicopter.

"Okay?" Shane wrapped his arm around Rafa's back. "Let me look at your stomach." He bent his head to poke and prod. "Seems okay. Bleeding has stopped. But you should rest."

"Let me drink before we go back." He gasped softly as he cupped his hands in the water, which felt positively icy now. After he gulped down a few handfuls, he sat back on his heels and looked at Shane, who kept one hand holding onto Rafa, always there to support him. There was so much he wanted to say, but all Rafa could do was hug him and savor the warmth of his body and breath.

The poor pilot was dead, yet in Shane's arms, damp and aching, Rafa felt wonderfully safe and loved. He couldn't deny himself the swell of gratitude that they were still alive, latching onto that hope like a life raft.

Chapter Thirteen

F UCK. THEY WEREN'T going to be found before dawn.

They weren't going to be found before dawn—and everything hurt. The tree bark scratched his back, but Shane hadn't moved since he'd gotten Rafa settled again between his legs. He'd lifted Rafa's shirt so they could press their bare skin together for warmth, careful he didn't aggravate any wounds. The cuts on Rafa's hands and arms fortunately seemed shallow enough, and the gash on his stomach had stabilized.

Still, they weren't rescued yet.

Trying to stave off panic, Shane had gotten used to every inhalation hurting. His ribs were likely bruised, but he didn't think they were broken. It didn't matter if they were, as long as Rafa was safe in his arms. God, he was tired, though. He ached to think of their warm bed back in Curl Curl.

You'll be there soon. You'll make it.

It was after midnight, and despite more distant thumping of helicopter rotors, the searchers hadn't gotten close. Shane knew that in the dark, it was next to impossible to spot anything even with searchlights, and without a visible crash site or rising smoke that could have been distantly sighted before the sun set, all the search team had to go on was the square area the chopper tour usually covered.

That was many, many miles.

The pilot had taken them over the lake because it had swelled with recent rain, which indicated it wasn't part of the normal tour. How much of his plan had he communicated with the tour staff? Had it been a spur-of-the-moment decision? How much latitude did the tour pilots have? The only person who could answer those questions at the moment was of course dead.

Because I didn't get him out in time.

Shuddering, Shane rubbed his cheek against Rafa's hair. Rafa was dozing off, and he jerked his head up. Shane murmured, "Sorry."

Camila was still awake, keeping watch over her husband, although she had to be exhausted. Ramon had lapsed into unconsciousness, mumbling sometimes and moaning raggedly.

Hernandez still hadn't woken, but Shane hoped her body was keeping her safe by stopping her from regaining consciousness. Still, hypothermia was a very real concern. It wasn't freezing, but it was quite cool compared to the heat of the day when the sun shone.

Why didn't I get him out in time?

Squeezing his eyes shut, he tried to banish the images of the sinking helicopter. It had been shockingly dark once the chopper had dropped below the surface, and he'd had to go on touch, his arms in front of him grasping for where he thought the pilot should be, the pressure of the water once the helicopter was completely submerged making his movements sluggish.

His heart had leapt when his fingers closed on the pilot's arm, but then he'd struggled to find the seatbelt release, his lungs burning with each passing second, panic beating against his ribcage, every instinct screaming to get back to the surface.

Still, he'd hunted for the release button, finally finding it and jabbing with his fingers, the need to breathe so great he knew he'd involuntarily gasp for air soon, and that he'd be dead if he did.

He'd yanked the man free and kicked desperately for the surface, eyes open, the water getting brighter, the sun a distant glow he aimed for, his skull and lungs aching. When he'd breathed again, the oxygen had tasted sweet, his head spinning with it.

A sob had almost burst free from his throat, but there'd been no time to celebrate his survival, not with the pilot—whose name he shamefully couldn't recall—limp and unresponsive.

Even while he'd done the mouth-to-mouth in the water, getting the man back to shore as fast as he could, Shane had known he was already dead. Still, he couldn't have lived with himself if he'd given up, so even as the compressions snapped one of the man's ribs, he'd kept going.

If I'd gotten his seatbelt off sooner…

He shuddered again, and Rafa tensed. "What is it?"

"Nothing." His pulse raced, and he took a slow breath, still savoring the oxygen and ignoring the throbbing pain in his ribs. Maybe they could make a fire… "Your parents haven't started smoking, have they? If we had a lighter, we could get a fire going."

Camila answered, her voice thin and tense. "No, we have not. I don't think Agent Hernandez does either. Perhaps… Well, perhaps Mr. Moir did?"

For a moment, Shane couldn't speak. Then he hoarsely asked, "That was his name?"

"Yes. Rich Moir, he said."

Rich Moir. He'd been middle-aged, around fifty. Were his parents still alive? Was he a father? *Why didn't I get him out in time?* He'd told Rafa they'd done all they could, but surely if Shane had been faster, *better…*

"We should check his pockets," Rafa whispered.

Shane kissed his head. "I'll do it. I'll check Hernandez too." He eased himself up, rubbing his hands over his arms and torso, ignoring the pain in his ribs.

First he checked Hernandez's pockets, along with her pulse, which was steady. No lighter in her pants or suit jacket, which was still a bit damp. Taking a deep breath, his ribs protesting, he approached Rich Moir.

The breast pockets of the man's white, short-sleeved dress shirt were empty. Shane stuck his fingers into a pants pocket, then the others, including the ones in the back. It felt like a horrible invasion, but it had to be done.

Empty, but for the damp, shredded remnants of a tissue. He stared at the white mess in his hand then shook it away, wiping his palm on his pants. Twigs snapped, and he looked up to find Rafa approaching.

Shane wanted to throw out his arms and hide the dead man from his sight, as foolish as that was. Rafa asked, "Anything?"

Shane shook his head. "Go back and rest. I'll see if I can find some dry sticks. Make a fire the old-fashioned way."

"I'll help you."

"No, you need to—"

"I need to help!" Rafa's eyes flashed in the moonlight. He lowered his voice. "I'm not useless. Don't treat me like I am."

"That's not..." Shane rubbed his face, shivering as a breeze rippled across the lake. "I'm sorry. I just want to take care of you."

Rafa dropped to his knees beside him, curling his arm around Shane's back and rubbing. "I know. And I love you for that. But I'm okay." His gaze fell to the dead man, and he shuddered. "I know I'm not trained for all this stuff like you are, but I can help. They need us to help them."

Us. Shane nodded. "You're right." As much as he wanted to protect Rafa and do everything himself, Rafa was tough. He was a man, and they *were* partners. And sitting there by the cold body of the person Shane hadn't saved, it was a relief not to be alone. A relief to feel Rafa's strong, warm grasp, to sag against him for a few moments and just breathe.

Then Shane nodded. "Let's see if we can start a fire."

They ventured into the trees, walking heavily to scare off

whatever creatures might be near. They kicked at the ground and came up with sticks that felt dry, so what the hell. Worth a shot. Returning to the others after gathering some twigs and leaves, they cleared out a little fire pit.

Shane squatted and started rubbing the sticks together, anchoring one and spinning the other between his palms like he'd seen someone do on TV.

"I don't think that's going to work," Camila noted.

"Me either," he replied.

Rafa sighed. "Glass half full, you guys."

Shane kept trying, although it was soon apparent it was no use. His hands ached, but he couldn't produce even the faintest whiff of smoke. He sat back on his heels, a tugging twinge in his torso with every breath. "Christ. This is harder than it looks."

"Let me try," Rafa said.

Shane wanted to argue that Rafa's hands were cut, but he bit his tongue and watched as Rafa spun one stick against the other in the bed of dried tinder.

Rafa grimaced. "Wow. This really is tough."

"Don't reopen those cuts," Camila said sharply.

Muttering under his breath, Rafa kept trying. Shane winced watching, knowing how painful it was, but Rafa didn't give up for long minutes.

Finally, Rafa sat back on his heels, breathing hard. "Shit. This is too hard."

"Language," his mother said absently.

Rafa and Shane shared a look, then laughed. It damn well hurt to laugh, but his heart sang to see a smile on Rafa's face, even for a few moments amidst the horrible reality that they were miles from rescue.

Their laughter cut off as Ramon wailed suddenly, thrashing on his back. Camila held him still, trying to soothe him, and Rafa crawled closer, holding his father's legs.

"It's okay, Dad. It's okay. We're here."

If they don't come in the morning...

Shane tried to banish the fear, and said, "We have to assume they won't find us before morning. We need to huddle up to prevent hypothermia."

Camila let out a ragged breath. "But he has to get to a hospital!" *He* obviously meant her husband. She waved a hand over Ramon. "He needs doctors! How did this happen? Why aren't they still looking?"

"I'm sure they are," Shane said, trying to sound reassuring. "They could show up any minute."

"Then why don't they?" she shouted, her voice cracking.

"They will, Mom. It's okay." Kneeling beside her, Rafa took her in his arms. For a moment, she was utterly rigid, but then she deflated, collapsing against her son, a sob escaping her tight lips. He held her tightly.

Ramon muttered words Shane couldn't understand, shifting restlessly and reaching up for the metal impaling him. Before Shane could get there, Camila had lunged and caught Ramon's hands.

"No, darling," she admonished, seemingly back in control. She sniffed loudly, then shook her head. "You're right, Mr. Kendrick. We must stay warm." As Ramon quieted for the moment, she moved up onto her knees, and Shane realized her feet were bare. If he'd noticed earlier, it hadn't registered. In the dark, her nail polish looked black but was probably red.

He asked, "Where are your shoes?"

"What?" She looked at him blankly before answering, "Oh. In the lake. They came off almost right away, I think. Jimmy Choos aren't meant for swimming."

Shane grabbed the socks they'd hung over a branch. After a few hours, they were still damp, but more dry than wet, which was something. "Better than nothing." He held his white sports socks out to her.

After a few moments of staring at the socks as if they were alien creatures, Camila nodded and took them, tugging the too-big cotton over her feet. "Thank you."

Shane tossed Rafa his socks, then draped Hernandez's jacket over her and tugged her socks onto her feet, which felt cold to the touch. He did another round of water with the sodden leather shoe. Ramon was too out of it to drink now, groaning and crying nonsensically again as Camila shushed him, petting his hair.

Shane debated whether they should move into the trees for more shelter, but the wind had thankfully stayed calm, little more than a breeze over the water, and the risk of moving Hernandez and Ramon more than they had to wasn't one Shane wanted to take.

Besides, on the one-in-a-million chance another chopper might find them in the dark, they had much better odds of being seen by the lake's edge and not under the cover of trees deeper into the woods.

Was he doing everything he could? Was he doing everything *right*? Rafa had said Shane was trained for this, but the Service hadn't drilled him in wilderness survival. He knew first aid, but that was about it. He knew it was important to keep warm and that rubbing skin to skin was the best way. But the idea of getting naked with Rafa's mother wasn't exactly appealing. He'd leave that suggestion for a last resort.

Should have watched more Bear Grylls.

The ground was dirt, stones, and twigs, but they had nothing to spread beneath them. With Hernandez and a groaning Ramon in the middle, Camila stretched out beside her husband, curled against him. Shane urged Rafa close to Hernandez, then spooned up behind him, lifting Rafa's shirt so their skin could press together.

This can't be real.

But it was. They were stuck. There was a dead man just out of sight, and if rescuers didn't come by morning, Hernandez and Rafa's father could die. Hell, they could all die.

Shane's lungs seized, the what-ifs scudding through his mind like machine-gun fire. It hurt to hold his breath, and he squeezed his eyes shut, exhaling slowly. He had to stay calm. There was no other option.

We have water. We can keep going for weeks with water. They'll find us long before that. They have to. They will. Every chopper in Australia will be here if need be.

Shane held Rafa close, trying to ignore Ramon's feverish, plaintive moans. Huddled there, sharing warmth, the only thing they could do was wait.

THEY WERE STILL stuck in the endless night, but at least it was more of a murky gray when Shane heard Camila get up and disappear into the trees. She returned a few minutes later, and he wondered if Camila Castillo had ever urinated in the woods before. Highly unlikely. Curled against a dozing, trembling Rafa, the thought almost made Shane laugh.

Almost.

He was still spooned up tightly behind Rafa, making sure he was as warm as possible, the rise and fall of his breathing reassuring. Shane's bare back was freezing, and he rolled his ankles and clenched his icy feet in his damp sneakers, keeping the blood flowing.

Beside Rafa, Hernandez was still breathing strongly with a steady pulse, mostly unconscious aside from soft murmurs and shudders. On his back, Ramon had moaned and cried out what felt like every few minutes, Camila and Rafa soothing him.

Ramon had gone quieter now, but in the moonlight, Shane

could see he was still breathing steadily, the terrible piece of shrapnel rising and falling with every inhalation and exhalation. It hadn't seemed to have pierced his lungs or any major organs, but the shock and risk of infection were obviously at a high level.

Rafa had only just dozed off, and Shane held him close, watching Camila pick her way to the water, rubbing her arms vigorously through her thin blouse. At least they seemed relatively protected in the valley, the wind still aside from a draft off the water as the night crept by with mind-numbing slowness.

Ensuring Rafa was napping comfortably—well, as comfortably as possible—Shane eased away from him and went to join Camila at the edge of the lake. He'd wake Rafa soon and get him up and moving around to make sure he was warm enough.

He chafed his bare arms, his palms still sore from the useless attempt at starting a fire. Crouching beside Camila, he joined her in cupping his hands in the cold water and drinking.

She whispered, "This night will never end."

"Sure feels that way. Do you know what time it is?" He nodded to the delicate gold watch on her wrist.

"Sadly not waterproof. But the sky seems a little brighter, doesn't it?"

"A little. Dawn's on the way. We'll make it."

She was quiet for a few moments, drinking a bit more water and shivering. Then she softly said, "I'm glad you're here."

For a second, Shane wasn't sure he'd heard her correctly. "I…"

Camila smiled ruefully. "I never thought I'd live to see the day either. But it's a comfort, having you here to take charge. After all these years, we're used to relying on the Secret Service. It's a relief that you're with us." She shuddered, sucking in a breath through her teeth.

Without letting himself stop to consider the pros and cons, Shane wrapped an arm around her back and rubbed.

"Thank you," she whispered, leaning into his side and tucking her socked feet under her, her arms crossed. "The truth is, I don't think I would have gotten out of that helicopter without your help, Mr. Kendrick. Certainly Ramon wouldn't have. I was trying to lift him, and the water was rushing over my head..." She trembled. "I thought that was it. Then you were there. We very well might be dead without you. So thank you. Truly. And for getting Rafa out first."

"You don't need to thank me."

She looked at him, her gaze steady. "I do." Then she peered back at the horizon, frowning. "What happens if they don't find us today?"

"They will." He rubbed her back steadily.

"You're very confident."

"Well, this is basically the Australian government's worst PR nightmare. Former president and first lady perish on sightseeing trip? Damn bad for tourism."

She huffed out a grim laugh. "True enough."

"And losing a protectee is the Service's biggest fear. They are moving heaven and earth to find you and Ramon. Trust me."

After a few moments, she said, "You must have been frightened. When you were shot and Rafa was taken."

He froze, his arm just under her shoulder blades. He swallowed thickly, images of mud and rain and disappearing taillights in the gloom filling his mind. He hoarsely muttered, "Yes."

"If that bullet had killed you... Do you think those men would have let Rafa go in the end?"

Perhaps he should have told her a pretty lie, but what was the point? "No."

She quivered against him, and Shane started rubbing her back again, trying not to imagine how Rafa would have suffered if Shane had died and the kidnappers had gotten away free and clear. Would they have started chopping off body parts to send to the president?

He squeezed his eyes shut for a moment, a tremor gripping him, his arm stopping its movement. Then Camila's hand squeezed his knee. He looked at her steady gaze, moonlight glinting off her eyes. She whispered, "You got him back. It's over now."

"But what if something else happens?" he blurted before he could stop himself. "My parents—"

Shut up. Just stop talking. Camila Castillo doesn't want to hear about your angst.

"That must have been awful, to lose them that way."

It was bizarre to hear genuine sympathy from her, but it thickened his throat and brought tears to his eyes. Jesus Christ, he could *not* start crying. Not trusting himself to speak, he nodded.

They'd been gone for years—and he was a grown man—but the ache of their loss swelled painfully. In that moment, he missed their guidance and love acutely, like a knife to the gut.

"What do you think they'd make of you and Rafa?"

That they never had the chance to meet the man Shane loved with all his heart *hurt*, and he couldn't answer, the lump in his throat too huge.

Brows drawn together, Camila turned her head to look more closely at him. She blinked, obvious surprise crossing her face. "I'm sure they'd love him. Everyone does." She returned her gaze to the lake, taking on a haughty tone. "And why wouldn't they? He's a wonderful young man. Of course he is; he has perfect parents."

Huffing out a laugh that was half a sob, Shane realized she was trying to joke. And God, he really loved her for it. He took a deep breath, the threat of tears receding like a wave returning to the ocean.

After clearing his throat, he squeezed her shoulders lightly in a thank you. "I'm sure they would have adored him. I wish… Well, so many things."

"You're a smart man," she said briskly, her tone no-nonsense again. "You know it wasn't your fault. Stop torturing yourself over what might have been. We all want to keep our loved ones safe. Letting my children go out into the world was a lot easier when they had Secret Service protection."

"I'll do everything in my power to keep Rafa safe. Always."

She was silent a moment, then said, "I believe you will." She shook her head. "I must say, you've proven to be a surprise."

It felt good to laugh, the low chuckle warming his chest. He started rubbing her back again slowly. "Coming from you, that's a ringing endorsement."

"Let's not get carried away, Mr. Kendrick. But I admit..."

Shane waited, wishing he didn't care so much about what she was going to say. After a few moments, he thought perhaps she wouldn't say anything at all.

But then she murmured, "My little boy's grown up. You and Rafa work well together."

He said, "Thank you," because he didn't know what else to say. For a few minutes, they sat in silence at the water's edge under the endless stars. He whispered, "It really is beautiful out here."

She looked up, as if noticing the night sky for the first time. "I suppose it is."

Ramon cried out, and Shane and Camila sprang up, returning to the others, getting back to business. Rafa was awake, talking to his father, holding his hands. He glanced up as Shane and Camila joined him, his brow creasing.

Shane gave him a smile and kissed his temple. With Camila, they kept watch over Ramon and Hernandez, huddled together, praying for dawn.

Chapter Fourteen

RAFA PULLED THE orange blanket tighter around him, gripping Shane's hand as the helicopter zoomed toward Adelaide. The relief when they'd heard the *thump-thump-thump* of rotors in the dawn had been a sweet surge, but even when a helicopter had eventually flown low over the valley, he hadn't let himself fully exhale until a rescuer had been lowered onto the shore.

Then there were more helicopters and people, wind in his eyes and a clamor that made his head pound. And now that he and Shane were in the back of a helicopter—medics attending to Agent Hernandez on a gurney in front of them, his parents on another chopper—Rafa tensed right back up.

Tasting bile, he stared out the window, remembering the moment the other helicopter had started spinning uncontrollably. That horrible pressure inside him as they'd plummeted, like he would be crushed. They would have been if they'd been flying higher.

As if reading his mind, Shane said, "It's okay. We're not going to crash again."

Rafa groaned and yelled over the noise of the helicopter, "Don't jinx it!"

Shane rapped his knuckles against his head. "Knock on wood."

Rafa had to laugh. Then he felt guilty, watching the medics examine Agent Hernandez, who was still unconscious. He'd tried to keep her warm during the night, rubbing her hands between his and pressing against her. Her pulse had seemed steady to him whenever he'd searched for it on her wrist, but he was hardly an expert.

It was strange to believe they'd really been found. Shane had assured them they'd be rescued once the sun rose, and sure enough. Rafa squeezed his hand now, thinking of the last time he and Shane had been rescued after almost dying.

God, "relief" wasn't strong enough a word to describe how he'd felt when Shane had lifted the lid of that box and pulled him into his arms.

"It's okay," Shane repeated.

"I know. You're here."

Shane kissed him tenderly, and Rafa leaned against him, closing his eyes for the rest of the flight, the rushing scenery kind of freaking him out.

The hospital was another blur of people and noise, and he hated being separated from Shane while doctors examined them. The nurses cleaned and bandaged a few of the small cuts on his neck, hands and arms, but most were already healing. The shallow gash on his stomach didn't need stitches.

Aside from feeling incredibly sore all over and like he could sleep for days, he was fine. He was starving yet strangely not hungry, and what he really wanted was a long, hot shower.

He hated wearing a hospital gown and being wheeled around, but they insisted on tests to make sure he didn't have any other injuries. As he got back in the wheelchair after standing for x-rays, he asked, "Any update on my dad?"

The orderly, a young guy with an easy grin, said, "He'll be right. No worries." He gave Rafa's shoulder a friendly squeeze. Rafa hoped he wasn't blowing smoke up his ass. He itched to be with Shane and his family, but let the hospital staff do all the tests and poking and prodding they wanted. Which took *forever*.

Finally, they took him to his mother's room, and he was barely in the door when Matthew was hugging him with his good arm. Rafa embraced him tightly, trying to be careful of Matthew's sling.

"Fuck, Raf. I was so scared." Trembling, Matthew's fingers dug into his back through the thin hospital robe he'd been given to wear over the gown.

Rafa breathed in his brother, who smelled like stale sweat and coffee. "I know. Me too."

"Fuck, I'm so glad you're okay."

Wearing a plush bathrobe over her hospital gown, Camila said, "*Language*," from where she sat up in the bed.

They ignored her, and Rafa asked, "Are you okay, Matty?" The dark circles under his eyes were huge, his hair a greasy mess.

"Aside from thinking you guys were dead all night, I'm awesome. Ade and Chris are on their way. They're freaking out, obviously. Shit, I can't believe Dad was *impaled*."

"I have to say he took it pretty well, all things considered." Rafa turned to Camila. "Mom, what did the doctors say? And you're okay?" He sat on the side of the bed and took her hand.

She squeezed tightly. "I'm fine. Sore ribs and lots of bruises, but nothing too serious. They extracted the metal safely from your father's chest. The surgeon's supposed to be here any minute to update us."

He exhaled. "Okay." *Please, God.*

"And what about you?" She frowned, trying to pull up his robe. "Your stomach?"

"Mom!" He batted her hands away. "Fine, thank you. Didn't even need stitches. They did x-rays and stuff, but I'm sure it's all clear."

She nodded. "I spoke to the doctor, and he wants us to stay the night for observation. Mr. Kendrick as well, I imagine.

They're readying the room next door for you both."

As much as Rafa hated the thought of a night in the hospital, at least he and Shane could be together. Something his mother seemed remarkably okay with. "Thanks."

"Sharing a room and they're not even married?" Matthew teased. "Pretty scandalous, Mom."

She leveled him with an impatient look. "It's a hospital. Two beds."

"How's Shane doing?" Matthew asked Rafa.

From the doorway, Shane said, "Bruised ribs and a few scrapes. Could have been a lot worse." He wore a crappy hospital robe over his gown too, and the same cheap slippers Rafa had. "Keeping me overnight just in case."

Matthew gave him a one-armed hug and said, "Glad you're okay, man."

"Thanks." Shane clapped Matthew's back lightly. "Good to see you."

Looking at Shane, Rafa thought he'd never get sick of the sight. *He's okay. We made it.* He got up and took Shane's hand, assuring him his injuries were minor.

The surgeon arrived, an older woman in colorful scrubs. An agent brought her inside, standing nearby as she said, "We were incredibly lucky the shrapnel didn't hit an artery or pierce his lung. We're keeping him in the ICU for now, but he's stable. Came through the surgery well. He does have a concussion and he'll need a good rest. It's going to take some time, but we expect him to make a full recovery."

Rafa exhaled again. "Can we see him?"

"In a few hours. One at a time. Now if you'll excuse me, I've got to scrub for my next patient."

Shane asked the agent lingering in the doorway, "What about Hernandez?"

"Head injury and a couple cracked ribs. But she'll make it."

Rafa sighed. "Thank God."

Shane asked, "Is the Service flying down her family?"

"Yes. Her parents are on the way." The man looked like he wanted to say something else to Shane, but then turned on his heel and left, shutting the door behind him.

In the ensuing silence, Matthew sat on the far side of Camila's bed, and Rafa and Shane pulled up guest chairs to the near side. Matthew cleared his throat.

"So, I hear you guys were quite the heroes."

"Huh?" Rafa said. "*Me?* No, it was Shane."

"It was both of you," Camila said forcefully. "You each performed admirably." She took Rafa's hand. "You were so brave, my darling. You really have grown up."

"You're totally the fave now," Matthew said. "Poor Chris has been demoted."

Camila huffed in exasperation. "I love you all equally! Why must you insist on this fiction that Christian is our favorite?"

Rafa and his brother shared an amused glance, and Rafa was about to tease her more when he realized she was quivering, tears filling her eyes. He squeezed her fingers. "Mom, Mom, it's okay. We're just giving you a hard time."

Matthew stared at her with wide eyes, reaching out to take her other hand. "We're only joking."

She took a shuddering breath, blinking rapidly. "I would just hate for you to really think that. Your father and I love you all so much. More than you can ever know. Please believe that."

"We do," Rafa said. "And we love you too." He leaned in and kissed her cheek.

"I think the exhaustion is getting to you," Matthew said. "You need to get some rest." He glanced at Rafa and Shane. "You should too. We all should."

A nurse tapped on the partly open door. "Couldn't have said it better myself. The room next door's ready. Let's get some food in your bellies before you have a nice sleep."

"Can't we see my dad first?" Rafa asked.

"It'll be hours, hon. He's all right, and you won't do him any good if you're asleep on your feet."

He reluctantly got up. At least he and Shane could be in the same room. "I really don't think I can sleep."

The nurse smiled kindly. "Let's just give it a try, mate."

WHEN RAFA WOKE, it was dark outside. He ached from head to toe, his whole body feeling pummeled and stiff. There was a low nightlight on above his bed, and he blinked up at it groggily. Where...?

Then it all flooded back like watching a movie on fast-forward—the train, the helicopter, the lake. Huddling together, waiting for rescue, his father screaming. The hospital.

Okay, apparently Rafa had been able to sleep after all. But what time was it? Rubbing his eyes, he focused on Shane's bed.

The empty bed.

Heart seizing, Rafa rocketed up. "Shane?" His bare feet slapped on the floor as he crossed to the little bathroom. Empty. "Shane!"

What if something happened? Maybe Shane had some horrible injury they hadn't spotted. Where was he? What if—

"Hey, hey." A plump, older nurse appeared in the doorway. "What's got you in such a tizzy, my love? Everything's all right."

"Where's Shane? He's supposed to be here!" His chest was too tight, his throat gone dry.

She gently took hold of Rafa's arm. "Settle, petal. He's right as rain. Went to sit with that security woman who was with you on the chopper. He didn't want to wake you."

Rafa forced himself to breathe, blood rushing in his ears.

Shane's fine. He's okay. Everything's all right. He managed to nod and mumble, "Sorry."

"Don't be. You've had a real time of it, haven't you? It's all right."

"How are my mom and dad?"

"She's sleeping finally. Your dad's doing well. Do you want to take a quick squiz at him? It's late, but they'll let you in for a couple minutes."

"Yes. I want to see him." His pulse raced again, the need to see his father alive and safe thrumming through him.

They let him stand by Ramon's bedside. Machines beeped, and he wasn't conscious, but his coloring looked healthier. Rafa hadn't realized just how pale his face had been.

When he squeezed his dad's hand, Ramon's eyes flickered open. Rafa wasn't sure at first if he could see him properly in the low light, but then he weakly squeezed Rafa's fingers and hoarsely murmured, "Rafalito."

"Yes, it's me. I'm here, Dad." Tears flooded his eyes.

His father looked at him as if there was so much he wanted to say, but the words were too much. Rafa gripped his hand. "It's okay, Dad. I know. I know. I love you."

Tears spilled down Ramon's cheeks, and Rafa kissed his forehead. "My Rafalito," he croaked, his eyes heavy.

He went under again, and the kindly nurse escorted Rafa back to his room, even though he would have rather stood there all night, just to make sure nothing went wrong.

Shane still wasn't back, and Rafa snuck into his mother's dim room, just to make sure she was all right. Matthew was asleep on a cot on the far side of the bed, propped up on pillows and snoring lightly.

Rafa tiptoed to the bed, his thin slippers quiet on the linoleum. As he neared, he realized Camila was awake and watching Matthew. She turned her head, frowning. She'd apparently had a shower and blow-dried her hair, which was straight and smooth. It was somehow reassuring.

"All right?" she whispered, reaching out her hand.

He took it and perched on the side of the bed, nodding. He kept his voice low. "I saw dad for a few minutes. He's doing pretty well, they said. I just wanted to check on you."

She smiled. "I'm fine, darling. You should be sleeping."

"So should you." He held her small, dry hand.

"I was, but something woke me." She sighed. "I'm just so relieved you're all right. It's still rather surreal that we survived."

"Yeah. I just wish the pilot had made it too."

Her face pinched. "I know. It doesn't seem fair. But you worked so hard to save him. I'm very proud of you."

He shrugged. "I didn't do much. Shane—"

"Don't sell yourself short. You stopped me from pulling out that metal." Her voice thickened. "I could have killed your father. I wasn't able to think, but you took charge. Thank you."

"I…" He flushed with pleasure at the praise. "Thanks. You did great, Mom. You got Dad to shore. It wasn't easy."

She whispered, "All those laps I've been swimming in our indoor pool since we left the White House paid off."

In the silence that fell, Rafa glanced at his brother, who still seemed to be sleeping. "It feels weird, being here," he murmured. "Like this is all some crappy dream."

"Yes. Oh, how I'm looking forward to being in my own bed again." In the faint light from the hallway, she looked positively wistful, an emotion Rafa didn't associate with his mother.

"Yeah. I miss my bed." *And cuddling with Shane.*

"It's…" She gave his hand a squeeze. "It's a lovely little home you've made. And I truly am sorry for the deplorable way I behaved that night."

She'd already apologized on the train, albeit briefly. His first instinct was to tell her it was okay, to make her feel better and say it wasn't a big deal. But… "It really sucked. It hurt a lot. But I believe you're sorry."

Tears glistened in her eyes, and she kept firm hold of his hand. "I never want to hurt you, darling. Not ever again. I know we'll likely never agree on everything, but please believe that."

"I do," he whispered, his throat thick and eyes burning.

"It's a difficult thing, when your babies grow up. You're a strong and brave young man, and I've underestimated you. I know you're not being taken advantage of. I see that now. I see how happy you are."

Rafa nodded, too emotional to say anything. He leaned down and kissed his mother's cheek.

They both jumped when Matthew whispered, "Don't worry. I'm still fucked up and need parental guidance."

Blinking back tears, Rafa laughed softly. "Thanks for taking one for the team. But you're going to be awesome. If it's what you want, you're going to be back in the pool and crushing it before you know it."

Camila reached out her left hand to the cot, and Matthew met her grasp as she said, "Your brother's right. Also, watch your language."

They all laughed, and when Rafa snuck back to his room, he couldn't stop smiling.

Shane wasn't back yet, but before Rafa could creep out again in search of him, a new cell phone buzzed on the table beside his bed. He assumed one of his parents' assistants had left it for him, and hopefully it wasn't going to be a reporter on the other end. "Hello?"

"Oh, thank God. One of your mother's minions gave us this number." Ashleigh's reassuring voice filled him with warm affection. "I'm here with Hadley. Is it okay if I put you on speaker?"

"Yeah, go ahead. It's so good to hear your voice. We're all

doing okay."

"So good to hear you too, babe. You realize you're giving me gray hair with all these 'adventures' you keep having." He could imagine the sarcastic air quotes she was using.

His sister-in-law added, "Me too. For a while there we were thinking the worst."

"We got really lucky." He sat gingerly on the side of the bed, the bruises over his body throbbing now that the shock had worn off.

"You really did. I mean, forget the whole crash part—sleeping out in the wild in Australia? You could have been eaten by dingoes. Or kangaroos. They're not trustworthy if you ask me. All that hopping. It's suspect."

He managed to smile. It was typical Ash, trying to make him laugh even at the worst of times. "At least it was only one night stuck outside."

Hadley said, "One night in the wild is *plenty* if you ask me. Especially in a country with poisonous snakes and spiders."

"Well, the US does have a few of those." Rafa smiled again.

Hadley answered, "One of the many reasons I live on the island of Manhattan. Here I just have to contend with rats the size of Chihuahuas."

Rafa chuckled. He'd always liked his sister-in-law. "I can't wait to see Chris and Ade tomorrow. Miss you guys too."

"I know. If I wasn't in the middle of this shoot, I'd be there," Hadley said.

Ashleigh added, "If you weren't okay, I'd tell Miranda to shove her Manolos where the sun don't shine and hop the first flight."

He laughed. "Don't do that, Ash. Wait, are you missing work right now? I have no idea what time it is."

"It's early morning over here," Ashleigh said. "I have to get to the office soon. I'm staying in Chris and Hadley's guest room.

Had to be with people who love you and your parents too. And we couldn't sleep until we talked to you and heard for ourselves that you're all okay."

Hadley said, "I'd better get a few hours sleep before my call time. Rest up, Raf. Give my best to Shane. Love you."

Rafa said his goodbyes to her, and Ashleigh took him off speakerphone. "Hey, babe. Seriously, stop almost dying, okay?"

He smiled. "I'll do my best."

"You and the stud muffin are okay?"

Rafa laughed again, and God, it felt so good. "We are. Shit, I really miss you."

"Hey, *you're* the one who decided to up and move halfway around the world." She sighed dramatically, then her tone became serious. "Are you really, *really* okay?"

"Yeah. I really am. Tired, but all right. The last couple days have been...rough." Being on the train seemed like a lifetime ago. "Before the crash, Shane and I got in a big fight, and—"

"Whoa, whoa. About what?"

He sighed. "I was an idiot. I accused him of cheating on me."

"*What?* He didn't, did he? Because I'd have to come down there and kick that stud muffin's meaty ass!"

"No, he didn't. I was insecure. We still need to talk about it all. The accident kind of took priority."

"Yeah, life and death is like that. Puts things in perspective."

"Yeah. Part of me wants to just forget the stupid fight and not bring it up."

"I feel you, babe. But talking about it is a good idea. Communication and all that shit. I hear it does wonders. Not that I would know, since my parents won't discuss anything outside the weather. They did text yesterday when they heard about the accident. I guess that's something. But it's like they want to have this superficial relationship where I never talk about being queer. Or even hint at it."

"Basically they want you back in the closet."

"Yep. So fuck that. And go talk to Shane. Don't put your feelings in the closet. Or something. I've been up all night—my analogy game is pretty weak right now."

"I'm sorry you were so worried. Can you take the morning off work?"

"My God, how would Miranda function? I'll be fine. Just need a huge coffee. Maybe five of them. I'll talk to you tomorrow, okay? Love you."

"Love you too. I'm… Thank you for always being my friend since the day we met. I'm so lucky."

"Well, shit, don't make me cry again. My eyes are puffy enough already. But same."

They hung up, and while Rafa was in the bathroom, Shane returned. He nudged open the door, which Rafa had left ajar. "Raf?"

"Hey." He spit toothpaste into the sink and smiled at Shane in the mirror, his stomach flip-flopping with a rush of affection. "Guess the Service dropped off our stuff."

"Great. We can get out of these hospital clothes." Shane took off his robe and gown, dropping them on the floor and closing the bathroom door behind him. He pressed up behind Rafa, kissing his head, Rafa's thin gown the only thing between them.

"How's Agent Hernandez?"

"She's sleeping. They think she should recover fully. She probably wouldn't want me there, but… You were fast asleep, and I had to make sure she was okay. Anything on your dad?" He leaned over and turned on the shower, still touching Rafa's arm with one hand, as if he couldn't bear to let him go.

"I got to see him for a few minutes. He woke up and he knew me. So that was good." Rafa turned to lean against the sink. He blew out a long breath. "I know my parents drive me crazy, but if anything happened to them…"

"I know." Shane stepped near again, slipping his hands under Rafa's thin gown and rubbing.

"Of course you do. Sorry." He pressed a kiss to Shane's neck, hugging him tightly. When Shane winced, he eased the pressure of his arms. "Oops. Forgot about your ribs." Under the bright lights, they were both bruised and battered, and he traced his fingers over the dark marks on Shane's torso.

"S'okay." Shane leaned back and kissed him gently, their lips dry. He tugged at the ties on Rafa's gown and pulled it from his body, dropping it in the corner. "Up for a steam? Might help."

"Yeah." He stretched, wincing. "I feel like someone went to town on me with a bag of rocks."

"Same." Shane leaned away to run his hand under the shower spray. "Hopefully this'll loosen us up."

With the hot water running, the small bathroom was getting steamy, and Rafa wanted nothing more than to get under the spray. The nurses would probably have to redo a couple of bandages on Rafa's cuts after the shower, but he hoped they wouldn't mind.

Still, a little voice—that sounded like Ash—nagged that they had to talk. He'd put it off on the train, and he had to deal with it. After clearing the air with his mom, he felt so much better, and he couldn't put it off any longer with Shane. He needed them to be a hundred percent back on firm ground.

There were so many things he wanted to say, and he had no idea where to start. Words crowded on his tongue, and he tried to find the right ones.

"Raf? What is it?"

As Shane's brow furrowed, Rafa blurted, "I'm so sorry."

Shane shook his head, still frowning. "For what?"

"The other night. On the train. For thinking even for a second that you could have cheated on me. I know you would never."

"Ah. Right." Shane half-smiled. "That seems like so long ago now." He cupped Rafa's cheek with his rough hand. "It's okay, baby. I should have told you about my history with Darnell. I fucked up. I honestly didn't think about it. The last time I slept with him was before I started on your detail. After I met you, even though we weren't together yet, I didn't want to be with anyone else. You were under my skin."

Rafa's heart soared, and his fingers grasped at Shane's biceps. They kissed, hard and definitively at first, then softly, with tender nips and licks until they had to catch their breath.

Shane leaned their foreheads together and whispered, "But I should have told you. And I should have been honest about the nightmares. I wanted to protect you above all else, and it wasn't fair."

His throat was painfully tight, and Rafa was tempted to just leave it at that and step under the water. *No. Get it all in the open.*

"I love that you want to take care of me. But when you won't talk to me about stuff that matters, it feels like... Like I'm good enough to fuck and surf with and hang out, but not good enough to really trust." Tears burned as he tried to keep control. "It makes me feel so *small*." His voice broke on the last word.

"Oh, baby." Shane wrapped his arms around Rafa, murmuring into his hair. "I'm so sorry. I never want you to feel like that again."

Rafa leaned against him gratefully, their naked skin warm and wonderful. Safe in Shane's embrace, he said a silent prayer of thanks that they were alive and together. Taking a deep breath, he asked, "What have you been dreaming about?"

Shane sighed, silent for a few moments, his arms tight around Rafa's back. "Sometimes the fire, and my parents. Sometimes the mud and rain outside that rest stop. You out of reach, calling to me. In pain because I couldn't get to you. Opening that box they stuffed you in..." His voice went gravelly. "Opening it to find you dead inside. With your eyes wide open. Skin cold when I pulled you out. Because I was too late. Because I failed you."

He clung to Shane, their naked, wounded bodies trembling despite the steam rising around them in the small bathroom, the tiles getting slick under Rafa's feet. "I'm here. It's all right."

"You were doing so well, and I didn't want to upset you." He brushed his knuckles over Rafa's cheek, his eyes tender. "You were the one who was kidnapped. Terrorized. But you're so strong. I thought if you weren't having nightmares, there was no excuse for me. I'm supposed to be—" His gaze skittered away.

"The big tough guy?"

Shane met Rafa's eyes sheepishly. "Yeah."

"My shrink said I'm 'resilient.' I guess I am, but that doesn't mean I'm not bothered by stuff sometimes."

"You really are resilient. It never ceases to amaze me."

Rafa plowed on. "But I still feel stuff. What happened was terrifying. I mean, even that word doesn't sound like enough. Waking up in that box…" He swallowed thickly, a sinking sensation gripping his stomach as he remembered. "I never knew what real fear was. I've been afraid of plenty of things, but when you think you might die, it's on a cellular level or something." He shivered. "Same with the helicopter. I knew we were crashing, and it was just…" He ran his hands over Shane's arms and back, making sure he was real, careful not to press too hard.

Shane held Rafa's waist, his breath warm on his lips as he whispered, "I thought that was it for us."

"You saved me again."

"No. You would have gotten out on your own."

He thought of the rising water and his parents. "Maybe. But I don't know about Mom and Dad, or Agent Hernandez. I would have gone back in for them. We might all be dead. It still doesn't feel real."

"You're all right." Shane nuzzled his cheek. "You're okay."

Memories seized him—sharp, violent images and sensations.

"In that box, one of the worst things was thinking you'd been shot. But you came for me. I'd probably be dead otherwise."

A visible tremor ran through Shane. "I don't know what I would have done. Who I'd be now. I'd have a very different life." He tightened his arms around Rafa's back, chest hair rough and reassuring.

Rafa looped his arms around his neck and kissed him softly, then rubbed his cheek against Shane's, reveling in the rasp of their stubble. "We're here. We're alive. Everything's going to be okay. You don't always have to be the tough guy." A thought surfaced, and he hesitated. "Am I too…" He struggled to find the right word.

Shane leaned back, brow furrowed. "You're perfect."

Rafa had to laugh. "I am not, and neither are you. But when we're together… You know, like when you take control and fuck me? Does it affect the way you see me?"

"What do you mean?"

"Like… I was afraid you might want, I dunno. A real man? A big manly man, like Darnell."

"Ah. You know, some big, buff guys love nothing more than to drop to their knees and beg for cock. Stereotypes are bullshit. You are the best, bravest man I know." His brows drew together. "When I came back from the States last week and you wanted to top… Was that about this?"

Rafa could feel his cheeks flushing, but kept his eyes on Shane's. "Uh-huh. I found out about your past with Darnell. I was jealous and hurt, and I wanted to—" He waved a hand.

Shane raised an eyebrow. "Stake your claim?"

He huffed out a laugh, more heat rushing to his face. "Yes. I wanted to prove that we're equals, I guess."

"We are always equals, no matter whose dick is in whose ass. If you want to switch up more often, we can."

"Maybe sometimes?" He bit his lip, trying to find the right

words. His limbs were heavy, and he traced his fingers up and down Shane's spine. "I loved being inside you. Feeling so close to you. But when you fuck me... It's hard to describe. Taking your cock makes me feel complete. *Right.* Like who I'm supposed to be. Who I repressed all those years. I mean, *I* knew who I was, but I had to hide it from everyone else but Ash."

"I understand." Shane squeezed Rafa's ass cheek gently. "You're so strong and beautiful. I'm incredibly lucky to have you."

"Sometimes I still can't believe it." He cringed. "God, thinking about that rest stop and jerking off in the bathroom stall. I never thought in a million years we'd ever end up here." Wriggling his hands between their bodies, he stroked Shane's hairy chest. "Can't believe I get to touch you. That you actually want me."

Shane took Rafa's face in his hands. "I want you forever."

Heart bursting with affection, Rafa said, "I want you too. And I love that you protect me. You always have, and I know you always will. But I want to protect you too. We're in this together."

"Absolutely." A little smile lifted Shane's lips. "Let's try to keep things in perspective in the future without almost dying."

A laugh shivered through Rafa, a moment of sweet release. "Yeah, we've had our fair share of near-death experiences. We're good."

Shane laughed, then groaned, putting a hand on his side. "Note to self, no laughing for a little while. Anyway, we're using up all the hospital's hot water. Better get in there."

Rafa stepped into the tub and stood under the shower, sighing into the hot water. "You can lean on me."

Catching Rafa's fingers, Shane climbed in and snuggled close.

Rafa thought fleetingly of the miserable, desperate kid he'd been at that rest stop, and wished he could go back in time to tell him all the pain would be worth it.

Chapter Fifteen

BITING BACK A groan, Shane blinked into the darkness. Around the edges of the blackout curtains in the hotel room he could see daylight, and there was an inch-wide shaft of weak light where they'd left the curtains a bit parted. Rafa was sprawled on his stomach beside him, sound asleep, parted lips visible.

He, Rafa, and Camila had been discharged after the one restless night in the hospital. Of course, they hadn't gone anywhere that day, staying close to Ramon as he continued to recover. But it had been wonderful to sleep last night in a real bed with Rafa at his side.

As much as he wanted to hold Rafa tightly and never let go, the extra-strength ibuprofen was wearing off and his sore ribs protested. Even in the dim light, he could make out the dark splotchy bruises on Rafa's body, and God, he hated them. They shouldn't make him feel like a failure, and he fought against the instinct.

Adriana and Christian's flight had been delayed by a storm, but they'd be arriving soon. Shane should probably wake Rafa so they could get back to the hospital, but a few more minutes wouldn't hurt. Rafa looked so peaceful, and Shane envied it.

No matter how he tried to clear his mind and relax, the same thought echoed. Initially after they'd been rescued, he'd been able to push aside the memory of Rich Moir's graying, cold skin. He could compartmentalize it and focus on Rafa, the Castillos, and Hernandez.

But now, he could feel ribs crack under his hands, clammy, lifeless lips under his, the puffs of air useless.

His chest tightened and he shifted on the soft mattress, unable to stop a grunt of pain as he tried to move to a different position. With a little snort and smack of lips, Rafa mumbled and woke, blinking at him.

"Hmm?" Rafa stretched, his naked limbs sliding over the sheets with a soft *shush-shush* sound. A few bruises were turning a paler purple. "Okay?"

Shane opened his mouth to say yes, of course he was fine. Nothing to worry about. He stopped. His throat was dry. "Can't stop thinking about the pilot."

Rafa seemed instantly wide awake, wriggling closer and resting his hand on Shane's chest. "You did all you could. You got him out. More than the rest of us would have been able to do." He hooked his foot over Shane's shin and rubbed slowly. "We did our best. We were in shock, and the helicopter was sinking, and… I don't know. Maybe I could have done something differently."

"Like what? No. You didn't do anything wrong."

"So if I didn't, then how come *you* did? Why do you have a different standard to uphold?"

He huffed, smiling softly. "Okay. I see your point."

"As much as you wish you could leap tall buildings in a single bound, you're not Superman. So don't go holing up in your mental Fortress of Solitude."

"That's really deep."

Rafa's puff of laughter ghosted over Shane's shoulder. "I thought so." He lightly drew his fingers down to Shane's belly. "How do you feel? Physically, I mean."

Again, he had to bite back the knee-jerk response of insisting he was fine. "Sore. You?"

"Yeah, sore, but a little better than yesterday." He inched closer, pressing his lips to Shane's left nipple. "How about if I kiss it all better?"

"Mmm. Sure you're up for it?"

"The question is whether you are." Rafa reached down and traced the curve of Shane's flaccid cock.

He chuckled, trying not to wince at the throb in his ribs. "I'm sure I could be persuaded."

"I really want to," Rafa whispered, as if he was telling a secret. He caressed Shane's balls and sensitive flesh, and Shane quivered. "I want to taste you. Breathe you in. Make you come. Just want to…feel you. Know we're still alive. Really *feel* it."

Shane brushed his hand over Rafa's head, his short hair sticking up. "Yeah. Please."

His teeth flashing in a smile in the semidarkness of the hotel room, Rafa kissed his way down Shane's body, his dry lips barely brushing his torso. He crawled between his legs, nudging them apart. Shane was only too happy to bend his knees and let them flop open.

At first, Rafa barely touched Shane's cock. He teased at the trail of hair leading down, nuzzling with his face before pressing kisses. He circled his fingers over Shane's inner thighs.

Shane's belly quivered, cock twitching and hardening. He moaned softly. "Feels good, baby."

Rafa grasped Shane's thickening shaft and ran his lips over it, then his stubbly cheeks. His hot exhalation on the tip sent goosebumps rippling. Shane moaned again. "So good." He lifted his hips eagerly.

"What do you want?" Rafa spread his hands over Shane's thighs, gentle on the bruises, ducking his head to kiss his balls.

"Oh, fuck." For some reason he couldn't name, Shane felt strangely vulnerable, splayed open like that. Words died in his throat.

Rafa murmured with a warm gust of air, "Tell me." Clearly he needed to hear it, and Shane had never been shy at all about talking during sex. Yet now he could only moan.

"Love your hairy balls," Rafa mumbled. "You're so hot." He licked his sac, lapping until Shane was shaking.

Lifting his head, Rafa licked his lips. "Do you need me?"

"Always." He traced his freckles with his fingertip. "More than you can imagine."

"Tell me. Tell me what you need."

Shane knew this was about more than sex, and he took a deep breath, ignoring the flare in his ribs. "Need your mouth. Need you to suck me." He wanted to grip Rafa's head and tug him down, but he kept his hands at his sides, fingers twitching. "Please. Need you, baby. No one else. Not ever. Just you."

Rafa swallowed him almost to the base, and the sudden hot pressure had Shane gasping. Rafa scraped his blunt nails over Shane's thighs, sucking forcefully, spit soon dripping from his lips. He bobbed his head, his lips and tongue finding all the right places.

Adrenaline coursed through Shane like fire in his veins, obliterating any pain from his ribs. His cock was like a raw nerve, all vibrating sensation, his balls tightening. He groaned. "Oh, baby."

The rest of the world and any lingering pain disappeared, Rafa's mouth on him the only thing left. When Rafa looked up, eyes feverish, Shane reached down to caress his face. Seeing his cock stretching Rafa's wet lips, filling him, spit dripping down his chin, made his head spin with a powerful sense of *rightness* he couldn't explain.

"You're so good, Raf. Oh, God." His balls tightening, he seized up and—

Rafa pulled off, squeezing the base of Shane's dick. His chest rising and falling, he caught his breath, smiling slyly as Shane grunted in frustration.

"You need to come?" Rafa asked innocently.

He groaned. "Now you're going to torture me?"

"Not for long." He kissed the slit of Shane's dick, his tongue teasing and sending sparks over his flesh. "Tell me what you want. Tell me what's in your head. I want to know everything." He ran his palms over Shane's trembling thighs.

"I promise I'll tell you." He caressed Rafa's head, missing the curls. "Right now? I want to come. Want to come in your mouth, baby. Want you to swallow it. So deep—"

Nostrils flaring, Rafa took Shane almost into his throat, sucking forcefully and digging the nails of one hand into Shane's thigh, a dull bolt of pain coupled with the heaven of his hot mouth.

Shane came with a shout, twisting his fingers into Rafa's short hair. Ecstasy rattled his body, muscles tensing as he emptied, loving the sight of Rafa slurping down every drop he could.

Lifting his head and sitting back on his heels, Rafa gulped in a breath. In the dim light, Shane could see how red his face was, a few white drops of cum splashed at the corners of his mouth.

Shane muttered, "So beautiful."

A smile curved Rafa's lips, and his tongue darted out to swipe at the spunk. His leaking cock stood hard and thick. Shane was utterly boneless on the mattress, but he needed to see Rafa come. He reached out a limp hand and said, "Come closer."

But Rafa shook his head. "Is that what you want? I don't think you *really* want to jerk me off right now."

He laughed softly despite his ribs. "Okay, you got me. I need to see you come, but I don't have the energy to help."

Rafa grinned. "Good thing I'm younger, huh, old man?" He wrapped his hand around his shaft and started working himself.

"Your cuts?"

"Barely feel them." He bit his lip, eyes closing. "Oh, shit. I'm so close."

Fuck, Rafa looked beautiful bringing himself off. Shane murmured, "You're so hot, baby. Look at you. You want to come on me? I want you to. Spray me with it."

"Yes," Rafa whimpered.

"Love watching you like this." Another truth poured out, the memory flowing freely. "That day at the rest stop, I wanted to watch you so badly. Wanted to break down that stall door and see you with your dick out. Kiss you and fuck you against the wall, slam my cock into you and fill you up. Make you come harder than you ever had. Be your first and show you how good it can be. Show you what you deserve."

"*Shane.*" Rafa whined, his hand flying, his panting filling the air.

"I need you to come. Please."

Crying out, Rafa toppled forward, holding himself up with his left hand on the mattress as he spurted onto Shane's stomach. Trembling, he jerked himself, eyes closed, sweat glistening on his brow, another ribbon of white painting Shane's skin.

Shane cupped his cheek. "That's it. That's so good."

Rafa collapsed between Shane's legs, mouth open on his belly, breath hot and wet. After a few moments, the rasp of Rafa's tongue traveled over Shane's stomach as he licked up his cum.

Shane groaned. "Are you going to give me a taste?"

On top of him now, Rafa shimmied up, supporting his weight on his hands beside Shane's shoulders as he captured his mouth in a deep, filthy kiss, sharing the salty musk.

They both groaned, and Shane met his tongue, licking and sucking—heat and sweat and cum filling his senses until he had to gasp in a breath.

Rafa flopped down beside him, chest heaving, a grin brightening his perfect face. "I love you. You make me feel so good."

"Ditto." He moved to give Rafa another kiss and hold him, but he couldn't hide the cringe as he shifted. "When I'm healed,

I'm going to fuck you all day and night."

Laughing, Rafa asked, "Are we going to eat? Or just all sex all the time?"

"Well, since you're such a talented chef, we'll find time for meals. Have to keep up our strength, after all."

"I'm not a chef yet," he said dismissively.

"*Yes*, you are. You might not have your degree yet, but you're a chef."

Rafa opened his mouth as if to argue, but then snapped it shut. He blew out a breath. "You're right. I am. I'm a good chef."

"Damned amazing chef. Damned amazing man. And I need you to believe that."

Rafa pressed a kiss to Shane's shoulder, and they took a few more minutes together in peace.

"OH MY *GAWD*!" Adriana launched herself at Rafa across the hospital room. He caught her with an *oomph*, grimacing, then hugging her back. Shane wanted to snap at her to be careful, but he bit his tongue. Yes, Rafa was bruised and sore, but he could handle an enthusiastic hug from his sister.

Ramon was in the bed in the center of the room, the back partly raised so he could sit. He was pale, and the eggs and fruit salad on his tray were only half-eaten, but he looked much better than he had.

Camila sat on a metal and plastic chair beside him. She was clearly tired, but her hair was glossy and neat, her blouse and pants pressed, trademark pearls back around her throat. He wondered how many strands she owned, but it was strangely reassuring to see her polished again.

Rafa disentangled himself from his sister and hugged Christian as Matthew hovered nearby. Rafa said, "It's so good to see you all.

Dad, how are you feeling? You look so much better!"

Shane stood back in the doorway as the Castillos talked over each other, Ramon insisting it hadn't been that bad, Matthew calling bullshit, and Camila admonishing him for language. Rafa and Adriana joined in the conversation, and Shane smiled to himself, barely able to make out a word.

He edged into the room, nodding to the expressionless agents stationed outside, closing the door behind him. Christian looked over and stepped forward, extending his hand and pumping Shane's enthusiastically. "I don't know if we were ever properly introduced. But of course Raf's told me a lot about you."

Shane smiled. "Likewise."

"I hear you and my brother were the heroes of the piece."

"We only did what was necessary. Rafa was amazing, though."

"I believe it," Christian said. "I think he's the bravest one of us all."

Shane was about to agree, but Adriana was flying at him. For a petite woman, she was surprisingly strong, and he inhaled sharply, pain flaring around his torso as she hugged him.

"Ade, he has bruised ribs! Go easy," Rafa said from where he'd perched on the side of Ramon's bed.

She let go, hand flying up to cover her mouth. "I'm so sorry!" She patted at her dark hair, which was pulled back in a ponytail. "Great first impression. I'm a wrinkled mess and I'm causing you bodily harm." She screwed up her face. "God, I probably stink too. I desperately need a shower."

"I know what it's like after those long-haul flights." Shane smiled at her. "You look beautiful." It was true. Her skinny jeans and blouse looked perfectly fine to him, and her hundred-watt smile reminded him of Rafa's.

He tugged at the hem of his button-down black shirt, which he'd worn in case the press were there to take pictures. He didn't want to look sloppy in the media if potential clients were watching. Rafa wore a green Henley and dark jeans, and he'd given the photographers a few tight smiles outside the hospital, gripping Shane's hand and ignoring their shouted fusillade of questions.

Adriana bit her lip. "I didn't hurt you too much, did I?"

"Not a bit," Shane lied. His ribs were going to ache regardless.

She grinned. "It's so good to really meet you finally. A real-life hero!"

"Not really." His skin itched with the prickling of everyone's gazes on him. The sensation reminded him of his early days on the job when he was eager to impress.

Sitting with long legs gracefully crossed in her designer slacks, Camila said, "Yes, I was telling them how you and Rafa took charge and saved our lives."

He scoffed. "We did what anyone would have done. I'm sure you would have been fine." He wasn't actually sure of that at all, but the praise made his stomach flutter and his face go hot. He didn't deserve it—he hadn't saved the pilot.

"A word of advice? Take the kudos from my mother when you can get them," Adriana said.

Clearing his throat, Shane said, "Well…thank you."

"You were so brave, Rafalito." Ramon beamed at Rafa. "We couldn't be more proud of the man you've become." To Rafa's siblings, he said, "You should have seen him—giving CPR, taking care of us with Shane." He glanced at Shane, then back at Rafa. "They work well together."

Adam's apple bobbing, Rafa opened and closed his mouth. His voice was thick when he murmured, "I love you, Dad."

Shane's heart swelled, and they all jumped at the knock on the door. Christian opened it, and they stared at one of the Castillos' assistants. The young man blinked owlishly, his cheeks pinking as he looked down at his crisp slacks and shirt as if expecting to see a big stain.

Christian smiled kindly. "Dennis. Come in."

"Hi." Small and studious-looking, Dennis smiled tentatively. "You wanted info on the pilot, so…" He thumbed open his phone and read off a few bullet points. "Wife's name is Janice, aged fifty-three. His mother is still alive, living in Alice Springs. Two children—Rebecca and Thomas, college students, one here in Adelaide and one in Melbourne."

"You've sent a flower arrangement?" Camila asked, not waiting for an answer. "And find out if the family would like to meet."

The thought had Shane's gut tightening. *Janice, Rebecca, and Thomas.* Faceless names of people suffering because he hadn't been fast enough. If only he'd been able to reach Rich Moir a minute sooner. Seconds, even…

"Do they know what caused the crash?" Camila asked.

Dennis said, "Not officially. Tail rotor malfunction seems likely based on what you described. They're pulling up the wreckage from the lake today. Had to get special equipment out there. The investigators from the transportation board are arriving here at the hospital shortly and want to speak to all of you."

Shane groaned internally. Of course he'd answer all their questions, but he wished he was back under the covers in the hotel with Rafa, just the two of them, peaceful with the curtains drawn.

Dennis left, and Adriana launched into a story about how she almost missed the flight from LA because of traffic and how worried she'd been. The rest of the Castillos nodded and listened and laughed, Camila with a decidedly long-suffering yet affectionate manner. She idly rubbed her husband's arm and toyed with his fingers, as if she just wanted to touch him and that sitting close wasn't enough. Shane found himself smiling watching her.

It was still bizarre to be with Rafa's family and not be standing against a wall in the corner. After so many years of, well, *lurking*, it was his instinct to hang back, with the Castillos especially. But Rafa got up and took hold of Shane's hand as his sister spoke.

Ramon and Camila didn't seem bothered by the hand-holding—although they kept their gazes on Adriana, so it was hard to say for sure. Shane couldn't help but feel out of place, as though he was intruding on a family reunion.

He wondered if it was normal to feel like that with in-laws, then scoffed mentally. He and Rafa weren't *married*—although the idea made his chest swell with warmth. It was silly, since Rafa was still so young. Surely they couldn't think about marriage until he'd finished school and established himself as a chef.

"Shane?" Rafa squeezed his fingers, looking at him expectant-ly.

His stomach flipped as he realized the Castillos were all watch-ing him. He smiled, heat prickling his neck. "Sorry. I was miles away." He scrambled for an explanation. "I was just wondering about Hernandez. I should go see her. Give you all time together."

Rafa frowned. "You don't have to go."

"I know, but I really do want to see how she is."

"Just know that you're..." Camila seemed to be searching for the right words. "Well, you're very welcome here, Shane."

He blinked at her, as did everyone else. "I, uh... Thank you."

As Rafa smiled, a face-scrunching, true smile, Matthew whis-tled softly. "It's 'Shane' now. This is serious progress, people."

Sighing, Camila rolled her eyes, and Ramon chuckled and said, "I'd take the money and run, Shane. Give Agent Hernandez our best. We'll see her later."

"Will do." He gave Rafa a wink, and Rafa was still grinning when Shane closed the door behind him.

He exhaled, ignoring the pain in his ribs. The other agents stationed outside the door side-eyed him. Head high, he asked, "Is Hernandez still in room three-twelve?" He braced, ready for attitude.

But one of them simply nodded, and their gaze on him as he walked down the hall didn't feel hostile. The door was ajar, and he stuck his head in, knocking lightly. Pale and looking small in the bed, Hernandez smiled faintly and said, "Kendrick. Come in."

There was another agent sitting by the bed, and he pushed back his chair with a scrape across the floor. Hernandez asked him, "Did you and Kendrick meet?"

"Not formally." The man stuck out his hand. "O'Leary."

We didn't formally meet because you've all been acting like I was crap you stepped in. But Shane shook his hand and nodded. He asked Hernandez, "How are you feeling?"

"Hell of a lot better than I was. I'm alive. Thanks to you and Valor, apparently."

He waved it off. "It was nothing."

"It wasn't fucking nothing, Kendrick. The way I hear it, I'd be dead if you hadn't fished me out before the chopper sunk."

"Rafa swam you to shore."

Her face creased, and she shuddered. "I don't remember any of it. It's not a good feeling. That powerlessness. But you both had my back."

He shrugged. "I would have done the same for anyone."

"I know. That's why you're a stand-up guy." Her voice went hoarse. "And you *were* my friend back in the day. I'm sorry I gave you the cold shoulder."

He offered her a little smile. "Apology accepted."

"Valor's a great kid. Rafa, I should say. Guess I shouldn't call him a kid either. You two are clearly crazy about each other, so good for you. You were always an exemplary agent, Kendrick."

"Until I wasn't." His grin was wry.

She huffed out a laugh. "I guess I was just disappointed. We all were. It made the Service a punchline. We were bitter."

"I get it. Trust me, I never expected to fall for a protectee. Never in a million years. But he's worth it. Worth everything."

O'Leary spoke up. "Good. God knows the Service can be a thankless job."

Hernandez reached for a cup of water, and Shane and O'Leary both made a move to help her. She glared. "Calm your tits. I can drink water unassisted." She did, lifting her head and shoulders, then flopping back down with a grimace. "But these dizzy spells can fuck off."

"I'll let you rest." After a moment's debate, Shane clasped her forearm, careful of the IV tube. "Take care. It was good to see you again."

"You too, Kendrick. Try to keep out of trouble for fuck's sake."

"Trying. Always trying."

Shane was still smiling when he walked into the hall. He'd only gone a few steps when a woman shakily asked, "Mr. Kendrick?"

"Yes." He stopped and regarded the woman. In her fifties, she was short and plump, her short hair dyed a red that didn't seem natural. Her eyes were red and puffy, and a somber, freckled young man stood next to her. Shane asked, "Can I help you?"

"I'm—my husband—"

His stomach lurched. "Mrs. Moir?"

She nodded. "Call me Jan. This is our boy, Thomas." Fresh tears spilled from her brown eyes. "Guess he's just mine now." The son squeezed his mother's shoulders as she trembled.

"I'm so sorry for your loss. I'm... Call me Shane, please." He braced. If this woman needed to yell at him and vent her grief, he'd gladly let her. It was the least he could do. "I'm sorry I couldn't save him. I tried, but..."

Jan jerked her head back. "Why would *you* be sorry? It was my Rich flying." She shook her head, swiping at tears. "He loved it so much, the bugger. Always made me nervous, but he was right at home up there in the sky." Her voice cracked. "He was so good at flying. I just don't know how this could have happened."

"I think the tail rotor went. It wasn't his fault. He was an excellent pilot. Completely in control. Then..."

"What?" Thomas asked, body rigid. "They won't tell us."

"We were flying lower, over the lake. Then there was a sound of metal screeching, really sudden. We started spinning out of control. Too close to the water to give him time to recover. I don't know if it would have been possible even if we were higher. I don't think it was his fault at all."

Jan shook with a sob. Then she nodded, sniffing. "We were afraid you'd all be angry. Blame him. I just wanted you to know that he was a good pilot. A good man. He always took such care! Was never reckless, was he, Tommy?"

"Never. He was such a bloody safety freak." Thomas pressed his lips together, clearly trying not to cry. "Used to drive us all nuts. I mean, who does fire drills in their house?" He laughed, eyes glistening.

Jan nodded. "That was my Rich."

Shane's eyes burned, and he swallowed hard. "I'm so sorry."

"They did say that you tried to save him." She sniffed. "Pulled him from the—the wreckage?"

He nodded. "He wasn't breathing. Rafa and I did CPR for a long time, but... It was too late. Maybe if I'd been able to get to him sooner, but he was farthest away from me, and..." He raised his hands helplessly, dropping them to his sides. "I'm sorry."

Jan reached out and grabbed his arm. "You've got nothing to be sorry for. Rich knew the risks. Don't you go climbing up on the cross. Someone needs the wood."

"That's what I've been trying to tell him," Rafa said from behind Shane.

Shane smiled gratefully, relieved to have him at his side again. He wanted to yank him into a hug and kiss to remind himself that Rafa was in one piece, but he settled for a hand on his lower back as he introduced him to Jan and Thomas.

Rafa shook Jan's hand and then clasped it in both of his. "I can't tell you how sorry I am. Is your daughter here as well?"

Thomas said, "She's fetching my Gran. Their flight gets in later today. This is a real shock. Obviously."

"Of course," Rafa said. "I know my family is eager to meet you. Are you up for it?"

Jan and her son shared a glance, and she nodded. "We weren't sure if you'd all be cursing Rich's name."

Rafa sucked in a breath. "No! Of course not. It wasn't his fault."

She nodded, tearing up again. "You've always seemed like such a nice boy. Bless you."

Rafa hugged her, and Shane loved him so damn much his chest was bursting with it.

"SOMETIMES, ROOM SERVICE and shit blowing up on TV is just what the doctor ordered." Rafa sighed contentedly and dropped his napkin on the plate balanced on his lap. "Is it weird that explosions are comforting right now?"

Beside him on the bed where they leaned against the headboard, Shane kissed his cheek. "No. Because that mayhem isn't real, and we know Captain America's about to save the day." He patted his stomach. "Your meat sauce is better, but pasta hit the spot."

Rafa snuggled against him, head on his shoulder as they watched Chris Evans battle the baddies on TV. They'd seen it before, but the familiarity was soothing.

After a few minutes, Rafa said, "I'm glad we got to meet his family. Rich Moir's, I mean."

"Yeah. Me too." The guilt hadn't magically vanished, but he felt mostly sadness now. "They're generous. Considering the rest of us survived, I'm not sure I would be in their shoes. It must seem so unfair."

"I guess that's life, right? Totally unfair. Makes you think about how easily it can all vanish. How much you can lose without any warning." He rubbed his cheek on Shane's shoulder. "But you know that."

"I do." Ignoring the protest from his ribs, he circled his arm around Rafa and drew him even closer. "Sometimes…"

"Mmm?"

He breathed in and out slowly. "Sometimes I think… Why *their* house? Why did my parents have faulty wiring that some contractor years before had screwed up? A time bomb in the walls, waiting to go off. Why did it have to happen in the middle of the night? When I wasn't there to help them?" He sighed. "I know, it wasn't my fault. I still wonder why. But I know there's no answer. It's just the way life goes." He thought of Alan and Jules and their doomed children. "Comes down to luck most of the time."

Rafa rubbed his palm over Shane's flannel-clad thigh. "It does. Which is why we have to make the most of every day." He chuckled. "I know it's super cliché, but it's true. I'm so glad to be here with you. I love you."

"I love you too, baby." He kissed the top of Rafa's head.

They watched the movie for a while in comfortable silence. Then Rafa said, "I really think he and Bucky should end up together. Clearly their love is precious."

"Clearly," he agreed as his new phone buzzed on the side table. Darnell's face filled the screen as a video call came in.

Rafa glanced over and paused the on-demand movie. "I'll just go…" He picked up his plate and started to move off the bed. "Say hi for me or whatever."

Shane reached out for his arm. "Stay. Please?" He slid his finger across the screen as Rafa settled back against the pillows tentatively. Shane smiled at his phone. "Hey, man."

"Hey, Greatest American Hero. Another day, another dramatic rescue. How are you doing?"

"Good." Shane turned the phone and held it so he and Rafa were both in frame. "Raf and I are chilling at the hotel. Watching the second Captain America movie."

"When are he and Bucky getting together? Because this thing with Peggy's grand-niece isn't working for me. Steve and Bucky are meant to be."

Rafa laughed. "I, um—I was just saying that."

"You know what they say about great minds." Darnell grinned. "How are you doing? And your folks?"

"Good. My dad's the worst off, but he'll be fine. They're going to discharge him in a few days hopefully, and my parents will have a private nurse to look after him."

"Glad to hear he's on the mend. The crash was scary stuff from the sound of it." Darnell shook his head. "When it was first reported that you were all missing, I really thought you were dead. So glad to be wrong."

Affection for his friend warmed Shane, and he smiled, going for a light tone. "Good thing you're often wrong."

Darnell's laughter boomed, low and joyous. "Ain't that the truth?" He turned his head and said to someone, "Yep. Coming." He faced the camera again. "Sorry. Have a suspect to interrogate. Pulling an all-nighter. But you know what they say about perps never sleeping."

Rafa laughed tentatively. "Do they say that?"

Darnell grinned. "They do now. You two take care of yourselves. Rafa, don't let him brood too much."

"I'm not brooding!" Shane protested.

"Sure. I believe you. Thousands wouldn't, but I do. Later."

The call ended, and Shane turned off his phone. Rafa said, "He's nice. Maybe he can come visit sometime. It would be cool to get to know him better."

"I'd like that." He nuzzled Rafa's cheek, still reveling in touching him and inhaling his unique scent. "Should we get back to Cap?"

"Mmm. Or, we could have a bath. Jerk each other off. Nothing too strenuous." He smiled softly. "I still want to touch you, like, all the time. To remember we're alive or something." He laughed. "It's stupid. I'm sure it'll fade."

Shane kissed him, tasting garlic and tomatoes and smoky onions as their tongues met. He smiled against Rafa's lips. "Let's hope not."

Epilogue

Eight months later

PADDLING OUT PAST the breakers, his shoulders aching but unable to resist one last ride, Rafa grinned to himself. Now that it was February, the kids were back in school and the beach was far less crowded. There wasn't a cloud in the sky, and his face was tight with salt and sun. His wetsuit had a high SPF, but no matter how much sunscreen he slathered on his face, his freckles still stood out.

But Shane loved kissing them, so there was that. Wet curls flopping in his face, Rafa turned and waited for a good wave. He watched Shane on the beach tugging his wetsuit down to his waist and drying his hairy chest with a towel.

There's a hot pocket.

He laughed to himself. That's what his classmate Ling, who constantly made up slang all her own, called Shane. Damo—somehow short for Damien—had agreed, even though he wasn't gay.

"I've bloody well got eyes, mate."

Feet dangling on either side of his board, Rafa laughed to himself again. He had *friends*. Along with weekly Skype sessions with Ashleigh, he had made actual real-life friends at the Cordon Bleu. Once they'd figured out he really could cook and didn't want special treatment, it had all fallen into place. He couldn't wait to get back to class next week when the new term began.

Ling had also helped get him a job at a fancy French restaurant downtown in Sydney. They were at the bottom of the ladder and spent hours a shift chopping veggies, but Rafa loved it. All his dreams were coming true.

He glanced over his shoulder and saw a set was coming in fast. Flopping down and paddling hard, he managed to catch it. At the last second, Rafa realized there was another surfer riding the wave to his left. He seemed to have come out of nowhere, and cursed loudly as he swerved and tumbled into the surf.

Rafa managed to keep his footing, riding the wave close to shore. In the shallows, he turned back to find the other surfer and apologize. He hoped he'd be able to spot the guy again and—

A tall young man in his twenties stormed toward him, and Rafa backed up instinctively, words tripping over his tongue. "I—I... Shit, I'm sorry!"

Ratty, wet hair plastered to his head, the man shoved Rafa with two strong hands on his chest. In a blink, Rafa was on his ass, water swirling around his waist, his heart pounding.

"That was my fucking wave!"

"I didn't see you! I'm sorry."

The guy loomed over him, long and thin, but wiry, his fists clenched. Then *he* was suddenly on his ass, Shane practically snarling, muscles flexing across his bare, broad back as he put himself between Rafa and the other surfer.

"Get the fuck away from him," Shane growled.

Another surfer appeared, his red hair practically glowing in the sun. "Back off, Wazza. Accidents happen."

Wazza shoved to his feet. "Little fucker snaked me!" He eyed Shane. "Needs his old man to fight his battles." He scooped up his board as Shane glared. To Rafa, he ordered, "Stay off my waves. Fucking tourist."

The redhead rolled his eyes. "He's been surfing this beach for months, you dickhead."

Shane practically vibrated, his jaw clenched, but he let Wazza stomp away, instead crouching by Rafa. "Are you hurt?"

"What? No." Cheeks hot, Rafa gently batted away Shane's hands and pushed to his feet, his board thumping against his calf, secured by its leash on his ankle. "It was nothing. I'm fine."

"He's always aggro," the redhead said. "Don't worry about him. Total bogan."

Rafa searched his ever-expanding mental dictionary of Aussie slang, but came up blank. He'd heard the term before, but didn't really get the meaning. "Bogan?"

"Yeah, you know. He's just…" The redhead waved his hand, then shrugged. "A real bogan."

That didn't clear up anything, but Rafa nodded anyway. "Thanks for your help."

"Anytime, mate. See you around!" He splashed off and paddled out.

Shane was still watching Wazza with clenched fists as if the guy was going to come back and pull a gun. Rafa elbowed him with a laugh. "I think the threat is contained. Ready to head home?"

"Yeah." Shane still stared at Wazza as they collected their stuff, looking back over his shoulder every so often as they walked up the few blocks to their bungalow. He'd worked long hours all week, planning the security for a big dinner event for one of his clients. He'd been wonderfully relaxed earlier on the beach, and Rafa hated seeing his shoulders so rigid.

In the kitchen, they chugged glasses of water, wetsuits peeled down to their waists. Shane was quiet and tense, and Rafa poked him in the chest. "Spill it."

"That asshole thought I was your father." He winced, chuckling. "Not great for my ego, I admit. I wanted to smash his crooked teeth out of his head."

Rafa teased, "Really? I couldn't tell." He circled his arms around Shane's waist and kissed him lightly. "I don't care what anyone else thinks. Especially not a bogan named Wazza. Whatever that means."

They laughed and kissed playfully, and Rafa leaned into Shane's warmth, rubbing against his hairy chest. Taking Rafa's face in his callused hands, Shane deepened the kiss, and the swirl of lazy desire in Rafa's belly sparked into a flame. His balls tingled with anticipation, their tongues meeting in a twisting dance.

Breaking the kiss to gulp in a breath, Rafa dipped his mouth to Shane's neck, nipping and sucking the tender skin there, making him moan. Rafa took his earlobe between his teeth, then whispered, "Give me some sugar, daddy."

They both laughed again and stripped off their shorts, grinning at each other. As Rafa took in Shane's hard, hairy body and thick cock, he quivered with a bolt of pleasure.

He's really mine.

Pushing aside a pile of dirty dishes with a clatter, Rafa bent over the kitchen counter. "Fuck me. Hard."

"Your wish is my command, baby." Shane's fingers were firm on his ass as he spread his cheeks and spit on Rafa's hole.

The edge of the counter dug into Rafa's lower belly, his hard cock crammed against the cupboards underneath. It wasn't exactly comfortable, but it spurred him on somehow. He spread his legs and pushed back. "Give it to me."

Shane spit again, a blob of wet saliva dripping down Rafa's crack. Then he dropped to his knees with a *thump* and buried his face in Rafa's ass, his stubble rough, tongue rasping wetly over his hole, circling it and pushing in.

"*Fuck*," Rafa gasped. "Oh yeah."

Shane's hot breath puffed over his flesh. "You want my cock? Need it?"

"Yes!" His right hand curled over the side of the sink, hanging on as he pushed back with his ass, his chin on the counter.

Spitting more, getting his hole dripping, Shane ate his ass. Then he shoved in a finger, fucking him with it. "That's not all, though. You're my cum slut, aren't you?"

Dick throbbing, Rafa moaned, "Yes." It was all his wildest fantasies come to life to be bent over and exposed, begging a man for his cock. And not just any man—the man of his *dreams*. And not just in any place—in their kitchen, their home.

Suddenly his eyes were wet with tears, and he couldn't breathe, his throat too thick. He swallowed hard. "Give me your cum, Shane. Please. Fuck me and fill me up."

"Such a slut for it. So hot." Shane stood and rustled around in a nearby drawer. Then he spread Rafa open wide and pushed the head of his thick, lubed shaft inside. "You're so beautiful. Love watching my cock inside you."

It burned wonderfully, and Rafa pressed his cheek to the counter. "All of it. Please."

Grunting, Shane shoved home, and Rafa cried out, digging his toes against the linoleum and squeezing with his inner muscles. Shane started fucking him, slamming in and out, their flesh slapping.

Rafa would probably have a bruise where the counter dug into his lower belly, and he didn't give a shit because nothing else mattered but the fire in his ass and through his veins as Shane fucked him the way he needed.

He rocked against the counter with each thrust, his dick so hard it was going to explode. Shane stroked rough hands over Rafa's shoulders. Then he took hold of his wrists and pulled his arms back by his hips the way Rafa loved it. He wasn't hanging onto anything, and it was like being suspended, totally powerless as Shane drilled his ass.

Rafa knew he *wasn't* powerless—Shane would stop immediately if he asked—but the sensation of being so thoroughly fucked by a stronger man, his arms restrained as he took that big cock, was an amazing surrender.

It made him so hot that he could trust Shane to take over completely. That Shane trusted him just as much. Saw him as an equal, no matter whose dick was in whose ass.

"Wish you had two cocks so you could fuck my mouth at the same time," Rafa gritted out, jerking with each thrust.

Shane laughed sharply, short of breath. "Me too." He hammered Rafa's ass. "Feel how deep I'm going? You like that?"

"*Yes.* Want your cum. All of it."

"It's yours, baby." He let go of Rafa's right wrist, but Rafa kept his arm back, his upper chest and cheek pressing against the counter. Shane reached below Rafa and jerked him, smearing the liquid leaking from his cock over his shaft. "You need to give me some first. Come on. Be a good boy."

Groaning, Rafa strained for release, the pressure in his ass and on his dick overwhelming. It had bothered him before, when people called him a boy, but now with Shane it turned him the hell on.

He whimpered as he came after a few more strokes, shaking with the pulses of sweet release, squeezing his eyes shut and seeing stars. The pleasure burned through him, and he opened his mouth on a silent cry.

Still shaking, he jerked in surprise as Shane's fingers slid into his mouth, filling it. They were slick with Rafa's semen, and he sucked greedily, moaning around them as Shane kept fucking his ass. It was the closest he could come to his lover having two cocks, and his dick spurted again as Shane hit his gland.

He was so full, and he squeezed Shane's dick hard. Shane muttered his name as he emptied inside him, and Rafa sucked his fingers, his mouth and ass both messy with cum. It was dirty and *perfect*, and he groaned helplessly as Shane bent over him, pressing wet kisses to his spine.

Slowly, Shane withdrew his fingers and cock, and Rafa whimpered, breathing hard. His knees were jelly, and he was relieved when Shane peeled him off the counter with strong hands, turning him and holding him close. He murmured against his curls, "I love you."

"Love you. I want to—" He bit off the words. He'd come up with the perfect plan for the weekend, so he shouldn't just blurt it out now. He leaned into Shane gratefully. "Shower? You might have to carry me."

With a laugh and a groan, Shane patted Rafa's ass. "We'll have to hobble over together. I might throw my back out after that."

When they were showered and dressed in shorts and tees, Rafa still itched to ask the question, the words impatient on his tongue, hovering at the tip. He waited until Shane was out of the bedroom to sneak the little box into his pocket.

With each beat of his heart, he felt like this was the right time. He'd planned on making a fancy French dinner on Saturday—lobster bisque, coq au vin, and a vanilla pear galette—but it didn't matter.

This was the time.

He'd made burger patties that morning, and as Shane heated the barbecue, Rafa threw together a salad and got out the ingredients for chocolate lava cakes. They were exceedingly easy to make, but Shane loved the gooey chocolate.

"Maybe simple is the way to go," Rafa muttered to himself as he grabbed the eggs. *Is this really the right time?* He buzzed with excitement and nerves.

He brought the burgers out, along with a couple of beers. As the meat cooked and the sun sank, they stood in easy silence in their yard, sipping from their bottles. A bird squawked, and the cooling night breeze ruffled Rafa's curls, carrying the brine of the sea. Oniony beef sizzled, and the sky streaked a deep reddish black.

Heart pounding, Rafa inhaled deeply.

"Doesn't get much better, does it?" Shane asked, rubbing a hand over Rafa's hip and kissing his cheek. "Want to watch *MasterChef?*"

He could only nod, afraid his voice would be nothing but a squeak. Shane frowned. "Okay?" He smoothed his palm over Rafa's butt. "Wasn't too rough?"

"No," he croaked before gulping his beer. He managed to exhale and give Shane a smile. "It doesn't get better."

In the living room, they ate their burgers and salad while the lava cakes baked. Rafa chewed and swallowed and tried to lose himself in the food and his favorite show. Apparently without success, because as he brought out dessert, Shane sighed and said, "Okay, what is it? You look like you're going to puke."

Rafa's head was light. "I actually might."

"What?" Shane's brow furrowed in that familiar, beautiful way. "Are you sick?" He put down his beer bottle and started to stand, but Rafa thrust the small plate at him before he could. Shane took it, glancing down at the round chocolate cake and silver fork, then doing a double take as he spotted the gold ring tucked on the side of the plate.

Rafa blurted, "I want to—what I mean is, will you marry me?"

Shane blinked at him. Then down at the ring, gooey chocolate inching toward it. Back up at Rafa. "You want to get married?"

Oh God. This wasn't the right time after all. Was this a huge mistake?

"Well, yeah. If you do. Maybe you don't? We've never really talked about it, which I guess is kind of stupid since I'm propos-ing." *Stop babbling!* "If you don't want to, it's totally cool." His cheeks burned, and he clenched and unclenched his hands, fidgeting as he stood by the couch.

Shane picked up the ring, holding it delicately between his fingers. When he looked back up, a huge smile split his face. "Of course I do. I thought about asking, but figured I should wait until you're done with school."

With a *whoosh*, Rafa exhaled and sat on the coffee table, his knees bumping Shane's. *He wants to marry me!*

"Raf? You still with me?" Shane nudged his knees.

"Uh-huh. You know, I thought about that—waiting to finish school—but why? Let's just do it. Have a little ceremony on the beach. We'll have to time it so it's not too close to the Olympics. Obviously Matty has to come, and he's swimming so amazingly that he's clearly making the team. We'll figure it out with his training and my parents' schedule. Give my family lots of notice. And our friends, obviously. Ash, Darnell, and Henry, especially."

He was rambling, and he took a breath. "It doesn't have to be fancy. And I'm not letting my parents invite all their political friends. As nice as the Australian prime minister was, she's not coming to our wedding."

"They're not going to like that. Wasn't Chris's wedding practically a state dinner?"

"Yep, and there's no way I'm letting that happen. We'll do it our way, and my parents can deal."

"Well, that is our unofficial motto."

Rafa's heart was about to burst. "Exactly. Screw what anyone else thinks. I want a small wedding on the beach, and I don't want to wait." He shrugged with a sly, teasing smile. "You're not getting any younger, so."

Barking out a laugh, Shane yanked him into a hug, Rafa practically on top of him. His breath tickled Rafa's ear. "It's true. Let's get married."

Joy pushed at Rafa's seams. They kissed until they were breathless, and then Shane gave him the gold band and held out his left hand, saying, "I guess we're not supposed to do it until the ceremony, but let's see how it fits."

Rafa had secretly measured his finger while Shane had been

fast asleep after a marathon fuck session. He exhaled happily as the ring fit, a little snug over Shane's second knuckle, but then resting perfectly.

Shane stared at it. "It's beautiful. But you need one too."

He pulled the other ring from his pocket and held it out. "I figured it would be cool if they matched."

Shane traced his finger over the faint etching in the gold of both rings. "Looks like a wave."

"Yeah. They're not super expensive or anything, but I thought it was cool. It fits us, you know? But if you don't like—"

Shane kissed him, all soft lips and love, then slid the ring onto Rafa's finger.

THE END

Afterword

Thank you so much for reading *Test of Valor*, and I hope you enjoyed it. I'd be grateful if you could take a few minutes to leave a review on Goodreads (or wherever you'd like!). Just a couple of sentences can really help other readers discover the book. Thank you!

Join the free gay romance newsletter!

My (mostly) monthly newsletter will keep you up to date on my latest releases and news from the world of LGBTQ romance. You'll also get access to exclusive giveaways, free reads, and much more. Join the mailing list today and you're automatically entered into my monthly giveaway.

Here's where you can find me online:
Website
www.keiraandrews.com
Facebook
facebook.com/keira.andrews.author
Facebook Reader Group
bit.ly/2gpTQpc
Instagram
instagram.com/keiraandrewsauthor
Goodreads
bit.ly/2k7kMj0
Amazon Author Page
amzn.to/2jWUfCL
Twitter
twitter.com/keiraandrews
BookBub
bookbub.com/authors/keira-andrews

Read more age-difference and adventure from Keira Andrews!

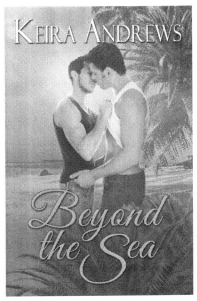

Beyond the Sea

Two straight guys. One desert island.

Even if it means quitting their boy band mid-tour, Troy Tanner isn't going to watch his little brother snort his future away after addiction destroyed their father. On a private jet taking him home from Australia, he and pilot Brian Sinclair soar above the vast South Pacific. Brian lost his passion for flying—and joy in life—after a traumatic crash, but now he and Troy must fight to survive when a cyclone strikes without warning.

Marooned a thousand miles from civilization, the turquoise water and white sand beach look like paradise. But although they can fish and make fire, the smallest infection or bacteria could be deadly. When the days turn into weeks with no sign of rescue, Troy and Brian grow closer, and friendship deepens into desire.

As they learn sexuality is about more than straight or gay and discover their true selves, the world they've built together is thrown into chaos. If Troy and Brian make it off the island, can their love endure?

This LGBT romance from Keira Andrews features bisexuality, finding love where you least expect it, eating way too many coconuts, and of course a happy ending.

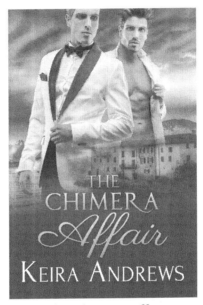

The Chimera Affair

His mission was seduction—not falling in love.

When young Sebastian Brambani meets a sexy and exciting older man, he's easily seduced. But for spy Kyle Grant, it's all business. Sebastian is simply a pawn in Kyle's mission to acquire a dangerous chemical weapon from Sebastian's criminal father. Kyle's life is his work for a shadowy international agency protecting the world from evil, and he can't worry about what will happen to Sebastian when the job is done.

Sebastian's unwitting role in Kyle's plan is the last straw for his ruthless father, who has been embarrassed by his gay son for the last time. But when Kyle discovers Sebastian could be the key to finding the deadly Chimera, he rescues him from a hired hitman and fights to keep him alive. Can a hardened spy and naïve college student take down a criminal kingpin, stay one step ahead of the killers on their trail—and fight the scorching attraction between them?

This gay romance from Keira Andrews features sexy spies, an age difference, a sheltered and passionate virgin, action and adventure, and of course a happy ending.

BONUS STORY INCLUDED: *The Argentine Seduction*, a sequel for Kyle and Sebastian featuring unexpected jealousy, protectiveness, and a dangerous mission in the simmering heat of Buenos Aires. (And of course a happy ending!)

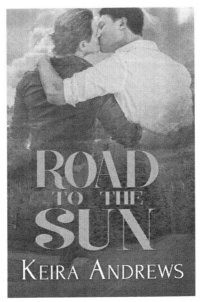

Road to the Sun

A desperate father. A lonely ranger. Unexpected love that can't be denied.

Jason Kellerman's life revolves around his eight-year-old daughter. Teenage curiosity with his best friend led to Maggie's birth, her mother tragically dying soon after. Insistent on raising his daughter himself, he was disowned by his wealthy family and has worked tirelessly to support Maggie—even bringing her west on a dream vacation. Only twenty-five, Jason hasn't had time to even think about romance. So the last thing he expects is to question his sexuality after meeting an undeniably attractive park ranger.

Ben Hettler's stuck. He loves working in the wild under Montana's big sky, but at forty-one, his love life is non-existent, his ex-boyfriend just married and adopted, and Ben's own dream of fatherhood feels impossibly out of reach. He's attracted to Jason, but what's the point? Besides the age difference and skittish Jason's lack of experience, they live thousands of miles apart. Ben wants more than a meaningless fling.

Then a hunted criminal takes Maggie hostage, throwing Jason and Ben together in a desperate and dangerous search through endless miles of mountain forest. If they rescue Maggie against all odds, can they build a new family together and find a place to call home?

Road to the Sun is a May-December gay romance from Keira Andrews featuring adventure, angst, coming out, sexual discovery, and of course a happy ending.

About the Author

After writing for years yet never really finding the right inspiration, Keira discovered her voice in gay romance, which has become a passion. She writes contemporary, historical, paranormal, and fantasy fiction, and—although she loves delicious angst along the way—Keira firmly believes in happy endings. For as Oscar Wilde once said, "The good ended happily, and the bad unhappily. That is what fiction means."

Find out more about Keira's books and sign up for her (mostly) monthly gay romance e-newsletter:

keiraandrews.com

Made in the USA
Middletown, DE
01 May 2018